THE GHOST SLAYERS

THE GHOST SLAYERS

Classic Tales of Occult Detection

Edited by
MIKE ASHLEY

BRITISH LIBRARY

This collection first published in 2022 by
The British Library
96 Euston Road
London NW1 2DB

Dates attributed to each story relate to first publication.

Cataloguing in Publication Data
A catalogue record for this publication is available from the British Library

ISBN 978 0 7123 5416 5
e-ISBN 978 0 7123 6749 3

The frontispiece illustration by John Swain accompanied the first appearance of 'The
Story of the Moor Road' by E. and H. Heron in *Pearson's Magazine* March 1898.

Cover design by Mauricio Villamayor with illustration by Sandra Gómez
Text design and typesetting by Tetragon, London
Printed in England by CPI Group (UK) Ltd, Croydon, CRO 4YY

CONTENTS

INTRODUCTION

In February 1882 the Society for Psychical Research (SPR) was founded in London. It was the first organisation to take a methodical, scientific approach to researching reports of psychic or spiritualist events. Amongst its early members were Henry Sidgwick, the first President, his brother-in-law the future Prime Minister, Arthur Balfour, the chief researchers Frederic Myers, Edmund Gurney and Frank Podmore, and the future Archbishop of Canterbury, Edward White Benson (father of the writer E. F. Benson). Myers, Gurney and Podmore undertook considerable research to produce the first study of psychic phenomena, *Phantasms of the Living*, published in 1886.

Their work provoked much interest in Victorian Britain and led to an interest in ghost-hunting. There had already been several stories involving those who investigate unusual phenomena, mostly doctors, such as Samuel Warren's anonymous doctor in his series "Passages from the Diary of a Late Physician", which began in 1830, or Sheridan Le Fanu's Dr. Martin Hesselius whose papers form the basis for the stories collected as *In a Glass Darkly* in 1872. But it was the SPR that became the main impetus for stories of occult detectives, with added interest as a result of the success of Arthur Conan Doyle's Sherlock Holmes stories. Holmes was not an occult detective—in fact he pooh-poohed the whole idea of the super-natural—but his cases were often unusual and it was only a small step from Holmes to investigators of the paranormal.

The first such literary investigator to appear not only in a series of stories but who purported to be associated with the SPR was Flaxman

Low, who appeared in a series of stories published by *Pearson's Magazine* in 1898 under the overall title "Real Ghost Stories". *Pearson's* went so far as to show fake photographs of the locations covered in each story. The series proved so popular that a second ran the following year and they were issued in book form as *Ghosts* at the end of 1899. There is a direct line of descent from Flaxman Low through other such psychic detectives as John Silence, Thomas Carnacki and Dr. Taverner through to the American Lucius Leffing, who was himself a self-confessed devotee of the Victorian era.

This anthology includes selections from across those classic years including some of the earliest investigations of Flaxman Low and John Silence and the far lesser-known exploits of Aylmer Vance, Mesmer Milann and Cosmo Thor. As you may expect there are a few haunted houses, though not haunted by the expected. And there's more unusual places to be haunted, such as an open road, a lighthouse and a valley in the depths of the Australian desert. The investigators have to have their wits about them, backed up by, as you will discover, a lifetime of experience.

But be prepared, just in case...

MIKE ASHLEY

A NOTE FROM THE PUBLISHER

The original short stories reprinted in the British Library Tales of the Weird series were written and published in a period ranging across the nineteenth and twentieth centuries. There are many elements of these stories which continue to entertain modern readers; however, in some cases there are also uses of language, instances of stereotyping and some attitudes expressed by narrators or characters which may not be endorsed by the publishing standards of today. We acknowledge therefore that some elements in the stories selected for reprinting may continue to make uncomfortable reading for some of our audience. With this series British Library Publishing aims to offer a new readership a chance to read some of the rare material of the British Library's collections in an affordable paperback format, to enjoy their merits and to look back into the worlds of the past two centuries as portrayed by their writers. It is not possible to separate these stories from the history of their writing and as such the following stories are presented as they were originally published with minor edits only, made for consistency of style and sense. We welcome feedback from our readers, which can be sent to the following address:

British Library Publishing
The British Library
96 Euston Road
London, NW1 2DB
United Kingdom

9

FLAXMAN LOW

in

THE STORY OF
THE MOOR ROAD

Kate and Hesketh Prichard

*When Flaxman Low was introduced to the public in "The Story of The
Spaniards, Hammersmith" (Pearson's Magazine, January 1898) readers
met the prototype of the psychic detective. He has offices in London, but is
often elsewhere which could be anywhere in the world—in that story it's
Vienna. He clearly has years of experience of the paranormal and he files
reports for the Psychical Research Society, as he calls it. Low is the true
professional and all who encounter him feel able to place their trust in him
to resolve what are sometimes the most unusual of hauntings or manifestations, as in the following story.*

*The original stories appeared under the names of E. & H. Heron which
masked the identities of a mother-and-son writing team, Kate and Hesketh
Prichard. They were a prolific pair. Kate (1851–1935) did most of the writing whilst Hesketh (1876–1922) came up with the ideas and they plotted
between them. He had been born in India, the son of a military officer who
had died just before Hesketh was born. They returned to England where
Hesketh underwent a public-school education and became something of an
adventurer, explorer, superb cricketer and excellent marksman. It is tragic
that his life was cut short by complications developed from malaria which
he had caught while in Panama in 1898, reporting on the construction of*

the Panama Canal. He and his mother created several popular characters for Pearson's Magazine, *notably the Spanish equivalent of Robin Hood, the brigand Don Q., whilst Hesketh alone wrote the series about the Canadian backwoodsman detective November Joe. However, in the world of supernatural fiction they remain immortal for Flaxman Low, and a series which began the fascination for the occult detective story.*

"The medical profession must always have its own peculiar offshoots," said Mr. Flaxman Low, "some are trades, some mere hobbies, others, again, are allied subjects of a serious and profound nature. Now, as a student of psychical phenomena, I account myself only two degrees removed from the ordinary general practitioner."

"How do you make that out?" returned Colonel Daimley, pushing the decanter of old port invitingly across the table.

"The nerve and brain specialist is the link between myself and the man you would send for if you had a touch of lumbago," replied Low with a slight smile. "Each division is but a higher grade of the same ladder—a step upwards into the unknown. I consider that I stand just one step above the specialist who makes a study of brain disease and insanity; he is at work on the disorders of the embodied spirit, while I deal with abnormal conditions of the free and detached spirit."

Colonel Daimley laughed aloud.

"That won't do, Low! No, no! First prove that your ghosts are sick."

"Certainly," replied Low gravely. "A very small proportion of spirits return as apparitions after the death of the body. Hence we may conclude that a ghost is a spirit in an abnormal condition. Abnormal conditions of the body usually indicate disease; why not of the spirit also?"

"That sounds fair enough," observed Lane Chaddam, the third man present. "Has the Colonel told you of our spook?"

The Colonel shook his handsome grey head in some irritation.

"You haven't convinced me yet, Lane, that it is a spook," he said drily. "Human nature is at the bottom of most things in this world according to my opinion."

"What spook is this?" asked Flaxman Low. "I heard nothing of it when I was down with you last year."

"It's a recent acquisition," replied Lane Chaddam. "I wish we were rid of it for my part."

"Have you seen it?" asked Low as he relit his long German pipe.

"Yes, and felt it!"

"What is it?"

"That's for you to say. He nearly broke my neck for me—that's all I can swear to."

Low knew Chaddam well. He was a long-limbed, athletic young fellow, with a good show of cups in his rooms, and was one of the various short-distance runners mentioned in the Badminton as having done the hundred in level time, and not the sort of man whose neck is easy to break.

"How did it happen?" asked Flaxman Low.

"About a fortnight ago," replied Chaddam. "I was flight-shooting near the burn where the hounds killed the otter last year. When the light began to fail, I thought I would come home by the old quarry, and pot anything that showed itself. As I walked along the far bank of the burn, I saw a man on the near side standing on the patch of sand below the reeds and watching me. As I came nearer I heard him coughing; it sounded like a sick cow. He stood still as if waiting for me. I thought it odd, because amongst the meres and water-meadows down there one never meets a stranger."

"Could you see him pretty clearly?"

"I saw his outline clearly, but not his face, because his back was toward the west. He was tall and jerry-built, so to speak, and had a little head no bigger than a child's, and he wore a fur cap with queer upstanding ears. When I came close, he suddenly slipped away; he jumped behind a big dyke, and I lost sight of him. But I didn't pay much attention; I had my gun, and I concluded it was a tramp."

"Tramps don't follow men of your size," observed Low with a smile.

"This fellow did, at any rate. When I got across to the spot where he had been standing—the sand is soft there—I looked for his tracks. I knew he was bound to have a big foot of his own considering his height. But there were no footprints!"

"No footprints? You mean it was too dark for you to see them?" broke in Colonel Daimley.

"I am sure I should have seen them had there been any," persisted Chaddam quietly. "Besides, a man can't take a leap as he did without leaving a good hole behind him. The sand was perfectly smooth, because there had been a strong east wind all day. After looking about and seeing no marks, I went on to the top of the knoll above the quarry. After a bit I felt I was followed, though I couldn't see anyone. You remember the thorn bush that overhangs the quarry pool? I stopped there and bent over the edge of the cliff to see if there was anything in the pool. As I stooped I felt a point like a steel puncheon catch me in the small of the back. I kicked off from the quarry wall as well as I could, so as to avoid the broken rocks below, and I just managed to clear them, but I fell into the water with a flop that knocked the wind out of me. However, I held on to the gun, and, after a minute, I climbed to a ledge under the cliff and waited to see what my friend on top would do next. He waited, too. I couldn't see him, but I heard him—he coughed up there in the dusk, the most ghastly noise I ever heard. The Colonel laughs at me, but it was about as nasty a half-hour as I care to have. In the end, I swam out across the pool and got home."

"I laugh at Lane," said the Colonel, "but all the same, it's a bad spot for a fall."

"You say he struck you in the back?" asked Flaxman Low, turning to Chaddam.

"Yes, and his finger was like a steel punch."

"What does Mrs. Daimley say to this affair?" went on Low presently.

"Not a word to my wife or Olivia, my dear Low!" exclaimed Colonel Daimley. "It would frighten them needlessly; besides, there would be an infernal fuss if we wanted to go flighting or anything after dark. I only fear for them, as they often drive into Nerbury by the Moor Road, which passes close by the quarry."

"Do they go in for their letters every evening as they used to do?"

"Just the same. And they won't take Stubbs with them, in spite of advice." The Colonel looked disconsolately at Low. "Women are angels, bless them! but they are the dickens to deal with because they always want to know why?"

"And now, Low, what have you to say about it?" asked Chaddam. "Have you told me all?"

"Yes. The only other thing is that Livy says she hears someone coughing in the spinney most nights."

"If all is as you say, Chaddam—pardon me, but in cases like this imagination is apt to play an unsuspected part—I should think that you have come upon a unique experience. What you have told me is not to be explained upon the lines of any ordinary theory."

After this they followed the ladies into the drawing-room, where they found Mrs. Daimley immersed in a novel as usual, and Livy looking pretty enough to account for the frequent presence of Lane Chaddam at Low Riddings. He was a distant cousin of the Colonel, and took advantage of his relationship to pay protracted visits to Northumberland.

Some years previous to the date of the above events, Colonel Daimley had bought and enlarged a substantial farmhouse which stood in a dip south of a lonely sweep of Northumbrian moors. It was a land of pale blue skies and far-off fringes of black and ragged pine trees.

From the house a lane led over the windswept shoulder of the upland down to a hollow spanned by a railway bridge, then up again across the high levels of the moors until at length it lost itself in the outskirts of the little town of Nerbury. This Moor Road was peculiarly lonely; it approached but one cottage the whole way, and ran very nearly over the doorstep of that one—a deserted-looking slip of a place between the railway bridge and the quarry. Beyond the quarry stretched acres of marshland, meadows and reedy meres, all of which had been manipulated with such ability by the Colonel, that the duck shooting on his land was the envy of the neighbourhood.

In spite of its loneliness the Moor Road was much frequented by the Daimleys, who preferred it to the high road, which was uninteresting and much longer. Mrs. Daimley and Olivia drove in of an evening to fetch their letters—being people with nothing on earth to do, they were naturally always in a hurry to get their letters—and they perpetually had parcels waiting for them at the station which required to be called for at all sorts of hours. Thus it will be seen that the fact of the quarry being haunted by Lane Chaddam's assailant, formed a very real danger to the inhabitants of Low Riddings.

At breakfast next day Livy said the tramp had been coughing in the spinney half the night.

"In what direction?" asked Flaxman Low.

Livy pointed to the window which looked on to the gate and the thick boundary hedge, the last still full of crisp ruddy leaves.

"You feel an interest in your tramp, Miss Daimley?"

"Of course, poor creature! I wanted to go out to look for him the other night, but they would not allow me."

"That was before we knew he was so interesting," said Chaddam. "I promise we'll catch him for you next time he comes."

And this was in fact the programme they tried to carry out, but although the coughing was heard in the spinney, no one even caught a glimpse of any living thing moving or hiding among the trees.

The next stage of the affair happened to be an experience of Livy. In some excitement she told the assembled family at dinner that she had just seen the coughing tramp.

Lane Chaddam changed colour.

"You don't mean to say, Livy, that you went to search for him alone?" he exclaimed half-angrily.

Flaxman Low and the Colonel wisely went on eating oyster patties without taking any apparent notice of the girl's news.

"Why shouldn't I?" asked Livy quickly, "but as it happens I saw him in Scully's cottage by the quarry this evening."

"What?" exclaimed Colonel Daimley, "in Scully's cottage. I'll see to that."

"Why? Are you all so prejudiced against my poor tramp?"

"On the contrary," replied Flaxman Low, "we all want to know what he's like."

"So odd-looking! I was driving home alone from the post when, as I passed the quarry cottage, I heard the cough. You know it is quite unmistakable; I looked up at the window and there he was. I have never seen anybody in the least like him. His face is ghastly pale and perfectly hairless, and he has such a little head. He stared at me so threateningly that I whipped up Lorelie."

"Were you frightened, then?"

"Not exactly, but he had such a wicked face that I drove away as fast as I could."

"I understood that you had arranged to send Stubbs for the letters?" said Colonel Daimley with some annoyance. "Why can't girls say what they mean?"

Livy made no reply, and after a pause Chaddam put a question.

"You must have passed along the Moor Road about seven o'clock?"

"Yes, it was after six when I left the Post-Office," replied Livy. "Why?"

"It was quite dark—how did you see the hairless man so plainly? I was round on the marshes all the evening, and I am quite certain there was no light at any time in Scully's cottage."

"I don't remember whether there was any light behind him in the room," returned Livy after a moment's consideration; "I only know that I saw his head and face quite plainly."

There was no more said on the subject at the time, though the Colonel forbade Livy to run any further risks by going alone on the Moor Road. After this the three men paraded the lane and lay in wait for the hairless tramp or ghost. On the second evening their watch was rewarded, when Chaddam came hurriedly into the smoking-room to say that the coughing could at that instant be heard in the hedge by the dining-room. It was still early, although the evening had closed in with clouds, and all outside was dark.

"I'll deal with him this time effectually!" exclaimed the Colonel. "I'll slip out the back way, and lie in the hedge down the road by the field gate. You two must chivy him out to me, and when he comes along, I'll have him against the sky-line and give him a charge of No. 4 if he shows fight."

The Colonel stole down the lane while the others beat the spinney and hedge, Flaxman Low very much chagrined at being forced to deal with an interesting problem in this rough and ready fashion. However, he saw that on this occasion at least it would be useless to oppose the Colonel's notions. When he and Chaddam met after beating the hedge they saw a tall figure shamble away rapidly down the lane towards the Colonel's hiding-place.

They stood still and waited for developments, but the minutes followed each other in intense stillness. Then they went to find the Colonel.

"Hullo, Colonel, anything wrong?" asked Chaddam on nearing the field gate.

The Colonel straightened himself with the help of Chaddam's arm.

"Did you see him?" he whispered.

"We thought so. Why did you not fire?"

"Because," said the Colonel in a husky voice, "I had no gun!"

"But you took it with you?"

"Yes."

Flaxman Low opened the lantern he carried, and, as the light swept round in a wide circle, something glinted on the grass. It was the stock of the Colonel's gun. A little further off they came upon the Damascus barrels bent and twisted into a ball like so much fine wire. Presently the Colonel explained.

"I saw him coming and meant to meet him, but I seemed dazed—I couldn't move! The gun was snatched from me, and I made no resistance—I don't know why." He took the gun barrels and examined them slowly, "I give in, Low, no human hand did that."

During dinner Flaxman Low said abruptly: "I suspect you have lately had an earthquake down here."

"How did you know?" asked Livy. "Have you been to the quarry?"

Low said he had not.

"It was such a poor little earthquake that even the papers did not think it worth while to mention it!" went on Livy. "We didn't feel any shock, and, in fact, knew nothing about it until Dr. Petterped told us."

"You had a landslip though?" went on Low.

Livy opened her pretty eyes.

"But you know all about it," she said. "Yes, the landslip was just by the old quarry."

"I should like to see the place tomorrow," observed Low.

Next day, therefore, when the Colonel went off to the coverts with a couple of neighbours, whom he had invited to join him, Flaxman Low accompanied Chaddam to examine the scene of the landslip.

From the edge of the upland, looking across the hollow crowded with reedy pools, they could see in the torn, reddish flank of the opposite slope the sharp tilt of the broken strata. To the right of this lay the old quarry, and about a hundred yards to the left the lonely house and the curving road.

Low descended into the hollow and spent a long time in the spongy ground between the back of the quarry and the lower edge of the newly-uncovered strata, using his little hammer freely, especially about one narrow black fissure, round which he sniffed and pottered in absorbed silence. Presently he called to Chaddam.

"There has been a slight explosion of gas—a rare gas, here," he said. "I hardly hoped to find traces of it, but it is unmistakeable."

"Very unmistakeable," agreed Chaddam, with a laugh. "You'd have said so had you been here when it happened."

"Ah, very satisfactory indeed. And that was a fortnight ago, you say?"

"Rather more now. It took place a couple of days before my fall into the quarry pool."

"Anyone ill near by—at that cottage for instance?" asked Low, as he joined Chaddam.

"Why? Was that gas poisonous? There's a man in the Colonel's employ named Scully in that cottage, who has had pneumonia, but he was on the mend when the landslip occurred. Since then he has grown steadily worse."

"Is there anyone with him?"

"Yes, the Daimleys sent for a woman to look after him. Scully's a very decent man. I often go in to see him."

"And so does the hairless man apparently," added Low.

"No, that's the queer part of it. Neither he nor the woman in charge have ever seen such a person as Livy described. I don't know what to think."

"The first thing to be done is to get the man from here at once," said Low decidedly. "Let's go in and see him."

They found Scully low and drowsy. The nurse shook her head at the two visitors in a despondent way.

"He grows weaker day by day," she said.

"Get him away from here at once," repeated Low, as they went out.

"We might have him up at Low Riddings, but he seems almost too weak to be moved," replied Chaddam doubtfully.

"My dear fellow, it's his only chance of life."

The Daimleys made arrangements for the reception of Scully, provided Dr. Thomson of Nerbury gave his consent to the removal. In the afternoon, therefore, Chaddam bicycled into Nerbury to see the doctor on the subject.

"If I were you, Chaddam," said Low before he started, "I'd be back by daylight."

Unfortunately Dr. Thomson was on his rounds, and did not return until after dark, by which time it was too late to remove Scully that evening. After leaving the doctor's house Chaddam went to the station to inquire about a box from Mudie's. The books having arrived, he took out a couple of volumes for Mrs. Daimley's present consumption, and was strapping them on in front of his bicycle, when it struck him that unless he went home by the Moor Road he would be late for dinner.

Accordingly he branched off into the bare track which led over the moors. The twilight had deepened into a fine, cold night, and a moon was swinging up into a pale, clear sky. The spread of heather, purple in the daytime, appeared jet black by moonlight, and across it he could see the white ribbon of road stretching ahead into the distance. The scents of the night were fresh in his nostrils, as he ran easily along the level with the breeze behind him.

He soon reached the incline past Scully's cottage. Well away to the left lay the quarry pool like a blotch of ink under its shadowing cliff. There was no light in the cottage, and it seemed even more deserted-looking than usual.

As Chaddam flashed under the bridge, he heard a cough, and glanced back over his shoulder.

A tall, loose-jointed form he had seen once before, was rearing itself up upon the railway bridge. There was something curiously unhuman about the lank outlines and the cant of the small head with its prick-eared cap showing out so clearly against the lighter sky behind.

When Chaddam looked again, he saw the thing on the bridge fling up its long arms and leap down on to the road some thirty feet below.

Then Chaddam rode. He began to think he had been a fool to come, and he counted that he was a good mile from home. At first he fancied he heard footfalls, then he fancied there were none. The hard road flew under him, all thoughts of economising his strength were lost, his single aim was to make the pace.

Suddenly his bicycle jerked violently, and he was shot over into the road. As he fell, he turned his head and was conscious of a little, bleached, bestial face, wet with fury, not ten yards behind!

He sprang to his feet, and ran up the road as he had never run before. He ran wonderfully, but he might as well have tried to race a cheetah. It was not a question of speed, the game was in the hands of this thing with the limbs of a starved Hercules, whose bony knees seemed to leap into its ghastly face at every stride. Chaddam topped the slope with a sickening sense of his own powerlessness. Already he saw Low Riddings in the distance, and a dim light came creeping along the road towards him. Another frantic spurt, and he had almost reached the light, when a hand closed like a vice on his shoulder, and seemed to fasten on the flesh. He rushed blindly on towards the house. He saw the door-handle gleam, and in another second he had pitched head foremost on to the knotted matting in the hall.

When he recovered his senses, his first question was: "Where is Low?"

"Didn't you meet him?" asked Livy. "I—that is, we were anxious about you as you were so late, and I was just going to meet you when Mr. Low came downstairs and insisted on going instead."

Chaddam stood up.

"I must follow him."

But as he spoke the front door opened, and Flaxman Low entered, and looked up at the clock.

"Eight-twenty," he said. "You're late, Chaddam."

Afterwards in the smoking-room he gave an account of what he had seen.

"I saw Chaddam racing up the road with a tall figure behind him. It stretched out its hand and grasped his shoulder. The next instant it stopped short as if it had been shot. It seemed to reel back and collapse, and then limped off into the hedge like a disappointed dog."

Chaddam stood up and began to take off his coat.

"Whatever the thing is, it is something out of the common. Look here!" he said, turning up his shirtsleeve over the point of his shoulder, where three singular marks were visible, irregularly placed as the fingers of a hand might fall. They were oblong in shape, about the size of a bean, and swollen in purple lumps well above the surface of the skin.

"Looks as if someone had been using a small cupping glass on you," remarked the Colonel uneasily. "What do you say to it, Low?"

"I say that since Chaddam has escaped with his life, I have only to congratulate him on what, in Europe certainly, is a unique adventure."

The Colonel threw his cigar into the fire.

"Such adventures are too dangerous for my taste," he said. "This creature has on two occasions murderously attacked Lane Chaddam, and it would, no doubt, have attacked Livy if it had had the chance.

We must leave this place at once, or we shall be murdered in our beds'!"

"I don't think, Colonel, that you will be troubled with this mysterious visitant again," replied Flaxman Low.

"Why not? Who or what is this horrible thing?"

"I believe it to be an Elemental Earth Spirit," returned Low. "No other solution fits the facts of the case."

"What is an Elemental?" resumed the Colonel irritably. "Remember, Low, I expect you to prove your theories so that a plain man may understand, if I am to stay on at Low Riddings."

"Eastern occultists describe wandering tribes of earth spirits, evil intelligences, possessing spirit as distinct from soul—all inimical to man."

"But how do you know that the thing on the Moor Road is an Elemental?"

"Because the points of resemblance are curiously remarkable. The occultists say that when these spirits materialise, they appear in grotesque and uncouth forms; secondly, that they are invariably bloodless and hairless; thirdly, they move with extraordinary rapidity, and leave no footprints; and, lastly, their agility and strength is superhuman. All these peculiarities have been observed in connection with the figure on the Moor Road."

"I admit that no man I have ever met with," commented Colonel Daimley, "could jump uninjured from a height of 30ft., race a bicycle, and twist up gun barrels like so much soft paper. So perhaps you're right. But can you tell me why or how it came here?"

"My conclusions," began Low, "may seem to you far-fetched and ridiculous, but you must give them the benefit of the fact that they precisely account for the otherwise unaccountable features which mark this affair. I connect this appearance with the earthquake and the sick man."

"What? Scully in league with the devil?" exclaimed the Colonel bluntly. "Why the man is too weak to leave his bed; besides, he is a short, thick-set fellow, entirely unlike our haunting friend."

"You mistake me, Colonel," said Low, in his quiet tones. "These Elementals cannot take form without drawing upon the resources of the living. They absorb the vitality of any ailing person until it is exhausted, and the person dies."

"Then they begin operations upon a fresh victim? A pleasant look-out to know we keep a well-attested vampire in the neighbourhood!"

"Vampires are a distinct race, with different methods; one being that the Elemental is a wanderer, and goes far afield to search for a new victim."

"But why should it want to kill me?" put in Chaddam.

"As I have told you, they are animated solely by a blind malignity to the human race, and you happened to be handy."

"But the earthquake, Low; where is the connection there?" demanded the Colonel, with the air of a man who intends to corner his opponent.

Flaxman Low lit one cigar at the end of another before he replied.

"At this point," he said, "my own theories and observations and those of the old occultists overlap. The occultists held that some of these spirits are imprisoned in the interior of the earth, but may be set free in consequence of those shiftings and disturbances which take place during an earthquake. This in more modern language simply means that Elementals are in some manner connected with certain of the primary strata. Now, my own researches have led me to conclude that atmospheric influences are intimately associated with spiritual phenomena. Some gases appear to be productive of such phenomena. One of these is generated when certain of the primary formations are newly exposed to the common air."

"This is almost beyond belief—I don't understand you," said the Colonel.

"I am sorry that I cannot give you all the links in my own chain of reasoning," returned Low. "Much is still obscure, but the evidence is sufficiently strong to convince me that in such a case of earthquake and landslip as has lately taken place here the phenomenon of an embodied Elemental might possibly be expected to follow, given the one necessary adjunct of a sick person in the near neighbourhood of the disturbance."

"But when this brute got hold of me, why didn't it finish me off?" asked Chaddam. "Or was it your coming that prevented it?"

Flaxman Low considered.

"No, I don't think I can flatter myself that my coming had anything to do with your escape. It was a near thing—how near you will understand when we hear further news of Scully in the morning."

A servant entered the room at this moment.

"The woman has come up from the cottage, sir, to say that Scully is dead."

"At what hour did he die?" asked Low.

"About ten minutes past eight, sir, she says."

"The hour agrees exactly," commented Low, when the man had left the room. "The figure stopped and collapsed so suddenly that I believed something of this kind must have happened."

"But surely this is a very unprecedented occurrence?"

"It is," said Flaxman Low. "But I can assure you that if you take the trouble to glance through the pages of the psychical periodicals you will find many statements at least as wonderful."

"But are they true?"

Flaxman Low shrugged his shoulders.

"At any rate," said he, "we know this is."

The Daimleys have spent many pleasant days at Low Riddings since then, but Chaddam—who has acquired a right to control Miss Livy's actions more or less—persists in his objection to any solitary expeditions to Nerbury along the Moor Road. For, although the figure has never been seen about Low Riddings since, some strange stories have lately appeared in the papers of a similar mysterious figure which has been met with more than once in the lonelier spots about North London. If it be true that this nameless wandering spirit, with the strength and activity of twenty men, still haunts our lonely roads, the sooner Mr. Flaxman Low exorcises it the better.

JOHN SILENCE

in

A PSYCHICAL INVASION

Algernon Blackwood

Following the popularity of Flaxman Low the fascination for the occult detective escalated with the publication of John Silence: Physician Extraordinary *in 1908. Algernon Blackwood (1869–1951) had originally written a series of essays on occult phenomena but his publisher, Eveleigh Nash, suggested he convert the articles into stories. Blackwood did so, introducing a detective who has undergone decades of specialist training in remote parts of the world and whose knowledge of the arcane is unprecedented. Blackwood has his own direct knowledge of investigating the paranormal. His father, who was head of the Post Office, employed Frank Podmore of the Society for Psychical Research and Podmore passed on to the younger Blackwood details on reported hauntings. It is known he investigated at least two such houses and probably more in his thirties when he became a member of the Hermetic Order of the Golden Dawn, which studied esoteric beliefs and rituals. An experienced traveller—like Hesketh Prichard—Blackwood brought to the genre an understanding of the supernatural and metaphysical which was unrivalled.*

This story was the first in the collection in which it was published and almost certainly one revised from Blackwood's original essay in which he was exploring how the mind can be opened to the paranormal through drugs— something Blackwood had experienced with almost fatal consequences when he was down-and-out in New York in the early 1890s. The later stories are clearly ones written as fiction and even include a Watson-like colleague called Hubbard, based on Blackwood's cousin and future brother-in-law, Arthur Hobart-Hampden (Hobart is pronounced Hubbard). As a result, reviewers labelled Silence as "a psychic Sherlock Holmes". Nash was delighted with the book and spared no expense promoting it with a huge advertising campaign so that no one in London could escape the lure of John Silence.

I

"**A**nd what is it makes you think I could be of use in this particular case?" asked Dr. John Silence, looking across somewhat sceptically at the Swedish lady in the chair facing him.

"Your sympathetic heart and your knowledge of occultism—"

"Oh, please—that dreadful word!" he interrupted, holding up a finger with a gesture of impatience.

"Well, then," she laughed, "your wonderful clairvoyant gift and your trained psychic knowledge of the processes by which a personality may be disintegrated and destroyed—these strange studies you've been experimenting with all these years—"

"If it's only a case of multiple personality I must really cry off," interrupted the doctor again hastily, a bored expression in his eyes.

"It's not that; now, please, be serious, for I want your help," she said; "and if I choose my words poorly you must be patient with my ignorance. The case I know will interest you, and no one else could deal with it so well. In fact, no ordinary professional man could deal with it at all, for I know of no treatment or medicine that can restore a lost sense of humour!"

"You begin to interest me with your 'case,'" he replied, and made himself comfortable to listen.

Mrs. Sivendson drew a sigh of contentment as she watched him go to the tube and heard him tell the servant he was not to be disturbed.

"I believe you have read my thoughts already," she said; "your intuitive knowledge of what goes on in other people's minds is positively uncanny."

Her friend shook his head and smiled as he drew his chair up to a convenient position and prepared to listen attentively to what she had to say. He closed his eyes, as he always did when he wished to absorb the real meaning of a recital that might be inadequately expressed, for by this method he found it easier to set himself in tune with the living thoughts that lay behind the broken words.

By his friends John Silence was regarded as an eccentric, because he was rich by accident, and by choice—a doctor. That a man of independent means should devote his time to doctoring, chiefly doctoring folk who could not pay, passed their comprehension entirely. The native nobility of a soul whose first desire was to help those who could not help themselves, puzzled them. After that, it irritated them, and, greatly to his own satisfaction, they left him to his own devices.

Dr. Silence was a free-lance, though, among doctors, having neither consulting-room, book keeper, nor professional manner. He took no fees, being at heart a genuine philanthropist, yet at the same time did no harm to his fellow-practitioners, because he only accepted unremunerative cases, and cases that interested him for some very special reason. He argued that the rich could pay, and the very poor could avail themselves of organised charity, but that a very large class of ill-paid, self-respecting workers, often followers of the arts, could not afford the price of a week's comforts merely to be told to travel. And it was these he desired to help: cases often requiring special and patient study—things no doctor can give for a guinea, and that no one would dream of expecting him to give.

But there was another side to his personality and practice, and one with which we are now more directly concerned; for the cases that especially appealed to him were of no ordinary kind, but rather of that intangible, elusive, and difficult nature best described as psychical afflictions; and, though he would have been the last person himself to approve of the title, it was beyond question that he was known more or less generally as the "Psychic Doctor."

In order to grapple with cases of this peculiar kind, he had submitted himself to a long and severe training, at once physical, mental, and spiritual. What precisely this training had been, or where undergone, no one seemed to know,—for he never spoke of it, as, indeed, he betrayed no single other characteristic of the charlatan,—but the fact that it had involved a total disappearance from the world for five years, and that after he returned and began his singular practice no one ever dreamed of applying to him the so easily acquired epithet of quack, spoke much for the seriousness of his strange quest and also for the genuineness of his attainments.

For the modern psychical researcher he felt the calm tolerance of the "man who knows." There was a trace of pity in his voice— contempt he never showed—when he spoke of their methods.

"This classification of results is uninspired work at best," he said once to me, when I had been his confidential assistant for some years. "It leads nowhere, and after a hundred years will lead nowhere. It is playing with the wrong end of a rather dangerous toy. Far better, it would be, to examine the causes, and then the results would so easily slip into place and explain themselves. For the sources are accessible, and open to all who have the courage to lead the life that alone makes practical investigation safe and possible."

And towards the question of clairvoyance, too, his attitude was significantly sane, for he knew how extremely rare the genuine power was, and that what is commonly called clairvoyance is nothing more than a keen power of visualising.

"It connotes a slightly increased sensibility, nothing more," he would say. "The true clairvoyant deplores his power, recognising that it adds a new horror to life, and is in the nature of an affliction. And you will find this always to be the real test."

Thus it was that John Silence, this singularly developed doctor, was able to select his cases with a clear knowledge of the difference between mere hysterical delusion and the kind of psychical affliction that claimed his special powers. It was never necessary for him to resort to the cheap mysteries of divination; for, as I have heard him observe, after the solution of some peculiarly intricate problem—

"Systems of divination, from geomancy down to reading by tea-leaves, are merely so many methods of obscuring the outer vision, in order that the inner vision may become open. Once the method is mastered, no system is necessary at all."

And the words were significant of the methods of this remarkable man, the keynote of whose power lay, perhaps, more than anything else, in the knowledge, first, that thought can act at a distance, and, secondly, that thought is dynamic and can accomplish material results.

"Learn how to *think*," he would have expressed it, "and you have learned to tap power at its source."

To look at—he was now past forty—he was sparely built, with speaking brown eyes in which shone the light of knowledge and self-confidence, while at the same time they made one think of that wondrous gentleness seen most often in the eyes of animals. A close beard concealed the mouth without disguising the grim determination of lips and jaw, and the face somehow conveyed an impression of transparency, almost of light, so delicately were the features refined away. On the fine forehead was that indefinable touch of peace that comes from identifying the mind with what is permanent in the soul, and letting the impermanent slip by without power to wound or distress; while, from his manner,—so gentle, quiet, sympathetic,—few could have guessed the strength of purpose that burned within like a great flame.

"I think I should describe it as a psychical case," continued the Swedish lady, obviously trying to explain herself very intelligently, "and just the kind you like. I mean a case where the cause is hidden deep down in some spiritual distress, and—"

"But the symptoms first, please, my dear Svenska," he interrupted, with a strangely compelling seriousness of manner, "and your deductions afterwards."

She turned round sharply on the edge of her chair and looked him in the face, lowering her voice to prevent her emotion betraying itself too obviously.

"In my opinion there's only one symptom," she half whispered, as though telling something disagreeable—"fear—simply fear."

"Physical fear?"

"I think not; though how can I say? I think it's a horror in the psychical region. It's no ordinary delusion; the man is quite sane; but he lives in mortal terror of something—"

"I don't know what you mean by his 'psychical region,'" said the doctor, with a smile; "though I suppose you wish me to understand that his spiritual, and not his mental, processes are affected. Anyhow, try and tell me briefly and pointedly what you know about the man, his symptoms, his need for help, *my* peculiar help, that is, and all that seems vital in the case. I promise to listen devotedly."

"I am trying," she continued earnestly, "but must do so in my own words and trust to your intelligence to disentangle as I go along.

He is a young author, and lives in a tiny house off Putney Heath somewhere. He writes humorous stories—quite a genre of his own: Pender—you must have heard the name—Felix Pender? Oh, the man had a great gift, and married on the strength of it; his future seemed assured. I say 'had,' for quite suddenly his talent utterly failed him. Worse, it became transformed into its opposite. He can no longer write a line in the old way that was bringing him success—"

Dr. Silence opened his eyes for a second and looked at her.

"He still writes, then? The force has not gone?" he asked briefly, and then closed his eyes again to listen.

"He works like a fury," she went on, "but produces nothing"—she hesitated a moment—"nothing that he can use or sell. His earnings have practically ceased, and he makes a precarious living by book-reviewing and odd jobs—very odd, some of them. Yet, I am certain his talent has not really deserted him finally, but is merely—"

Again Mrs. Sivendson hesitated for the appropriate word.

"In abeyance," he suggested, without opening his eyes.

"Obliterated," she went on, after a moment to weigh the word, "merely obliterated by something else—"

"By some *one* else?"

"I wish I knew. All I can say is that he is haunted, and temporarily his sense of humour is shrouded—gone—replaced by something dreadful that writes other things. Unless something competent is done, he will simply starve to death. Yet he is afraid to go to a doctor for fear of being pronounced insane; and, anyhow, a man can hardly ask a doctor to take a guinea to restore a vanished sense of humour, can he?"

"Has he tried any one at all—?"

"Not doctors yet. He tried some clergymen and religious people; but they *know* so little and have so little intelligent sympathy.

And most of them are so busy balancing on their own little pedestals—"

John Silence stopped her tirade with a gesture.

"And how is it that you know so much about him?" he asked gently.

"I know Mrs. Pender well—I knew her before she married him—"

"And is she a cause, perhaps?"

"Not in the least. She is devoted; a woman very well educated, though without being really intelligent, and with so little sense of humour herself that she always laughs at the wrong places. But she has nothing to do with the cause of his distress; and, indeed, has chiefly guessed it from observing him, rather than from what little he has told her. And he, you know, is a really lovable fellow, hard-working, patient—altogether worth saving."

Dr. Silence opened his eyes and went over to ring for tea. He did not know very much more about the case of the humorist than when he first sat down to listen; but he realised that no amount of words from his Swedish friend would help to reveal the real facts. A personal interview with the author himself could alone do that.

"All humorists are worth saving," he said with a smile, as she poured out tea. "We can't afford to lose a single one in these strenuous days. I will go and see your friend at the first opportunity."

She thanked him elaborately, effusively, with many words, and he, with much difficulty, kept the conversation thenceforward strictly to the teapot.

And, as a result of this conversation, and a little more he had gathered by means best known to himself and his secretary, he was whizzing in his motor-car one afternoon a few days later up the Putney Hill to have his first interview with Felix Pender, the humorous writer who was the victim of some mysterious malady in his "psychical region" that had obliterated his sense of the comic and threatened to wreck his life and destroy his talent. And his desire to help was probably of equal strength with his desire to know and to investigate.

The motor stopped with a deep purring sound, as though a great black panther lay concealed within its hood, and the doctor—the "psychic doctor," as he was sometimes called—stepped out through the gathering fog, and walked across the tiny garden that held a blackened fir tree and a stunted laurel shrubbery. The house was very small, and it was some time before any one answered the bell. Then, suddenly, a light appeared in the hall, and he saw a pretty little woman standing on the top step begging him to come in. She was dressed in grey, and the gaslight fell on a mass of deliberately brushed light hair. Stuffed, dusty birds, and a shabby array of African spears, hung on the wall behind her. A hat-rack, with a bronze plate full of very large cards, led his eye swiftly to a dark staircase beyond. Mrs. Pender had round eyes like a child's, and she greeted him with an effusiveness that barely concealed her emotion, yet strove to appear naturally cordial. Evidently she had been looking out for his arrival, and had outrun the servant girl. She was a little breathless.

"I hope you've not been kept waiting—I think it's *most* good of you to come—" she began, and then stopped sharp when she saw his face in the gaslight. There was something in Dr. Silence's look that did not encourage mere talk. He was in earnest now, if ever man was.

"Good evening, Mrs. Pender," he said, with a quiet smile that won confidence, yet deprecated unnecessary words, "the fog delayed me a little. I am glad to see you."

They went into a dingy sitting-room at the back of the house, neatly furnished but depressing. Books stood in a row upon the mantelpiece. The fire had evidently just been lit. It smoked in great puffs into the room.

"Mrs. Sivendson said she thought you might be able to come," ventured the little woman again, looking up engagingly into his face and betraying anxiety and eagerness in every gesture. "But I hardly dared to believe it. I think it is really too good of you. My husband's case is so peculiar that—well, you know, I am quite sure any *ordinary* doctor would say at once the asylum—"

"Isn't he in, then?" asked Dr. Silence gently.

"In the asylum?" she gasped. "Oh dear, no—not yet!"

"In the house, I meant," he laughed.

She gave a great sigh.

"He'll be back any minute now," she replied, obviously relieved to see him laugh; "but the fact is, we didn't expect you so early—I mean, my husband hardly thought you would come at all."

"I am always delighted to come—when I am really wanted, and can be of help," he said quickly; "and, perhaps, it's all for the best that your husband is out, for now that we are alone you can tell me something about his difficulties. So far, you know, I have heard very little."

Her voice trembled as she thanked him, and when he came and took a chair close beside her she actually had difficulty in finding words with which to begin.

"In the first place," she began timidly, and then continuing with a nervous incoherent rush of words, "he will be simply delighted that you've really come, because he said you were the only person he would consent to see at all—the only doctor, I mean. But, of course, he doesn't know how frightened I am, or how much I have noticed. He pretends with me that it's just a nervous breakdown, and I'm sure he doesn't realise all the odd things I've noticed him doing. But the main thing, I suppose—"

"Yes, the main thing, Mrs. Pender," he said encouragingly, noticing her hesitation.

"—is that he thinks we are not alone in the house. That's the chief thing."

"Tell me more facts—just facts."

"It began last summer when I came back from Ireland; he had been here alone for six weeks, and I thought him looking tired and queer—ragged and scattered about the face, if you know what I mean, and his manner worn out. He said he had been writing hard, but his inspiration had somehow failed him, and he was dissatisfied with his work. His sense of humour was leaving him, or changing into something else, he said. There was something in the house, he declared, that"—she emphasised the words—"prevented his feeling funny."

"Something in the house that prevented his feeling funny," repeated the doctor. "Ah, now we're getting to the heart of it!"

"Yes," she resumed vaguely; "that's what he kept saying."

"And what was it he *did* that you thought strange?" he asked sympathetically. "Be brief, or he may be here before you finish."

"Very small things, but significant it seemed to me. He changed his workroom from the library, as we call it, to the sitting-room. He said all his characters became wrong and terrible in the library; they altered, so that he felt like writing tragedies—vile, debased tragedies, the tragedies of broken souls. But now he says the same of the smoking-room, and he's gone back to the library."

"Ah!"

"You see, there's so little I can tell you," she went on, with increasing speed and countless gestures. "I mean it's only very small things he does and says that are queer. What frightens me is that he assumes there is some one else in the house all the time—some one

I never see. He does not actually say so, but on the stairs I've seen him standing aside to let some one pass; I've seen him open a door to let some one in or out; and often in our bedroom he puts chairs about as though for some one else to sit in. Oh—oh yes, and once or twice," she cried—"once or twice—"

She paused, and looked about her with a startled air.

"Yes?"

"Once or twice," she resumed hurriedly, as though she heard a sound that alarmed her, "I've heard him running—coming in and out of the rooms breathless as if something were after him—"

The door opened while she was still speaking, cutting her words off in the middle, and a man came into the room. He was dark and clean-shaven, sallow rather, with the eyes of imagination, and dark hair growing scantily about the temples. He was dressed in a shabby tweed suit, and wore an untidy flannel collar at the neck. The dominant expression of his face was startled—hunted; an expression that might any moment leap into the dreadful stare of terror and announce a total loss of self-control.

The moment he saw his visitor a smile spread over his worn features, and he advanced to shake hands.

"I hoped you would come; Mrs. Sivendson said you might be able to find time," he said simply. His voice was thin and reedy. "I am very glad to see you, Dr. Silence. It is 'Doctor,' is it not?"

"Well, I am entitled to the description," laughed the other, "but I rarely get it. You know, I do not practise as a regular thing; that is, I only take cases that specially interest me, or—"

He did not finish the sentence, for the men exchanged a glance of sympathy that rendered it unnecessary.

"I have heard of your great kindness."

"It's my hobby," said the other quickly, "and my privilege."

"I trust you will still think so when you have heard what I have to tell you," continued the author, a little wearily. He led the way across the hall into the little smoking-room where they could talk freely and undisturbed.

In the smoking-room, the door shut and privacy about them, Pender's attitude changed somewhat, and his manner became very grave. The doctor sat opposite, where he could watch his face. Already, he saw, it looked more haggard. Evidently it cost him much to refer to his trouble at all.

"What I have is, in my belief, a profound spiritual affliction," he began quite bluntly, looking straight into the other's eyes.

"I saw that at once," Dr. Silence said.

"Yes, you saw that, of course; my atmosphere must convey that much to any one with psychic perceptions. Besides which, I feel sure from all I've heard, that you are really a soul-doctor, are you not, more than a healer merely of the body?"

"You think of me too highly," returned the other; "though I prefer cases, as you know, in which the spirit is disturbed first, the body afterwards."

"I understand, yes. Well, I have experienced a curious disturbance in—*not* in my physical region primarily. I mean my nerves are all right, and my body is all right. I have no delusions exactly, but my spirit is tortured by a calamitous fear which first came upon me in a strange manner."

John Silence leaned forward a moment and took the speaker's hand and held it in his own for a few brief seconds, closing his eyes as he did so. He was not feeling his pulse, or doing any of the things that doctors ordinarily do; he was merely absorbing into himself the main note of the man's mental condition, so as to get completely his own point of view, and thus be able to treat his case with true sympathy. A very close observer might perhaps have noticed that a slight tremor ran through his frame after he had held the hand for a few seconds.

"Tell me quite frankly, Mr. Pender," he said soothingly, releasing the hand, and with deep attention in his manner, "tell me all the steps that led to the beginning of this invasion. I mean tell me what the particular drug was, and why you took it, and how it affected you—"

"Then you know it began with a drug!" cried the author, with undisguised astonishment.

"I only know from what I observe in you, and in its effect upon myself. You are in a surprising psychical condition. Certain portions of your atmosphere are vibrating at a far greater rate than others. This is the effect of a drug, but of no ordinary drug. Allow me to finish, please. If the higher rate of vibration spreads all over, you will become, of course, permanently cognisant of a much larger world than the one you know normally. If, on the other hand, the rapid portion sinks back to the usual rate, you will lose these occasional increased perceptions you now have."

"You amaze me!" exclaimed the author; "for your words exactly describe what I have been feeling—"

"I mention this only in passing, and to give you confidence before you approach the account of your real affliction," continued the doctor. "All perception, as you know, is the result of vibrations; and clairvoyance simply means becoming sensitive to an increased scale of vibrations. The awakening of the inner senses we hear so much about means no more than that. Your partial clairvoyance is easily explained. The only thing that puzzles me is how you managed to procure the drug, for it is not easy to get in pure form, and no adulterated tincture could have given you the terrific impetus I see you have acquired. But, please proceed now and tell me your story in your own way."

"This *Cannabis indica*," the author went on, "came into my possession last autumn while my wife was away. I need not explain how I got it, for that has no importance; but it was the genuine fluid extract, and I could not resist the temptation to make an experiment. One of its effects, as you know, is to induce torrential laughter—"

"Yes; sometimes."

"—I am a writer of humorous tales, and I wished to increase my own sense of laughter—to see the ludicrous from an abnormal point of view. I wished to study it a bit, if possible, and—"

"Tell me!"

"I took an experimental dose. I starved for six hours to hasten the effect, locked myself into this room, and gave orders not to be disturbed. Then I swallowed the stuff and waited."

"And the effect?"

"I waited one hour, two, three, four, five hours. Nothing happened. No laughter came, but only a great weariness instead. Nothing in the room or in my thoughts came within a hundred miles of a humorous aspect."

"Always a most uncertain drug," interrupted the doctor. "We make very small use of it on that account."

"At two o'clock in the morning I felt so hungry and tired that I decided to give up the experiment and wait no longer. I drank some milk and went upstairs to bed. I felt flat and disappointed. I fell asleep at once and must have slept for about an hour, when I awoke suddenly with a great noise in my ears. It was the noise of my own laughter! I was simply shaking with merriment. At first I was bewildered and thought I had been laughing in dreams, but a moment later I remembered the drug, and was delighted to think that after all I had got an effect. It had been working all along, only I had miscalculated the time. The only unpleasant thing *then* was an odd feeling that I had not waked naturally, but had been wakened by some one else—deliberately. This came to me as a certainty in the middle of my noisy laughter and distressed me."

"Any impression who it could have been?" asked the doctor, now listening with close attention to every word, very much on the alert.

Pender hesitated and tried to smile. He brushed his hair from his forehead with a nervous gesture.

"You must tell me all your impressions, even your fancies; they are quite as important as your certainties."

"I had a vague idea that it was some one connected with my forgotten dream, some one who had been at me in my sleep, some one of great strength and great ability—of great force—quite an unusual personality—and, I was certain, too—a woman."

"A good woman?" asked John Silence quietly.

Pender started a little at the question and his sallow face flushed; it seemed to surprise him. But he shook his head quickly with an indefinable look of horror.

"Evil," he answered briefly, "appallingly evil, and yet mingled with the sheer wickedness of it was also a certain perverseness—the perversity of the unbalanced mind."

He hesitated a moment and looked up sharply at his interlocutor. A shade of suspicion showed itself in his eyes.

"No," laughed the doctor, "you need not fear that I'm merely humouring you, or think you mad. Far from it. Your story interests me exceedingly and you furnish me unconsciously with a number of clues as you tell it. You see, I possess some knowledge of my own as to these psychic byways."

"I was shaking with such violent laughter," continued the narrator, reassured in a moment, "though with no clear idea what was amusing me, that I had the greatest difficulty in getting up for the matches, and was afraid I should frighten the servants overhead with my explosions. When the gas was lit I found the room empty, of course, and the door locked as usual. Then I half dressed and went out on to the landing, my hilarity better under control, and proceeded to go downstairs. I wished to record my sensations. I stuffed a handkerchief into my mouth so as not to scream aloud and communicate my hysterics to the entire household."

"And the presence of this—this—?"

"It was hanging about me all the time," said Pender, "but for the moment it seemed to have withdrawn. Probably, too, my laughter killed all other emotions."

"And how long did you take getting downstairs?"

"I was just coming to that. I see you know all my 'symptoms' in advance, as it were; for, of course, I thought I should never get to the bottom. Each step seemed to take five minutes, and crossing the narrow hall at the foot of the stairs—well, I could have sworn it was half an hour's journey had not my watch certified that it was a few seconds. Yet I walked fast and tried to push on. It was no good. I walked apparently without advancing, and at that rate it would have taken me a week to get down Putney Hill."

"An experimental dose radically alters the scale of time and space sometimes—"

"But, when at last I got into my study and lit the gas, the change came horridly, and sudden as a flash of lightning. It was like a douche of icy water, and in the middle of this storm of laughter—"

"Yes; what?" asked the doctor, leaning forward and peering into his eyes.

"—I was overwhelmed with terror," said Pender, lowering his reedy voice at the mere recollection of it.

He paused a moment and mopped his forehead. The scared, hunted look in his eyes now dominated the whole face. Yet, all the time, the corners of his mouth hinted of possible laughter as though the recollection of that merriment still amused him. The combination of fear and laughter in his face was very curious, and lent great conviction to his story; it also lent a bizarre expression of horror to his gestures.

"Terror, was it?" repeated the doctor soothingly.

"Yes, terror; for, though the Thing that woke me seemed to have gone, the memory of it still frightened me, and I collapsed into a chair. Then I locked the door and tried to reason with myself, but the drug made my movements so prolonged that it took me five minutes to reach the door, and another five to get back to the chair again. The laughter, too, kept bubbling up inside me—great wholesome laughter that shook me like gusts of wind—so that even my terror almost made me laugh. Oh, but I may tell you, Dr. Silence, it was altogether vile, that mixture of fear and laughter, altogether vile!

"Then, all at once, the things in the room again presented their funny side to me and set me off laughing more furiously than ever. The bookcase was ludicrous, the arm-chair a perfect clown, the way the clock looked at me on the mantelpiece too comic for words; the arrangement of papers and inkstand on the desk tickled me till I roared and shook and held my sides and the tears streamed down my cheeks. And that footstool! Oh, that absurd footstool!"

He lay back in his chair, laughing to himself and holding up his hands at the thought of it, and at the sight of him Dr. Silence laughed too.

"Go on, please," he said, "I quite understand. I know something myself of the hashish laughter."

The author pulled himself together and resumed, his face growing quickly grave again.

"So, you see, side by side with this extravagant, apparently causeless merriment, there was also an extravagant, apparently causeless terror. The drug produced the laughter, I knew; but what brought in the terror I could not imagine. Everywhere behind the fun lay the fear. It was terror masked by cap and bells; and I became the playground for two opposing emotions, armed and fighting to the death. Gradually, then, the impression grew in me that this fear was caused by the invasion—so you called it just now—of the 'person' who had wakened me: she was utterly evil; inimical to my soul, or at least to all in me that wished for good. There I stood, sweating and trembling, laughing at everything in the room, yet all the while with this white terror mastering my heart. And this creature was putting—putting her—"

He hesitated again, using his handkerchief freely.

"Putting what?"

"—putting ideas into my mind," he went on glancing nervously about the room. "Actually tapping my thought-stream so as to switch off the usual current and inject her own. How mad that sounds! I know it, but it's true. It's the only way I can express it. Moreover, while the operation terrified me, the skill with which it was accomplished filled me afresh with laughter at the clumsiness of men by comparison. Our ignorant, bungling methods of teaching the minds of others, of inculcating ideas, and so on, overwhelmed me with laughter when I understood this superior and diabolical method. Yet my laughter seemed hollow and ghastly, and ideas of evil and tragedy trod close upon the heels of the comic. Oh, doctor, I tell you again, it was unnerving!"

John Silence sat with his head thrust forward to catch every word of the story which the other continued to pour out in nervous, jerky sentences and lowered voice.

"You *saw* nothing—no one—all this time?" he asked.

"Not with my eyes. There was no visual hallucination. But in my mind there began to grow the vivid picture of a woman—large, dark-skinned, with white teeth and masculine features, and one eye—the left—so drooping as to appear almost closed. Oh, such a face—!"

"A face you would recognise again?"

Pender laughed dreadfully.

"I wish I could forget it," he whispered, "I only wish I could forget it!" Then he sat forward in his chair suddenly, and grasped the doctor's hand with an emotional gesture.

"I *must* tell you how grateful I am for your patience and sympathy," he cried, with a tremor in his voice, "and—that you do not think me mad. I have told no one else a quarter of all this, and the mere freedom of speech—the relief of sharing my affliction with another—has helped me already more than I can possibly say."

Dr. Silence pressed his hand and looked steadily into the frightened eyes. His voice was very gentle when he replied.

"Your case, you know, is very singular, but of absorbing interest to me," he said, "for it threatens, not your physical existence, but the temple of your psychical existence—the inner life. Your mind would not be permanently affected here and now, in this world; but in the existence after the body is left behind, you might wake up with your spirit so twisted, so distorted, so befouled, that you would be *spiritually insane*—a far more radical condition than merely being insane here."

There came a strange hush over the room, and between the two men sitting there facing one another.

"Do you really mean—Good Lord!" stammered the author as soon as he could find his tongue.

"What I mean in detail will keep till a little later, and I need only say now that I should not have spoken in this way unless I were quite positive of being able to help you. Oh, there's no doubt as to that, believe me. In the first place, I am very familiar with the workings of this extraordinary drug, this drug which has had the chance effect of opening you up to the forces of another region; and, in the second, I have a firm belief in the reality of super-sensuous occurrences as well as considerable knowledge of psychic processes acquired by long and painful experiment. The rest is, or should be, merely sympathetic treatment and practical application. The hashish has partially opened another world to you by increasing your rate of psychical vibration, and thus rendering you abnormally sensitive. Ancient forces attached to this house have attacked you. For the moment I am only puzzled as to their precise nature; for were they of an ordinary character, I should myself be psychic enough to feel them. Yet I am conscious of feeling nothing as yet. But now, please continue, Mr. Pender, and tell me the rest of your wonderful story; and when you have finished, I will talk about the means of cure."

Pender shifted his chair a little closer to the friendly doctor and then went on in the same nervous voice with his narrative.

"After making some notes of my impressions I finally got upstairs again to bed. It was four o'clock in the morning. I laughed all the way up—at the grotesque banisters, the droll physiognomy of the staircase window, the burlesque grouping of the furniture, and the memory of that outrageous footstool in the room below; but nothing more happened to alarm or disturb me, and I woke late in the morning after a dreamless sleep, none the worse for my experiment except for a slight headache and a coldness of the extremities due to lowered circulation."

"Fear gone, too?" asked the doctor.

"I seemed to have forgotten it, or at least ascribed it to mere nervousness. Its reality had gone, anyhow for the time, and all that day I wrote and wrote and wrote. My sense of laughter seemed wonderfully quickened and my characters acted without effort out of the heart of true humour. I was exceedingly pleased with this result of my experiment. But when the stenographer had taken her departure and I came to read over the pages she had typed out, I recalled her sudden glances of surprise and the odd way she had looked up at me while I was dictating. I was amazed at what I read and could hardly believe I had uttered it."

"And why?"

"It was so distorted. The words, indeed, were mine so far as I could remember, but the meanings seemed strange. It frightened me. The sense was so altered. At the very places where my characters were intended to tickle the ribs, only curious emotions of sinister amusement resulted. Dreadful innuendoes had managed to creep into the phrases. There was laughter of a kind, but it was bizarre, horrible, distressing; and my attempt at analysis only increased my dismay. The story, as it read then, made me shudder, for by virtue of these slight changes it had come somehow to hold the soul of horror, of horror disguised as merriment. The framework of humour was there, if you understand me, but the characters had turned sinister, and their laughter was evil."

"Can you show me this writing?"

The author shook his head.

"I destroyed it," he whispered. "But, in the end, though of course much perturbed about it, I persuaded myself that it was due to some after-effect of the drug, a sort of reaction that gave a twist to my mind and made me read macabre interpretations into words and situations that did not properly hold them."

"And, meanwhile, did the presence of this person leave you?"

"No; that stayed more or less. When my mind was actively employed I forgot it, but when idle, dreaming, or doing nothing in particular, there she was beside me, influencing my mind horribly—"

"In what way, precisely?" interrupted the doctor.

"Evil, scheming thoughts came to me, visions of crime, hateful pictures of wickedness, and the kind of bad imagination that so far has been foreign, indeed impossible, to my normal nature—"

"The pressure of the Dark Powers upon the personality," murmured the doctor, making a quick note.

"Eh? I didn't quite catch—"

"Pray, go on. I am merely making notes; you shall know their purport fully later."

"Even when my wife returned I was still aware of this Presence in the house; it associated itself with my inner personality in most intimate fashion; and outwardly I always felt oddly constrained to be polite and respectful towards it—to open doors, provide chairs and hold myself carefully deferential when it was about. It became very compelling at last, and, if I failed in any little particular, I seemed to know that it pursued me about the house, from one room to another, haunting my very soul in its inmost abode. It certainly came before my wife so far as my attentions were concerned.

"But, let me first finish the story of my experimental dose, for I took it again the third night, and underwent a very similar experience, delayed like the first in coming, and then carrying me off my feet when it did come with a rush of this false demon-laughter. This time, however, there was a reversal of the changed scale of space and time; it shortened instead of lengthened, so that I dressed and got downstairs in about twenty seconds, and the couple of hours I stayed and worked in the study passed literally like a period of ten minutes."

"That is often true of an overdose," interjected the doctor, "and you may go a mile in a few minutes, or a few yards in a quarter of an hour. It is quite incomprehensible to those who have never experienced it, and is a curious proof that time and space are merely forms of thought."

"This time," Pender went on, talking more and more rapidly in his excitement, "another extraordinary effect came to me, and I experienced a curious changing of the senses, so that I perceived external things through one large main sense-channel instead of through the five divisions known as sight, smell, touch, and so forth. You will, I know, understand me when I tell you that I *heard* sights and *saw* sounds. No language can make this comprehensible, of course, and I can only say, for instance, that the striking of the clock I saw as a visible picture in the air before me. I saw the sounds of the tinkling bell. And in precisely the same way I heard the colours in the room, especially the colours of those books in the shelf behind you. Those red bindings I heard in deep sounds, and the yellow covers of the French bindings next to them made a shrill, piercing note not unlike the chattering of starlings. That brown bookcase muttered, and those green curtains opposite kept up a constant sort of rippling sound like the lower notes of a wood-horn. But I only was conscious of these sounds when I looked steadily at the different objects, and thought about them. The room, you understand, was not full of a chorus of notes; but when I concentrated my mind upon a colour, I heard, as well as saw, it."

"That is a known, though rarely-obtained, effect of *Cannabis indica*," observed the doctor. "And it provoked laughter again, did it?"

"Only the muttering of the cupboard-bookcase made me laugh. It was so like a great animal trying to get itself noticed, and made me think of a performing bear—which is full of a kind of pathetic humour, you know. But this mingling of the senses produced no confusion in my brain. On the contrary, I was unusually clear-headed and experienced an intensification of consciousness, and felt marvellously alive and keen-minded.

"Moreover, when I took up a pencil in obedience to an impulse to sketch—a talent not normally mine—I found that I could draw nothing but heads, nothing, in fact, but one head—always the same—the head of a dark-skinned woman, with huge and terrible features and a very drooping left eye; and so well drawn, too, that I was amazed, as you may imagine—"

"And the expression of the face—?"

Pender hesitated a moment for words, casting about with his hands in the air and hunching his shoulders. A perceptible shudder ran over him.

"What I can only describe as—*blackness*," he replied in a low tone; "the face of a dark and evil soul."

"You destroyed that, too?" queried the doctor sharply.

"No; I have kept the drawings," he said, with a laugh, and rose to get them from a drawer in the writing-desk behind him.

"Here is all that remains of the pictures, you see," he added, pushing a number of loose sheets under the doctor's eyes; "nothing but a few scrawly lines. That's all I found the next morning. I had really drawn no heads at all—nothing but those lines and blots and wriggles. The pictures were entirely subjective, and existed only in my mind which constructed them out of a few wild strokes of the pen. Like the altered scale of space and time it was a complete delusion. These all passed, of course, with the passing of the drug's effects. But the other thing did not pass. I mean, the presence of that Dark Soul remained with me. It is here still. It is real. I don't know how I can escape from it."

"It is attached to the house, not to you personally. You must leave the house."

"Yes. Only I cannot afford to leave the house, for my work is my sole means of support, and—well, you see, since this change I cannot even write. They are horrible, these mirthless tales I now write, with their mockery of laughter, their diabolical suggestion. Horrible! I shall go mad if this continues."

He screwed his face up and looked about the room as though he expected to see some haunting shape.

"The influence in this house, induced by my experiment, has killed in a flash, in a sudden stroke, the sources of my humour, and, though I still go on writing funny tales—I have a certain name, you know—my inspiration has dried up, and much of what I write I have to burn—yes, doctor, to burn, before any one sees it."

"As utterly alien to your own mind and personality?"

"Utterly! As though some one else had written it—"

"Ah!"

"And shocking!" He passed his hand over his eyes a moment and let the breath escape softly through his teeth. "Yet most damnably clever in the consummate way the vile suggestions are insinuated under cover of a kind of high drollery. My stenographer left me, of course—and I've been afraid to take another—"

John Silence got up and began to walk about the room leisurely without speaking; he appeared to be examining the pictures on the wall and reading the names of the books lying about. Presently he paused on the hearthrug, with his back to the fire, and turned to look his patient quietly in the eyes. Pender's face was grey and drawn; the hunted expression dominated it; the long recital had told upon him.

"Thank you, Mr. Pender," he said, a curious glow showing about his fine, quiet face, "thank you for the sincerity and frankness of your account. But I think now there is nothing further I need ask you." He indulged in a long scrutiny of the author's haggard features, drawing purposely the man's eyes to his own and then meeting them with a look of power and confidence calculated to inspire even the feeblest soul with courage. "And, to begin with," he added, smiling pleasantly, "let me assure you without delay that you need have no alarm, for you are no more insane or deluded than I myself am—"

Pender heaved a deep sigh and tried to return the smile.

"—and this is simply a case, so far as I can judge at present, of a very singular psychical invasion, and a very sinister one, too, if you perhaps understand what I mean—"

"It's an odd expression; you used it before, you know," said the author wearily, yet eagerly listening to every word of the diagnosis, and deeply touched by the intelligent sympathy which did not at once indicate the lunatic asylum.

"Possibly," returned the other, "and an odd affliction too, you'll allow, yet one not unknown to the nations of antiquity, nor to those moderns, perhaps, who recognise the freedom of action under certain pathogenic conditions between this world and another."

"And you think," asked Pender hastily, "that it is all primarily due to the *Cannabis*? There is nothing radically amiss with myself—nothing incurable, or—?"

"Due entirely to the overdose," Dr. Silence replied emphatically, "to the drug's direct action upon your psychical being. It rendered you ultra-sensitive and made you respond to an increased rate of vibration. And, let me tell you, Mr. Pender, that your experiment might have had results far more dire. It has brought you into touch with a somewhat singular class of Invisible, but of one, I think, chiefly human in character. You might, however, just as easily have been drawn out of human range altogether, and the results of such a contingency would have been exceedingly terrible. Indeed, you would not now be here to tell the tale. I need not alarm you on that score, but mention it as a warning you will not misunderstand or underrate after what you have been through.

"You look puzzled. You do not quite gather what I am driving at; and it is not to be expected that you should, for you, I suppose, are the nominal Christian with the nominal Christian's lofty standard of ethics, and his utter ignorance of spiritual possibilities. Beyond a somewhat childish understanding of 'spiritual wickedness in high places,' you probably have no conception of what is possible once you break down the slender gulf that is mercifully fixed between you and that Outer World. But my studies and training have taken me far outside these orthodox trips, and I have made experiments that I could scarcely speak to you about in language that would be intelligible to you."

He paused a moment to note the breathless interest of Pender's face and manner. Every word he uttered was calculated; he knew exactly the value and effect of the emotions he desired to waken in the heart of the afflicted being before him.

"And from certain knowledge I have gained through various experiences," he continued calmly, "I can diagnose your case as I said before to be one of psychical invasion."

"And the nature of this—er—invasion?" stammered the bewildered writer of humorous tales.

"There is no reason why I should not say at once that I do not yet quite know," replied Dr. Silence. "I may first have to make one or two experiments—"

"On me?" gasped Pender, catching his breath.

"Not exactly," the doctor said, with a grave smile, "but with your assistance, perhaps. I shall want to test the conditions of the house—to ascertain, if possible, the character of the forces, of this strange personality that has been haunting you—"

"At present you have no idea exactly who—what—why—" asked the other in a wild flurry of interest, dread and amazement.

"I have a very good idea, but no proof rather," returned the doctor. "The effects of the drug in altering the scale of time and space, and merging the senses have nothing primarily to do with the invasion. They come to any one who is fool enough to take an experimental dose. It is the other features of your case that are unusual. You see, you are now in touch with certain violent emotions, desires, purposes, still active in this house, that were produced in the past by some powerful and evil personality that lived here. How long ago, or why they still persist so forcibly, I cannot positively say. But I should judge that they are merely forces acting automatically with the momentum of their terrific original impetus."

"Not directed by a living being, a conscious will, you mean?"

"Possibly not—but none the less dangerous on that account, and more difficult to deal with. I cannot explain to you in a few minutes the nature of such things, for you have not made the studies that would enable you to follow me; but I have reason to believe that on the dissolution at death of a human being, its forces may still persist and continue to act in a blind, unconscious fashion. As a rule they speedily dissipate themselves, but in the case of a very powerful personality they may last a long time. And, in some cases—of which I incline to think this is one—these forces may coalesce with certain non-human entities who thus continue their life indefinitely and increase their strength to an unbelievable degree. If the original personality was evil, the beings attracted to the left-over forces will also be evil. In this case, I think there has been an unusual and dreadful aggrandisement of the thoughts and purposes left behind long ago by a woman of consummate wickedness and great personal power of character and intellect. Now, do you begin to see what I am driving at a little?"

Pender stared fixedly at his companion, plain horror showing in his eyes. But he found nothing to say, and the doctor continued—

"In your case, predisposed by the action of the drug, you have experienced the rush of these forces in undiluted strength. They wholly obliterate in you the sense of humour, fancy, imagination,—all that makes for cheerfulness and hope. They seek, though perhaps automatically only, to oust your own thoughts and establish themselves in their place. You are the victim of a psychical invasion. At the same time, you have become clairvoyant in the true sense. You are also a clairvoyant victim."

Pender mopped his face and sighed. He left his chair and went over to the fireplace to warm himself.

"You must think me a quack to talk like this, or a madman," laughed Dr. Silence. "But never mind that. I have come to help you, and I can help you if you will do what I tell you. It is very simple: you must leave this house at once. Oh, never mind the difficulties; we will deal with those together. I can place another house at your disposal, or I would take the lease here off your hands, and later have it pulled down. Your case interests me greatly, and I mean to see you through, so that you have no anxiety, and can drop back into your old groove of work tomorrow! The drug has provided you, and therefore me, with a short-cut to a very interesting experience. I am grateful to you."

The author poked the fire vigorously, emotion rising in him like a tide. He glanced towards the door nervously.

"There is no need to alarm your wife or to tell her the details of our conversation," pursued the other quietly. "Let her know that you will soon be in possession again of your sense of humour and your health, and explain that I am lending you another house for six months. Meanwhile I may have the right to use this house for a night or two for my experiment. Is that understood between us?"

"I can only thank you from the bottom of my heart," stammered Pender, unable to find words to express his gratitude.

Then he hesitated for a moment, searching the doctor's face anxiously.

"And your experiment with the house?" he said at length.

"Of the simplest character, my dear Mr. Pender. Although I am myself an artificially trained psychic, and consequently aware of the presence of discarnate entities as a rule, I have so far felt nothing here at all. This makes me sure that the forces acting here are of an unusual description. What I propose to do is to make an experiment with a view of drawing out this evil, coaxing it from its lair, so to speak, in order that it may *exhaust itself through me* and become dissipated for ever. I have already been inoculated," he added; "I consider myself to be immune."

"Heavens above!" gasped the author, collapsing on to a chair.

"Hell beneath! might be a more appropriate exclamation," the doctor laughed. "But, seriously, Mr. Pender, this is what I propose to do—with your permission."

"Of course, of course," cried the other, "you have my permission and my best wishes for success. I can see no possible objection, but—"

"But what?"

"I pray to Heaven you will not undertake this experiment alone, will you?"

"Oh dear, no; not alone."

"You will take a companion with good nerves, and reliable in case of disaster, won't you?"

"I shall bring two companions," the doctor said.

"Ah, that's better. I feel easier. I am sure you must have among your acquaintances men who—"

"I shall not think of bringing men, Mr. Pender."

The other looked up sharply.

"No, or women either; or children."

"I don't understand. Who will you bring, then?"

"Animals," explained the doctor, unable to prevent a smile at his companion's expression of surprise—"two animals, a cat and a dog."

Pender stared as if his eyes would drop out upon the floor, and then led the way without another word into the adjoining room where his wife was awaiting them for tea.

II

A few days later the humorist and his wife, with minds greatly relieved, moved into a small furnished house placed at their free disposal in another part of London; and John Silence, intent upon his approaching experiment, made ready to spend a night in the empty house on the top of Putney Hill. Only two rooms were prepared for occupation: the study on the ground floor and the bedroom immediately above it; all other doors were to be locked, and no servant was to be left in the house. The motor had orders to call for him at nine o'clock the following morning.

And, meanwhile, his secretary had instructions to look up the past history and associations of the place, and learn everything he could concerning the character of former occupants, recent or remote.

The animals, by whose sensitiveness he intended to test any unusual conditions in the atmosphere of the building, Dr. Silence selected with care and judgement. He believed (and had already made curious experiments to prove it) that animals were more often, and more truly, clairvoyant than human beings. Many of them, he felt convinced, possessed powers of perception far superior to that mere keenness of the senses common to all dwellers in the wilds where the senses grow specially alert; they had what he termed "animal clairvoyance," and from his experiments with horses, dogs, cats, and even birds, he had drawn certain deductions, which, however, need not be referred to in detail here.

Cats, in particular, he believed, were almost continuously conscious of a larger field of vision, too detailed even for a photographic camera, and quite beyond the reach of normal human organs. He had, further, observed that while dogs were usually terrified in the presence of such phenomena, cats on the other hand were soothed and satisfied. They welcomed manifestations as something belonging peculiarly to their own region.

He selected his animals, therefore, with wisdom so that they might afford a differing test, each in its own way, and that one should not merely communicate its own excitement to the other. He took a dog and a cat.

The cat he chose, now full grown, had lived with him since kittenhood, a kittenhood of perplexing sweetness and audacious mischief. Wayward it was and fanciful, ever playing its own mysterious games in the corners of the room, jumping at invisible nothings, leaping sideways into the air and falling with tiny moccasined feet on to another part of the carpet, yet with an air of dignified earnestness which showed that the performance was necessary to its own well-being, and not done merely to impress a stupid human audience. In the middle of elaborate washing it would look up, startled, as though to stare at the approach of some Invisible, cocking its little head sideways and putting out a velvet pad to inspect cautiously. Then it would get absent-minded, and stare with equal intentness in another direction (just to confuse the onlookers), and suddenly go on furiously washing its body again, but in quite a new place. Except for a white patch on its breast it was coal black. And its name was—Smoke.

"Smoke" described its temperament as well as its appearance. Its movements, its individuality, its posing as a little furry mass of concealed mysteries, its elfin-like elusiveness, all combined to justify its name; and a subtle painter might have pictured it as a wisp of floating smoke, the fire below betraying itself at two points only—the glowing eyes.

All its forces ran to intelligence—secret intelligence, the wordless, incalculable intuition of the Cat. It was, indeed, *the* cat for the business in hand.

The selection of the dog was not so simple, for the doctor owned many; but after much deliberation he chose a collie, called Flame from his yellow coat. True, it was a trifle old, and stiff in the joints, and even beginning to grow deaf, but, on the other hand, it was a very particular friend of Smoke's, and had fathered it from kittenhood upwards so that a subtle understanding existed between them. It was this that turned the balance in its favour, this and its courage. Moreover, though good-tempered, it was a terrible fighter, and its anger when provoked by a righteous cause was a fury of fire, and irresistible.

It had come to him quite young, straight from the shepherd, with the air of the hills yet in its nostrils, and was then little more than skin and bones and teeth. For a collie it was sturdily built, its nose blunter than most, its yellow hair stiff rather than silky, and it had full eyes, unlike the slit eyes of its breed. Only its master could touch it, for it ignored strangers, and despised their pattings—when any dared to pat it. There was something patriarchal about the old beast. He was in earnest, and went through life with tremendous energy and big things in view, as though he had the reputation of his whole race to uphold. And to watch him fighting against odds was to understand why he was terrible.

In his relations with Smoke he was always absurdly gentle; also he was fatherly; and at the same time betrayed a certain diffidence or shyness. He recognised that Smoke called for strong yet respectful management. The cat's circuitous methods puzzled him, and his elaborate pretences perhaps shocked the dog's liking for direct, undisguised action. Yet, while he failed to comprehend these tortuous feline mysteries, he was never contemptuous or condescending; and he presided over the safety of his furry black friend somewhat as a father, loving but intuitive, might superintend the vagaries of a wayward and talented child. And, in return, Smoke rewarded him with exhibitions of fascinating and audacious mischief.

And these brief descriptions of their characters are necessary for the proper understanding of what subsequently took place.

With Smoke sleeping in the folds of his fur coat, and the collie lying watchful on the seat opposite, John Silence went down in his motor after dinner on the night of November 15th.

And the fog was so dense that they were obliged to travel at quarter speed the entire way.

It was after ten o'clock when he dismissed the motor and entered the dingy little house with the latchkey provided by Pender. He found the hall gas turned low, and a fire in the study. Books and food had also been placed ready by the servant according to instructions. Coils of fog rushed in after him through the opened door and filled the hall and passage with its cold discomfort.

The first thing Dr. Silence did was to lock up Smoke in the study with a saucer of milk before the fire, and then make a search of the house with Flame. The dog ran cheerfully behind him all the way while he tried the doors of the other rooms to make sure they were locked. He nosed about into corners and made little excursions on his own account. His manner was expectant. He knew there must be something unusual about the proceeding, because it was contrary to the habits of his whole life not to be asleep at this hour on the mat in front of the fire. He kept looking up into his master's face, as door after door was tried, with an expression of intelligent sympathy, but at the same time a certain air of disapproval. Yet everything his master did was good in his eyes, and he betrayed as little impatience as possible with all this unnecessary journeying to and fro. If the doctor was pleased to play this sort of game at such an hour of the night, it was surely not for him to object. So he played it too; and was very busy and earnest about it into the bargain.

After an uneventful search they came down again to the study, and here Dr. Silence discovered Smoke washing his face calmly in front of the fire. The saucer of milk was licked dry and clean; the preliminary examination that cats always make in new surroundings had evidently been satisfactorily concluded. He drew an arm-chair up to the fire, stirred the coals into a blaze, arranged the table and lamp to his satisfaction for reading, and then prepared surreptitiously to watch the animals. He wished to observe them carefully without their being aware of it.

Now, in spite of their respective ages, it was the regular custom of these two to play together every night before sleep. Smoke always made the advances, beginning with grave impudence to pat the dog's tail, and Flame played cumbrously, with condescension. It was his duty, rather than pleasure; he was glad when it was over, and sometimes he was very determined and refused to play at all.

And this night was one of the occasions on which he was firm.

The doctor, looking cautiously over the top of his book, watched the cat begin the performance. It started by gazing with an innocent expression at the dog where he lay with nose on paws and eyes wide open in the middle of the floor. Then it got up and made as though it meant to walk to the door, going deliberately and very softly. Flame's eyes followed it until it was beyond the range of sight, and then the cat turned sharply and began patting his tail tentatively with one paw. The tail moved slightly in reply, and Smoke changed paws and tapped it again. The dog, however, did not rise to play as was his wont, and the cat fell to patting it briskly with both paws. Flame still lay motionless.

This puzzled and bored the cat, and it went round and stared hard into its friend's face to see what was the matter. Perhaps some inarticulate message flashed from the dog's eyes into its own little brain, making it understand that the programme for the night had better not begin with play. Perhaps it only realised that its friend was immovable. But, whatever the reason, its usual persistence thenceforward deserted it, and it made no further attempts at persuasion. Smoke yielded at once to the dog's mood; it sat down where it was and began to wash.

But the washing, the doctor noted, was by no means its real purpose; it only used it to mask something else; it stopped at the most busy and furious moments and began to stare about the room. Its thoughts wandered absurdly. It peered intently at the curtains; at the shadowy corners; at empty space above; leaving its body in curiously awkward positions for whole minutes together. Then it turned sharply and stared with a sudden signal of intelligence at the dog, and Flame at once rose somewhat stiffly to his feet and began to wander aimlessly and restlessly to and fro about the floor. Smoke followed him, padding quietly at his heels. Between them they made what seemed to be a deliberate search of the room.

And, here, as he watched them, noting carefully every detail of the performance over the top of his book, yet making no effort to interfere, it seemed to the doctor that the first beginnings of a faint distress betrayed themselves in the collie, and in the cat the stirrings of a vague excitement.

He observed them closely. The fog was thick in the air, and the tobacco smoke from his pipe added to its density; the furniture at the far end stood mistily, and where the shadows congregated in hanging clouds under the ceiling, it was difficult to see clearly at all; the lamplight only reached to a level of five feet from the floor, above which came layers of comparative darkness, so that the room appeared twice as lofty as it actually was. By means of the lamp and the fire, however, the carpet was everywhere clearly visible.

The animals made their silent tour of the floor, sometimes the dog leading, sometimes the cat; occasionally they looked at one another as though exchanging signals; and once or twice, in spite of the limited space, he lost sight of one or other among the fog and the shadows. Their curiosity, it appeared to him, was something more than the excitement lurking in the unknown territory of a strange room; yet, so far, it was impossible to test this, and he purposely kept his mind quietly receptive lest the smallest mental excitement on his part should communicate itself to the animals and thus destroy the value of their independent behaviour.

They made a very thorough journey, leaving no piece of furniture unexamined, or unsmelt. Flame led the way, walking slowly with lowered head, and Smoke followed demurely at his heels, making a transparent pretence of not being interested, yet missing nothing. And, at length, they returned, the old collie first, and came to rest on the mat before the fire. Flame rested his muzzle on his master's knee, smiling beatifically while he patted the yellow head and spoke his name; and Smoke, coming a little later, pretending he came by chance, looked from the empty saucer to his face, lapped up the milk when it was given him to the last drop, and then sprang upon his knees and curled round for the sleep it had fully earned and intended to enjoy.

Silence descended upon the room. Only the breathing of the dog upon the mat came through the deep stillness, like the pulse of time marking the minutes; and the steady drip, drip of the fog outside upon the window-ledges dismally testified to the inclemency of the night beyond. And the soft crashings of the coals as the fire settled down into the grate became less and less audible as the fire sank and the flames resigned their fierceness.

It was now well after eleven o'clock, and Dr. Silence devoted himself again to his book. He read the words on the printed page and took in their meaning superficially, yet without starting into life the correlations of thought and suggestion that should accompany interesting reading. Underneath, all the while, his mental energies were absorbed in watching, listening, waiting for what might come. He was not over sanguine himself, yet he did not wish to be taken by surprise. Moreover, the animals, his sensitive barometers, had incontinently gone to sleep.

After reading a dozen pages, however, he realised that his mind was really occupied in reviewing the features of Pender's extraordinary story, and that it was no longer necessary to steady his imagination by studying the dull paragraphs detailed in the pages before him. He laid down his book accordingly, and allowed his thoughts to dwell upon the features of the Case. Speculations as to the meaning, however, he rigorously suppressed, knowing that such thoughts would act upon his imagination like wind upon the glowing embers of a fire.

As the night wore on the silence grew deeper and deeper, and only at rare intervals he heard the sound of wheels on the main road a hundred yards away, where the horses went at a walking pace owing to the density of the fog. The echo of pedestrian footsteps no longer reached him, the clamour of occasional voices no longer came down the side street. The night, muffled by fog, shrouded by veils of ultimate mystery, hung about the haunted villa like a doom. Nothing in the house stirred. Stillness, in a thick blanket, lay over the upper storeys. Only the mist in the room grew more dense, he thought, and the damp cold more penetrating. Certainly, from time to time, he shivered.

The collie, now deep in slumber, moved occasionally,—grunted, sighed, or twitched his legs in dreams. Smoke lay on his knees, a pool of warm, black fur, only the closest observation detecting the movement of his sleek sides. It was difficult to distinguish exactly where his head and body joined in that circle of glistening hair; only a black satin nose and a tiny tip of pink tongue betrayed the secret.

Dr. Silence watched him, and felt comfortable. The collie's breathing was soothing. The fire was well built, and would burn for another two hours without attention. He was not conscious of the least nervousness. He particularly wished to remain in his ordinary and normal state of mind, and to force nothing. If sleep came naturally, he would let it come—and even welcome it. The coldness of the room, when the fire died down later, would be sure to wake him again; and it would then be time enough to carry these sleeping barometers up to bed. From various psychic premonitions he knew quite well that the night would not pass without adventure; but he did not wish to force its arrival; and he wished to remain normal, and let the animals remain normal, so that, when it came, it would be unattended by excitement or by any straining of the attention. Many experiments had made him wise. And, for the rest, he had no fear.

Accordingly, after a time, he did fall asleep as he had expected, and the last thing he remembered, before oblivion slipped up over his eyes like soft wool, was the picture of Flame stretching all four legs at once, and sighing noisily as he sought a more comfortable position for his paws and muzzle upon the mat.

It was a good deal later when he became aware that a weight lay upon his chest, and that something was pencilling over his face and mouth. A soft touch on the cheek woke him. Something was patting him.

He sat up with a jerk, and found himself staring straight into a pair of brilliant eyes, half green, half black. Smoke's face lay level with his own; and the cat had climbed up with its front paws upon his chest.

The lamp had burned low and the fire was nearly out, yet Dr. Silence saw in a moment that the cat was in an excited state. It kneaded with its front paws into his chest, shifting from one to the other. He felt them prodding against him. It lifted a leg very carefully and patted his cheek gingerly. Its fur, he saw, was standing ridgewise upon its back; the ears were flattened back somewhat; the tail was switching sharply. The cat, of course, had wakened him with a purpose, and the instant he realised this, he set it upon the arm of the chair and sprang up with a quick turn to face the empty room behind him. By some curious instinct, his arms of their own accord assumed an attitude of defence in front of him, as though to ward off something that threatened his safety. Yet nothing was visible. Only shapes of fog hung about rather heavily in the air, moving slightly to and fro.

His mind was now fully alert, and the last vestiges of sleep gone. He turned the lamp higher and peered about him. Two things he became aware of at once: one, that Smoke, while excited, was *pleasurably* excited; the other, that the collie was no longer visible upon the mat at his feet. He had crept away to the corner of the wall farthest from the window, and lay watching the room with wide-open eyes, in which lurked plainly something of alarm.

Something in the dog's behaviour instantly struck Dr. Silence as unusual, and, calling him by name, he moved across to pat him. Flame got up, wagged his tail, and came over slowly to the rug, uttering a low sound that was half growl, half whine. He was evidently perturbed about something, and his master was proceeding to administer comfort when his attention was suddenly drawn to the antics of his other four-footed companion, the cat.

And what he saw filled him with something like amazement.

Smoke had jumped down from the back of the arm-chair and now occupied the middle of the carpet, where, with tail erect and legs stiff as ramrods, it was steadily pacing backwards and forwards in a narrow space, uttering, as it did so, those curious little guttural sounds of pleasure that only an animal of the feline species knows how to make expressive of supreme happiness. Its stiffened legs and arched back made it appear larger than usual, and the black visage wore a smile of beatific joy. Its eyes blazed magnificently; it was in an ecstasy.

At the end of every few paces it turned sharply and stalked back again along the same line, padding softly, and purring like a roll of little muffled drums. It behaved precisely as though it were rubbing against the ankles of some one who remained invisible. A thrill ran down the doctor's spine as he stood and stared. His experiment was growing interesting at last.

He called the collie's attention to his friend's performance to see whether he too was aware of anything standing there upon the carpet, and the dog's behaviour was significant and corroborative. He came as far as his master's knees and then stopped dead, refusing to investigate closely. In vain Dr. Silence urged him; he wagged his tail, whined a little, and stood in a half-crouching attitude, staring alternately at the cat and at his master's face. He was, apparently, both puzzled and alarmed, and the whine went deeper and deeper down into his throat till it changed into an ugly snarl of awakening anger.

Then the doctor called to him in a tone of command he had never known to be disregarded; but still the dog, though springing up in response, declined to move nearer. He made tentative motions, pranced a little like a dog about to take to water, pretended to bark, and ran to and fro on the carpet. So far there was no actual fear in his manner, but he was uneasy and anxious, and nothing would induce him to go within touching distance of the walking cat. Once he made a complete circuit, but always carefully out of reach; and in the end he returned to his master's legs and rubbed vigorously against him. Flame did not like the performance at all: that much was quite clear.

For several minutes John Silence watched the performance of the cat with profound attention and without interfering. Then he called to the animal by name.

"Smoke, you mysterious beastie, what in the world are you about?" he said, in a coaxing tone.

The cat looked up at him for a moment, smiling in its ecstasy, blinking its eyes, but too happy to pause. He spoke to it again. He called to it several times, and each time it turned upon him its blazing eyes, drunk with inner delight, opening and shutting its lips, its body large and rigid with excitement. Yet it never for one instant paused in its short journeys to and fro.

He noted exactly what it did: it walked, he saw, the same number of paces each time, some six or seven steps, and then it turned sharply and retraced them. By the pattern of the great roses in the carpet he measured it. It kept to the same direction and the same line. It behaved precisely as though it were rubbing against something solid. Undoubtedly, there was something standing there on that strip of carpet, something invisible to the doctor, something that alarmed the dog, yet caused the cat unspeakable pleasure.

"Smokie!" he called again, "Smokie, you black mystery, what is it excites you so?"

Again the cat looked up at him for a brief second, and then continued its sentry-walk, blissfully happy, intensely preoccupied. And, for an instant, as he watched it, the doctor was aware that a faint uneasiness stirred in the depths of his own being, focusing itself for the moment upon this curious behaviour of the uncanny creature before him.

75

There rose in him quite a new realisation of the mystery connected with the whole feline tribe, but especially with that common member of it, the domestic cat—their hidden lives, their strange aloofness, their incalculable subtlety. How utterly remote from anything that human beings understood lay the sources of their elusive activities. As he watched the indescribable bearing of the little creature mincing along the strip of carpet under his eyes, coquetting with the powers of darkness, welcoming, maybe, some fearsome visitor, there stirred in his heart a feeling strangely akin to awe. Its indifference to human kind, its serene superiority to the obvious, struck him forcibly with fresh meaning; so remote, so inaccessible seemed the secret purposes of its real life, so alien to the blundering honesty of other animals. Its absolute poise of bearing brought into his mind the opium-eater's words that "no dignity is perfect which does not at some point ally itself with the mysterious"; and he became suddenly aware that the presence of the dog in this foggy, haunted room on the top of Putney Hill was uncommonly welcome to him. He was glad to feel that Flame's dependable personality was with him. The savage growling at his heels was a pleasant sound. He was glad to hear it. That marching cat made him uneasy.

Finding that Smoke paid no further attention to his words, the doctor decided upon action. Would it rub against his leg, too? He would take it by surprise and see.

He stepped quickly forward and placed himself upon the exact strip of carpet where it walked.

But no cat is ever taken by surprise! The moment he occupied the space of the Intruder, setting his feet on the woven roses midway in the line of travel, Smoke suddenly stopped purring and sat down. It lifted up its face with the most innocent stare imaginable of its green eyes. He could have sworn it laughed. It was a perfect child again. In a single second it had resumed its simple, domestic manner; and it gazed at him in such a way that he almost felt Smoke was the normal being, and *his* was the eccentric behaviour that was being watched. It was consummate, the manner in which it brought about this change so easily and so quickly.

"Superb little actor!" he laughed in spite of himself, and stooped to stroke the shining black back. But, in a flash, as he touched its fur, the cat turned and spat at him viciously, striking at his hand with one paw. Then, with a hurried scutter of feet, it shot like a shadow across the floor and a moment later was calmly sitting over by the window-curtains washing its face as though nothing interested it in the whole world but the cleanness of its cheeks and whiskers.

John Silence straightened himself up and drew a long breath. He realised that the performance was temporarily at an end. The collie, meanwhile, who had watched the whole proceeding with marked disapproval, had now lain down again upon the mat by the fire, no longer growling. It seemed to the doctor just as though something that had entered the room while he slept, alarming the dog, yet bringing happiness to the cat, had now gone out again, leaving all as it was before. Whatever it was that excited its blissful attentions had retreated for the moment.

He realised this intuitively. Smoke evidently realised it, too, for presently he deigned to march back to the fireplace and jump upon his master's knees. Dr. Silence, patient and determined, settled down once more to his book. The animals soon slept; the fire blazed cheerfully; and the cold fog from outside poured into the room through every available chink and cranny.

For a long time silence and peace reigned in the room and Dr. Silence availed himself of the quietness to make careful notes of what had happened. He entered for future use in other cases an exhaustive analysis of what he had observed, especially with regard to the effect upon the two animals. It is impossible here, nor would it be intelligible to the reader unversed in the knowledge of the region known to a scientifically trained psychic like Dr. Silence, to detail these observations. But to him it was clear, up to a certain point—and for the rest he must still wait and watch. So far, at least, he realised that while he slept in the chair—that is, while his will was dormant—the room had suffered intrusion from what he recognised as an intensely active Force, and might later be forced to acknowledge as something more than merely a blind force, namely, a distinct personality.

So far it had affected himself scarcely at all, but had acted directly upon the simpler organisms of the animals. It stimulated keenly the centres of the cat's psychic being, inducing a state of instant happiness (intensifying its consciousness probably in the same way a drug or stimulant intensifies that of a human being); whereas it alarmed the less sensitive dog, causing it to feel a vague apprehension and distress.

His own sudden action and exhibition of energy had served to disperse it temporarily, yet he felt convinced—the indications were not lacking even while he sat there making notes—that it still remained near to him, conditionally if not spatially, and was, as it were, gathering force for a second attack.

And, further, he intuitively understood that the relations between the two animals had undergone a subtle change: that the cat had become immeasurably superior, confident, sure of itself in its own peculiar region, whereas Flame had been weakened by an attack he could not comprehend and knew not how to reply to. Though not yet afraid, he was defiant—ready to act against a fear that he felt to be approaching. He was no longer fatherly and protective towards the cat. Smoke held the key to the situation; and both he and the cat knew it.

Thus, as the minutes passed, John Silence sat and waited, keenly on the alert, wondering how soon the attack would be renewed, and at what point it would be diverted from the animals and directed upon himself.

The book lay on the floor beside him, his notes were complete. With one hand on the cat's fur, and the dog's front paws resting against his feet, the three of them dozed comfortably before the hot fire while the night wore on and the silence deepened towards midnight.

It was well after one o'clock in the morning when Dr. Silence turned the lamp out and lighted the candle preparatory to going up to bed. Then Smoke suddenly woke with a loud sharp purr and sat up. It neither stretched, washed nor turned: it listened. And the doctor, watching it, realised that a certain indefinable change had come about that very moment in the room. A swift readjustment of the forces within the four walls had taken place—a new disposition of their personal equations. The balance was destroyed, the former harmony gone. Smoke, most sensitive of barometers, had been the first to feel it, but the dog was not slow to follow suit, for on looking down he noted that Flame was no longer asleep. He was lying with eyes wide open, and that same instant he sat up on his great haunches and began to growl.

Dr. Silence was in the act of taking the matches to re-light the lamp when an audible movement in the room behind made him pause. Smoke leaped down from his knee and moved forward a few paces across the carpet. Then it stopped and stared fixedly; and the doctor stood up on the rug to watch.

As he rose the sound was repeated, and he discovered that it was not in the room as he first thought, but outside, and that it came from more directions than one. There was a rushing, sweeping noise against the window-panes, and simultaneously a sound of something brushing against the door—out in the hall. Smoke advanced sedately across the carpet, twitching his tail, and sat down within a foot of the door. The influence that had destroyed the harmonious conditions of the room had apparently moved in advance of its cause. Clearly, something was about to happen.

For the first time that night John Silence hesitated; the thought of that dark narrow hall-way, choked with fog, and destitute of human comfort, was unpleasant. He became aware of a faint creeping of his flesh. He knew, of course, that the actual opening of the door was not necessary to the invasion of the room that was about to take place, since neither doors nor windows, nor any other solid barriers could interpose an obstacle to what was seeking entrance. Yet the opening of the door would be significant and symbolic, and he distinctly shrank from it.

But for a moment only. Smoke, turning with a show of impatience, recalled him to his purpose, and he moved past the sitting, watching creature, and deliberately opened the door to its full width.

What subsequently happened, happened in the feeble and flickering light of the solitary candle on the mantelpiece.

Through the opened door he saw the hall, dimly lit and thick with fog. Nothing, of course, was visible—nothing but the hat-stand, the African spears in dark lines upon the wall and the high-backed wooden chair standing grotesquely underneath on the oilcloth floor. For one instant the fog seemed to move and thicken oddly; but he set that down to the score of the imagination. The door had opened upon nothing.

Yet Smoke apparently thought otherwise, and the deep growling of the collie from the mat at the back of the room seemed to confirm his judgement.

For, proud and self-possessed, the cat had again risen to his feet, and having advanced to the door, was now ushering some one slowly into the room. Nothing could have been more evident. He paced from side to side, bowing his little head with great *empressement* and holding his stiffened tail aloft like a flagstaff. He turned this way and that, mincing to and fro, and showing signs of supreme satisfaction. He was in his element. He welcomed the intrusion, and apparently reckoned that his companions, the doctor and the dog, would welcome it likewise.

The Intruder had returned for a second attack.

Dr. Silence moved slowly backwards and took up his position on the hearthrug, keying himself up to a condition of concentrated attention.

He noted that Flame stood beside him, facing the room, with body motionless, and head moving swiftly from side to side with a curious swaying movement. His eyes were wide open, his back rigid, his neck and jaws thrust forward, his legs tense and ready to leap. Savage, ready for attack or defence, yet dreadfully puzzled and perhaps already a little cowed, he stood and stared, the hair on his spine and sides positively bristling outwards as though a wind played through them. In the dim firelight he looked like a great yellow-haired wolf, silent, eyes shooting dark fire, exceedingly formidable. It was Flame, the terrible.

Smoke, meanwhile, advanced from the door towards the middle of the room, adopting the very slow pace of an invisible companion. A few feet away it stopped and began to smile and blink its eyes. There was something deliberately coaxing in its attitude as it stood there undecided on the carpet, clearly wishing to effect some sort of introduction between the Intruder and its canine friend and ally. It assumed its most winning manners, purring, smiling, looking persuasively from one to the other, and making quick tentative steps first in one direction and then in the other. There had always existed such perfect understanding between them in everything. Surely Flame would appreciate Smoke's intentions now, and acquiesce.

But the old collie made no advances. He bared his teeth, lifting his lips till the gums showed, and stood stockstill with fixed eyes and heaving sides. The doctor moved a little farther back, watching intently the smallest movement, and it was just then he divined suddenly from the cat's behaviour and attitude that it was not only a single companion it had ushered into the room, but *several*. It kept crossing over from one to the other, looking up at each in turn. It sought to win over the dog to friendliness with them all. The original Intruder had come back with reinforcements. And at the same time he further realised that the Intruder was something more than a blindly acting force, impersonal though destructive. It was a Personality, and moreover a great personality. And it was accompanied for the purposes of assistance by a host of other personalities, minor in degree, but similar in kind.

He braced himself in the corner against the mantelpiece and waited, his whole being roused to defence, for he was now fully aware that the attack had spread to include himself as well as the animals, and he must be on the alert. He strained his eyes through the foggy atmosphere, trying in vain to see what the cat and dog saw; but the candlelight threw an uncertain and flickering light across the room and his eyes discerned nothing. On the floor Smoke moved softly in front of him like a black shadow, his eyes gleaming as he turned his head, still trying with many insinuating gestures and much purring to bring about the introductions he desired.

But it was all in vain. Flame stood riveted to one spot, motionless as a figure carved in stone.

Some minutes passed, during which only the cat moved, and then there came a sharp change. Flame began to back towards the wall. He moved his head from side to side as he went, sometimes turning to snap at something almost behind him. *They* were advancing upon him, trying to surround him. His distress became very marked from now onwards, and it seemed to the doctor that his anger merged into genuine terror and became overwhelmed by it. The savage growl sounded perilously like a whine, and more than once he tried to dive past his master's legs, as though hunting for a way of escape. He was trying to avoid something that everywhere blocked the way.

This terror of the indomitable fighter impressed the doctor enormously; yet also painfully; stirring his impatience; for he had never before seen the dog show signs of giving in, and it distressed him to witness it. He knew, however, that he was not giving in easily, and understood that it was really impossible for him to gauge the animal's sensations properly at all. What Flame felt, and saw, must be terrible indeed to turn him all at once into a coward. He faced something that made him afraid of more than his life merely. The doctor spoke a few quick words of encouragement to him, and stroked the bristling hair. But without much success. The collie seemed already beyond the reach of comfort such as that, and the collapse of the old dog followed indeed very speedily after this.

And Smoke, meanwhile, remained behind, watching the advance, but not joining in it; sitting, pleased and expectant, considering that all was going well and as it wished. It was kneading on the carpet with its front paws—slowly, laboriously, as though its feet were dipped in treacle. The sound its claws made as they caught in the threads was distinctly audible. It was still smiling, blinking, purring.

Suddenly the collie uttered a poignant short bark and leaped heavily to one side. His bared teeth traced a line of whiteness through the gloom. The next instant he dashed past his master's legs, almost upsetting his balance, and shot out into the room, where he went blundering wildly against walls and furniture. But that bark was significant; the doctor had heard it before and knew what it meant: for it was the cry of the fighter against odds and it meant that the old beast had found his courage again. Possibly it was only the courage of despair, but at any rate the fighting would be terrific. And Dr. Silence understood, too, that he dared not interfere. Flame must fight his own enemies in his own way.

But the cat, too, had heard that dreadful bark; and it, too, had understood. This was more than it had bargained for. Across the dim shadows of that haunted room there must have passed some secret signal of distress between the animals. Smoke stood up and looked swiftly about him. He uttered a piteous meow and trotted smartly away into the greater darkness by the windows. What his object was only those endowed with the spirit-like intelligence of cats might know. But, at any rate, he had at last ranged himself on the side of his friend. And the little beast meant business.

At the same moment the collie managed to gain the door. The doctor saw him rush through into the hall like a flash of yellow light. He shot across the oilcloth, and tore up the stairs, but in another second he appeared again, flying down the steps and landing at the bottom in a tumbling heap, whining, cringing, terrified. The doctor saw him slink back into the room again and crawl round by the wall towards the cat. Was, then, even the staircase occupied?

Did *They* stand also in the hall? Was the whole house crowded from floor to ceiling?

The thought came to add to the keen distress he felt at the sight of the collie's discomfiture. And, indeed, his own personal distress had increased in a marked degree during the past minutes, and continued to increase steadily to the climax. He recognised that the drain on his own vitality grew steadily, and that the attack was now directed against himself even more than against the defeated dog, and the too much deceived cat.

It all seemed so rapid and uncalculated after that—the events that took place in this little modern room at the top of Putney Hill between midnight and sunrise—that Dr. Silence was hardly able to follow and remember it all. It came about with such uncanny swiftness and terror; the light was so uncertain; the movements of the black cat so difficult to follow on the dark carpet, and the doctor himself so weary and taken by surprise—that he found it almost impossible to observe accurately, or to recall afterwards precisely what it was he had seen or in what order the incidents had taken place. He never could understand what defect of vision on his part made it seem as though the cat had duplicated itself at first, and then increased indefinitely, so that there were at least a dozen of them darting silently about the floor, leaping softly on to chairs and tables, passing like shadows from the open door to the end of the room, all black as sin, with brilliant green eyes flashing fire in all directions. It was like the reflections from a score of mirrors placed round the walls at different angles. Nor could he make out at the time why the size of the room seemed to have altered, grown much larger, and why it extended away behind him where ordinarily the wall should have been. The snarling of the enraged and terrified collie sounded sometimes so far away; the ceiling seemed to have raised itself so much higher than before, and much of the furniture had changed in appearance and shifted marvellously.

It was all so confused and confusing, as though the little room he knew had become merged and transformed into the dimensions of quite another chamber, that came to him, with its host of cats and its strange distances, in a sort of vision.

But these changes came about a little later, and at a time when his attention was so concentrated upon the proceedings of Smoke and the collie, that he only observed them, as it were, subconsciously. And the excitement, the flickering candlelight, the distress he felt for the collie, and the distorting atmosphere of fog were the poorest possible allies to careful observation.

At first he was only aware that the dog was repeating his short dangerous bark from time to time, snapping viciously at the empty air, a foot or so from the ground. Once, indeed, he sprang upwards and forwards, working furiously with teeth and paws, and with a noise like wolves fighting, but only to dash back the next minute against the wall behind him. Then, after lying still for a bit, he rose to a crouching position as though to spring again, snarling horribly and making short half-circles with lowered head. And Smoke all the while meowed piteously by the window as though trying to draw the attack upon himself.

Then it was that the rush of the whole dreadful business seemed to turn aside from the dog and direct itself upon his own person. The collie had made another spring and fallen back with a crash into the corner, where he made noise enough in his savage rage to waken the dead before he fell to whining and then finally lay still. And directly afterwards the doctor's own distress became intolerably acute. He had made a half movement forward to come to the rescue when a veil that was denser than mere fog seemed to drop down over the scene, draping room, walls, animals and fire in a mist of darkness and folding also about his own mind. Other forms moved silently across the field of vision, forms that he recognised from previous experiments, and welcomed not. Unholy thoughts began to crowd into his brain, sinister suggestions of evil presented themselves seductively. Ice seemed to settle about his heart, and his mind trembled. He began to lose memory—memory of his identity, of where he was, of what he ought to do. The very foundations of his strength were shaken. His will seemed paralysed.

And it was then that the room filled with this horde of cats, all dark as the night, all silent, all with lamping eyes of green fire. The dimensions of the place altered and shifted. He was in a much larger space. The whining of the dog sounded far away, and all about him the cats flew busily to and fro, silently playing their tearing, rushing game of evil, weaving the pattern of their dark purpose upon the floor. He strove hard to collect himself and remember the words of power he had made use of before in similar dread positions where his dangerous practice had sometimes led; but he could recall nothing consecutively; a mist lay over his mind and memory; he felt dazed and his forces scattered. The deeps within were too troubled for healing power to come out of them.

It was glamour, of course, he realised afterwards, the strong glamour thrown upon his imagination by some powerful personality behind the veil; but at the time he was not sufficiently aware of this and, as with all true glamour, was unable to grasp where the true ended and the false began. He was caught momentarily in the same vortex that had sought to lure the cat to destruction through its delight, and threatened utterly to overwhelm the dog through its terror.

There came a sound in the chimney behind him like wind booming and tearing its way down. The windows rattled. The candle flickered and went out The glacial atmosphere closed round him with the cold of death, and a great rushing sound swept by overhead as though the ceiling had lifted to a great height. He heard the door shut. Far away it sounded. He felt lost, shelterless in the depths of his soul. Yet still he held out and resisted while the climax of the fight came nearer and nearer... He had stepped into the stream of forces awakened by Pender and he knew that he must withstand them to the end or come to a conclusion that it was not good for a man to come to. Something from the region of utter cold was upon him.

And then quite suddenly, through the confused mists about him, there slowly rose up the Personality that had been all the time directing the battle. Some force entered his being that shook him as the tempest shakes a leaf, and close against his eyes—clean level with his face—he found himself staring into the wreck of a vast dark Countenance, a countenance that was terrible even in its ruin.

For ruined it was, and terrible it was, and the mark of spiritual evil was branded everywhere upon its broken features. Eyes, face and hair rose level with his own, and for a space of time he never could properly measure, or determine, these two, a man and a woman, looked straight into each other's visages and down into each other's hearts.

And John Silence, the soul with the good, unselfish motive, held his own against the dark discarnate woman whose motive was pure evil, and whose soul was on the side of the Dark Powers.

It was the climax that touched the depth of power within him and began to restore him slowly to his own. He was conscious, of course, of effort, and yet it seemed no superhuman one, for he had recognised the character of his opponent's power, and he called upon the good within him to meet and overcome it. The inner forces stirred and trembled in response to his call. They did not at first come readily as was their habit, for under the spell of glamour they had already been diabolically lulled into inactivity, but come they eventually did, rising out of the inner spiritual nature he had learned with so much time and pain to awaken to life. And power and confidence came with them. He began to breathe deeply and regularly, and at the same time to absorb into himself the forces opposed to him, and to *turn them to his own account*. By ceasing to resist, and allowing the deadly stream to pour into him unopposed, he used the very power supplied by his adversary and thus enormously increased his own.

For this spiritual alchemy he had learned. He understood that force ultimately is everywhere one and the same; it is the motive behind that makes it good or evil; and his motive was entirely unselfish. He knew—provided he was not first robbed of self-control—how vicariously to absorb these evil radiations into himself and change them magically into his own good purposes. And, since his motive was pure and his soul fearless, they could not work him harm.

Thus he stood in the main stream of evil unwittingly attracted by Pender, deflecting its course upon himself; and after passing through the purifying filter of his own unselfishness these energies could only add to his store of experience, of knowledge, and therefore of power. And, as his self-control returned to him, he gradually accomplished this purpose, even though trembling while he did so.

Yet the struggle was severe, and in spite of the freezing chill of the air, the perspiration poured down his face. Then, by slow degrees, the dark and dreadful countenance faded, the glamour passed from his soul, the normal proportions returned to walls and ceiling, the forms melted back into the fog, and the whirl of rushing shadow-cats disappeared whence they came.

And with the return of the consciousness of his own identity John Silence was restored to the full control of his own will-power. In a deep, modulated voice he began to utter certain rhythmical sounds that slowly rolled through the air like a rising sea, filling the room with powerful vibratory activities that whelmed all irregularities of lesser vibrations in its own swelling tone. He made certain sigils, gestures and movements at the same time. For several minutes he continued to utter these words, until at length the growing volume dominated the whole room and mastered the manifestation of all that opposed it. For just as he understood the spiritual alchemy that can transmute evil forces by raising them into higher channels, so he knew from long study the occult use of sound, and its direct effect upon the plastic region wherein the powers of spiritual evil work their fell purposes. Harmony was restored first of all to his own soul, and thence to the room and all its occupants.

And, after himself, the first to recognise it was the old dog lying in his corner. Flame began suddenly uttering sounds of pleasure, that "something" between a growl and a grunt that dogs make upon being restored to their master's confidence. Dr. Silence heard the thumping of the collie's tail against the ground. And the grunt and the thumping touched the depth of affection in the man's heart, and gave him some inkling of what agonies the dumb creature had suffered.

Next, from the shadows by the window, a somewhat shrill purring announced the restoration of the cat to its normal state. Smoke was advancing across the carpet. He seemed very pleased with himself, and smiled with an expression of supreme innocence. He was no shadow-cat, but real and full of his usual and perfect self-possession. He marched along, picking his way delicately, but with a stately dignity that suggested his ancestry with the majesty of Egypt. His eyes no longer glared; they shone steadily before him; they radiated, not excitement, but knowledge. Clearly he was anxious to make amends for the mischief to which he had unwittingly lent himself owing to his subtle and electric constitution.

Still uttering his sharp high purrings he marched up to his master and rubbed vigorously against his legs. Then he stood on his hind feet and pawed his knees and stared beseechingly up into his face. He turned his head towards the corner where the collie still lay, thumping his tail feebly and pathetically.

John Silence understood. He bent down and stroked the creature's living fur, noting the line of bright blue sparks that followed the motion of his hand down its back. And then they advanced together towards the corner where the dog was.

Smoke went first and put his nose gently against his friend's muzzle, purring while he rubbed, and uttering little soft sounds of affection in his throat. The doctor lit the candle and brought it over. He saw the collie lying on its side against the wall; it was utterly exhausted, and foam still hung about its jaws. Its tail and eyes responded to the sound of its name, but it was evidently very weak and overcome. Smoke continued to rub against its cheek and nose and eyes, sometimes even standing on its body and kneading into the thick yellow hair. Flame replied from time to time by little licks of the tongue, most of them curiously misdirected.

But Dr. Silence felt intuitively that something disastrous had happened, and his heart was wrung. He stroked the dear body, feeling it over for bruises or broken bones, but finding none. He fed it with what remained of the sandwiches and milk, but the creature clumsily upset the saucer and lost the sandwiches between its paws, so that the doctor had to feed it with his own hand. And all the while Smoke meowed piteously.

Then John Silence began to understand. He went across to the farther side of the room and called aloud to it.

"Flame, old man! come!"

At any other time the dog would have been upon him in an instant, barking and leaping to the shoulder. And even now he got up, though heavily and awkwardly, to his feet. He started to run, wagging his tail more briskly. He collided first with a chair, and then ran straight into a table. Smoke trotted close at his side, trying his very best to guide him. But it was useless. Dr. Silence had to lift him up into his own arms and carry him like a baby. For he was blind.

III

It was a week later when John Silence called to see the author in his new house, and found him well on the way to recovery and already busy again with his writing. The haunted look had left his eyes, and he seemed cheerful and confident.

"Humour restored?" laughed the doctor, as soon as they were comfortably settled in the room overlooking the Park.

"I've had no trouble since I left that dreadful place," returned Pender gratefully; "and thanks to you—"

The doctor stopped him with a gesture.

"Never mind that," he said, "we'll discuss your new plans afterwards, and my scheme for relieving you of the house and helping you settle elsewhere. Of course it must be pulled down, for it's not fit for any sensitive person to live in, and any other tenant might be afflicted in the same way you were. Although, personally, I think the evil has exhausted itself by now."

He told the astonished author something of his experiences in it with the animals.

"I don't pretend to understand," Pender said, when the account was finished, "but I and my wife are intensely relieved to be free of it all. Only I must say I should like to know something of the former history of the house. When we took it six months ago I heard no word against it."

Dr. Silence drew a typewritten paper from his pocket.

"I can satisfy your curiosity to some extent," he said, running his eye over the sheets, and then replacing them in his coat; "for by my secretary's investigations I have been able to check certain information obtained in the hypnotic trance by a 'sensitive' who helps me in such cases. The former occupant who haunted you appears to have been a woman of singularly atrocious life and character who finally suffered death by hanging, after a series of crimes that appalled the whole of England and only came to light by the merest chance. She came to her end in the year 1798, for it was not this particular house she lived in, but a much larger one that then stood upon the site it now occupies, and was then, of course, not in London, but in the country. She was a person of intellect, possessed of a powerful, trained will, and of consummate audacity, and I am convinced availed herself of the resources of the lower magic to attain her ends. This goes far to explain the virulence of the attack upon yourself, and why she is still able to carry on after death the evil practices that formed her main purpose during life."

"You think that after death a soul can still consciously direct—" gasped the author.

"I think, as I told you before, that the forces of a powerful personality may still persist after death in the line of their original momentum," replied the doctor; "and that strong thoughts and purposes can still react upon suitably prepared brains long after their originators have passed away.

"If you knew anything of magic," he pursued, "you would know that thought is dynamic, and that it may call into existence forms and pictures that may well exist for hundreds of years. For, not far removed from the region of our human life, is another region where floats the waste and drift of all the centuries, the limbo of the shells of the dead; a densely populated region crammed with horror and abomination of all descriptions, and sometimes galvanised into active life again by the will of a trained manipulator, a mind versed in the practices of lower magic. That this woman understood its vile commerce, I am persuaded, and the forces she set going during her life have simply been accumulating ever since, and would have continued to do so had they not been drawn down upon yourself, and afterwards discharged and satisfied through me.

"Anything might have brought down the attack, for, besides drugs, there are certain violent emotions, certain moods of the soul, certain spiritual fevers, if I may so call them, which directly open the inner being to a cognisance of this astral region I have mentioned. In your case it happened to be a peculiarly potent drug that did it.

"But now, tell me," he added, after a pause, handing to the perplexed author a pencil-drawing he had made of the dark countenance that had appeared to him during the night on Putney Hill—"tell me if you recognise this face?"

Pender looked at the drawing closely, greatly astonished. He shuddered a little as he looked.

"Undoubtedly," he said, "it is the face I kept trying to draw—dark, with the great mouth and jaw, and the drooping eye. That is the woman."

Dr. Silence then produced from his pocket-book an old-fashioned woodcut of the same person which his secretary had unearthed from the records of the Newgate Calendar. The woodcut and the pencil drawing were two different aspects of the same dreadful visage. The men compared them for some moments in silence.

"It makes me thank God for the limitations of our senses," said Pender quietly, with a sigh; "continuous clairvoyance must be a sore affliction."

"It is indeed," returned John Silence significantly, "and if all the people nowadays who claim to be clairvoyant were really so, the statistics of suicide and lunacy would be considerably higher than they are. It is little wonder," he added, "that your sense of humour was clouded, with the mind-forces of that dead monster trying to use your brain for their dissemination. You have had an interesting adventure, Mr. Felix Pender, and, let me add, a fortunate escape."

The author was about to renew his thanks when there came a sound of scratching at the door, and the doctor sprang up quickly.

"It's time for me to go. I left my dog on the step, but I suppose—"

Before he had time to open the door, it had yielded to the pressure behind it and flew wide open to admit a great yellow-haired collie. The dog, wagging his tail and contorting his whole body with delight, tore across the floor and tried to leap up upon his owner's breast. And there was laughter and happiness in the old eyes; for they were clear again as the day.

THOMAS CARNACKI

in

THE SEARCHER OF
THE END HOUSE

William Hope Hodgson

Like Prichard and Blackwood, William Hope Hodgson (1877–1918) was a traveller and adventurer, though in his case mostly at sea. He had run away to join the merchant navy when he was twelve but was brought back home and only formally indentured when he was fourteen (and claimed to be fifteen) in 1891. He was at sea for nine years and travelled around the world three times. He received a medal from the Royal Humane Society when he rescued a fellow seaman who had fallen into shark-infested waters. While at sea he had kept fit with body-building exercises, so when he returned home in 1899 he established a Keep-Fit school in Blackburn, Lancashire. He wrote about body-building for Sandow's Magazine *and, acquiring the taste for publication, turned to writing fiction. These included two novels set at sea;* The Boats of the "Glen Carrig" *(1907) and* The Ghost Ship *(1909), the cosmic extravaganza* The House on the Borderland *(1908) and the unique* The Night Land *(1912). He wrote many short stories including the series about Carnacki the Ghost-Finder, several of which first appeared in* The Idler *magazine in 1910. We don't learn Carnacki's first name in these stories but when Hodgson applied for the stories to be copyrighted in the United States he referred to his detective as "Thomas". Searching for a book publisher, Hodgson was approached by Eveleigh Nash. Blackwood had chosen not to write any further John Silence stories but their popularity prompted Nash to seek another author and the result was* Carnacki, the Ghost-Finder, *published in 1913.*

Hodgson's life was tragically cut short when he was killed at the Battle of Kemmel near Ypres in April 1918, aged only forty.

I t was still evening, as I remember, and the four of us, Jessop, Arkright, Taylor and I, looked disappointedly at Carnacki, where he sat silent in his great chair.

We had come in response to the usual card of invitation, which—as you know—we have come to consider as a sure prelude to a good story; and now, after telling us the short incident of the Three Straw Platters, he had lapsed into a contented silence, and the night not half gone, as I have hinted.

However, as it chanced, some pitying fate jogged Carnacki's elbow, or his memory, and he began again, in his queer level way:—

"The 'Straw Platters' business reminds me of the 'Searcher' Case, which I have sometimes thought might interest you. It was some time ago, in fact a deuce of a long time ago, that the thing happened; and my experience of what I might term 'curious' things was very small at that time.

"I was living with my mother when it occurred, in a small house just outside of Appledorn, on the South Coast. The house was the last of a row of detached cottage villas, each house standing in its own garden; and very dainty little places they were, very old, and most of them smothered in roses; and all with those quaint old leaded windows, and doors of genuine oak. You must try to picture them for the sake of their complete niceness.

"Now I must remind you at the beginning that my mother and I had lived in that little house for two years; and in the whole of that time there had not been a single peculiar happening to worry us.

"And then, something happened.

"It was about two o'clock one morning, as I was finishing some letters, that I heard the door of my mother's bedroom open, and she came to the top of the stairs, and knocked on the banisters.

"'All right, dear,' I called; for I suppose she was merely reminding me that I should have been in bed long ago; then I heard her go back to her room, and I hurried my work, for fear she should lie awake, until she heard me safe up to my room.

"When I was finished, I lit my candle, put out the lamp, and went upstairs. As I came opposite the door of my mother's room, I saw that it was open, called good night to her, very softly, and asked whether I should close the door. As there was no answer, I knew that she had dropped off to sleep again, and I closed the door very gently, and turned into my room, just across the passage. As I did so, I experienced a momentary, half-aware sense of a faint, peculiar, disagreeable odour in the passage; but it was not until the following night that I *realised* I had noticed a smell that offended me. You follow me? It is so often like that—one suddenly knows a thing that really recorded itself on one's consciousness, perhaps a year before.

"The next morning at breakfast, I mentioned casually to my mother that she had 'dropped off,' and I had shut the door for her. To my surprise, she assured me she had never been out of her room. I reminded her about the two raps she had given upon the banister; but she still was certain I must be mistaken; and in the end I teased her, saying she had grown so accustomed to my bad habit of sitting up late, that she had come to call me in her sleep. Of course, she denied this, and I let the matter drop; but I was more than a little puzzled, and did not know whether to believe my own explanation, or to take the mater's, which was to put the noises down to the mice, and the open door to the fact that she couldn't have properly latched it, when she went to bed. I suppose, away in the subconscious part of me, I had a stirring of less reasonable thoughts; but certainly, I had no real uneasiness at that time.

"The next night there came a further development. About two thirty a.m., I heard my mother's door open, just as on the previous night, and immediately afterwards she rapped sharply, on the banister, as it seemed to me. I stopped my work and called up that I would not be long. As she made no reply, and I did not hear her go back to bed, I had a quick sense of wonder whether she might not be doing it in her sleep, after all, just as I had said.

"With the thought, I stood up, and taking the lamp from the table, began to go toward the door, which was open into the passage. It was then I got a sudden nasty sort of thrill; for it came to me, all at once, that my mother never knocked, when I sat up too late; she always called. You will understand I was not really frightened in any way; only vaguely uneasy, and pretty sure she must really be doing the thing in her sleep.

"I went quickly up the stairs, and when I came to the top, my mother was not there; but her door was open. I had a bewildered sense though believing she must have gone quietly back to bed, without my hearing her. I entered her room and found her sleeping quietly and naturally; for the vague sense of trouble in me was sufficiently strong to make me go over to look at her.

"When I was sure that she was perfectly right in every way, I was still a little bothered; but much more inclined to think my suspicion correct and that she had gone quietly back to bed in her sleep, without knowing what she had been doing. This was the most reasonable thing to think, as you must see.

"And then it came to me, suddenly, that vague, queer, mildewy smell in the room; and it was in that instant I became aware I had smelt the same strange, uncertain smell the night before in the passage.

"I was definitely uneasy now, and began to search my mother's room; though with no aim or clear thought of anything, except to assure myself that there was nothing in the room. All the time, you know, I never *expected really* to find anything; only my uneasiness had to be assured.

"In the middle of my search my mother woke up, and of course I had to explain. I told her about her door opening, and the knocks on the banister, and that I had come up and found her asleep. I said nothing about the smell, which was not very distinct; but told her that the thing happening twice had made me a bit nervous, and possibly fanciful, and I thought I would take a look 'round, just to feel satisfied.

"I have thought since that the reason I made no mention of the smell, was not only that I did not want to frighten my mother, for I was scarcely that myself; but because I had only a vague half-knowledge that I associated the smell with fancies too indefinite and peculiar to bear talking about. You will understand that I am able *now* to analyse and put the thing into words; but *then* I did not even know my chief reason for saying nothing; let alone appreciate its possible significance.

"It was my mother, after all, who put part of my vague sensations into words:—

"'What a disagreeable smell!' she exclaimed, and was silent a moment, looking at me. Then:—'You feel there's something wrong?' still looking at me, very quietly but with a little, nervous note of questioning expectancy.

"'I don't know,' I said. 'I can't understand it, unless you've really been walking about in your sleep.'

"'The smell,' she said.

"'Yes,' I replied. 'That's what puzzles me too. I'll take a walk through the house; but I don't suppose it's anything.'

"I lit her candle, and taking the lamp, I went through the other bedrooms, and afterwards all over the house, including the three underground cellars, which was a little trying to the nerves, seeing that I was more nervous than I would admit.

"Then I went back to my mother, and told her there was really nothing to bother about; and, you know, in the end, we talked ourselves into believing it was nothing. My mother would not agree that she might have been sleepwalking; but she was ready to put the door opening down to the fault of the latch, which certainly snicked very lightly. As for the knocks, they might be the old warped woodwork of the house cracking a bit, or a mouse rattling a piece of loose plaster. The smell was more difficult to explain; but finally we agreed that it might easily be the queer night smell of the moist earth, coming in through the open window of my mother's room, from the back garden, or—for that matter—from the little churchyard beyond the big wall at the bottom of the garden.

"And so we quietened down, and finally I went to bed, and to sleep.

"I think this is certainly a lesson on the way we humans can delude ourselves; for there was not one of these explanations that my reason could really accept. Try to imagine yourself in the same circumstances, and you will see how absurd our attempts to explain the happenings really were.

"In the morning, when I came down to breakfast, we talked it all over again, and whilst we agreed that it was strange, we also agreed that we had begun to imagine funny things in the backs of our minds, which now we felt half ashamed to admit. This is very strange when you come to look into it; but very human.

"And then that night again my mother's door was slammed once more just after midnight. I caught up the lamp, and when I reached her door, I found it shut. I opened it quickly, and went in, to find my mother lying with her eyes open, and rather nervous; having been waked by the bang of the door. But what upset me more than anything, was the fact that there was a disgusting smell in the passage and in her room.

"Whilst I was asking her whether she was all right, a door slammed twice downstairs; and you can imagine how it made me feel. My mother and I looked at one another; and then I lit her candle, and taking the poker from the fender, went downstairs with the lamp, beginning to feel really nervous. The cumulative effect of so many queer happenings was getting hold of me; and all the *apparently* reasonable explanations seemed futile.

"The horrible smell seemed to be very strong in the downstairs passage; also in the front room and the cellars; but chiefly in the passage. I made a very thorough search of the house, and when I had finished, I knew that all the lower windows and doors were properly shut and fastened, and that there was no living thing in the house, beyond our two selves. Then I went up to my mother's room again, and we talked the thing over for an hour or more, and in the end came to the conclusion that we might, after all, be reading too much into a number of little things; but, you know, inside of us, we did not believe this.

"Later, when we had talked ourselves into a more comfortable state of mind, I said good night, and went off to bed; and presently managed to get to sleep.

"In the early hours of the morning, whilst it was still dark, I was waked by a loud noise. I sat up in bed, and listened. And from downstairs, I heard:—bang, bang, bang, one door after another being slammed; at least, that is the impression the sounds gave to me.

"I jumped out of bed, with the tingle and shiver of sudden fright on me; and at the same moment, as I lit my candle, my door was pushed slowly open; I had left it unlatched, so as not to feel that my mother was quite shut off from me.

"'Who's there?' I shouted out, in a voice twice as deep as my natural one, and with a queer breathlessness, that sudden fright so often gives one. 'Who's there?'

"Then I heard my mother saying:—

"'It's me, Thomas. Whatever is happening downstairs?'

"She was in the room by this, and I saw she had her bedroom poker in one hand, and her candle in the other. I could have smiled at her, had it not been for the extraordinary sounds downstairs.

"I got into my slippers, and reached down an old sword bayonet from the wall; then I picked up my candle, and begged my mother not to come; but I knew it would be little use, if she had made up her mind; and she had, with the result that she acted as a sort of rearguard for me, during our search. I know, in some ways, I was very glad to have her with me, as you will understand.

"By this time, the door slamming had ceased, and there seemed, probably because of the contrast, to be an appalling silence in the house. However, I led the way, holding my candle high, and keeping the sword bayonet very handy. Downstairs we found all the doors wide open; although the outer doors and the windows were closed all right. I began to wonder whether the noises had been made by the doors after all. Of one thing only were we sure, and that was, there was no living thing in the house, beside ourselves, while everywhere throughout the house, there was the taint of that disgusting odour.

"Of course it was absurd to try to make believe any longer. There was something strange about the house; and as soon as it was daylight, I set my mother to packing; and soon after breakfast, I saw her off by train.

"Then I set to work to try to clear up the mystery. I went first to the landlord, and told him all the circumstances. From him, I found that twelve or fifteen years back, the house had got rather a curious name from three or four tenants; with the result that it had remained empty a long while; in the end he had let it at a low rent to a Captain Tobias, on the one condition that he should hold his tongue, if he saw anything peculiar. The landlord's idea—as he told me frankly—was to free the house from these tales of 'something queer,' by keeping a tenant in it, and then to sell it for the best price he could get.

"However, when Captain Tobias left, after a ten years' tenancy, there was no longer any talk about the house; so when I offered to take it on a five years' lease, he had jumped at the offer. This was the whole story; so he gave me to understand. When I pressed him for details of the supposed peculiar happenings in the house, all those years back, he said the tenants had talked about a woman who always moved about the house at night. Some tenants never saw anything; but others would not stay out the first month's tenancy.

"One thing the landlord was particular to point out, that no tenant had ever complained about knockings, or door slamming. As for the smell, he seemed positively indignant about it; but why, I don't suppose he knew himself, except that he probably had some vague feeling that it was an indirect accusation on my part that the drains were not right.

"In the end, I suggested that he should come down and spend the night with me. He agreed at once, especially as I told him I intended to keep the whole business quiet, and try to get to the bottom of the curious affair; for he was anxious to keep the rumour of the haunting from getting about.

"About three o'clock that afternoon, he came down, and we made a thorough search of the house, which, however, revealed nothing unusual. Afterwards, the landlord made one or two tests, which showed him the drainage was in perfect order; after that we made our preparations for sitting up all night.

"First, we borrowed two policemen's dark lanterns from the station nearby, and where the superintendent and I were friendly, and as soon as it was really dusk, the landlord went up to his house for his gun. I had the sword bayonet I have told you about; and when the landlord got back, we sat talking in my study until nearly midnight.

"Then we lit the lanterns and went upstairs. We placed the lanterns, gun and bayonet handy on the table; then I shut and sealed the bedroom doors; afterwards we took our seats, and turned off the lights.

"From then until two o'clock, nothing happened; but a little after two, as I found by holding my watch near the faint glow of the closed lanterns, I had a time of extraordinary nervousness; and I bent toward the landlord, and whispered to him that I had a queer feeling something was about to happen, and to be ready with his lantern; at the same time I reached out toward mine. In the very instant I made this movement, the darkness which filled the passage seemed to become suddenly of a dull violet colour; not, as if a light had been shone; but as if the natural blackness of the night had changed colour. And then, coming through this violet night, through this violet-coloured gloom, came a little naked Child, running. In an extraordinary way, the Child seemed not to be distinct from the surrounding gloom; but almost as if it were a concentration of that extraordinary atmosphere; as if that gloomy colour which had changed the night, came from the Child. It seems impossible to make clear to you; but try to understand it.

"The Child went past me, running, with the natural movement of the legs of a chubby human child, but in an absolute and inconceivable silence. It was a very small Child, and must have passed under the table; but I saw the Child through the table, as if it had been only a slightly darker shadow than the coloured gloom. In the same instant, I saw that a fluctuating glimmer of violet light outlined the metal of the gun-barrels and the blade of the sword bayonet, making them seem like faint shapes of glimmering light, floating unsupported where the tabletop should have shown solid.

"Now, curiously, as I saw these things, I was subconsciously aware that I heard the anxious breathing of the landlord, quite clear and laboured, close to my elbow, where he waited nervously with his hands on the lantern. I realised in that moment that he saw nothing; but waited in the darkness, for my warning to come true.

"Even as I took heed of these minor things, I saw the Child jump to one side, and hide behind some half-seen object that was certainly nothing belonging to the passage. I stared, intently, with a most extraordinary thrill of expectant wonder, with fright making goose flesh of my back. And even as I stared, I solved for myself the less important problem of what the two black clouds were that hung over a part of the table. I think it very curious and interesting, the double working of the mind, often so much more apparent during times of stress. The two clouds came from two faintly shining shapes, which I knew must be the metal of the lanterns; and the things that looked black to the sight with which I was then seeing, could be nothing else but what to normal human sight is known as light. This phenomenon I have always remembered. I have twice seen a somewhat similar thing; in the Dark Light Case and in that trouble of Maetheson's, which you know about.

"Even as I understood this matter of the lights, I was looking to my left, to understand why the Child was hiding. And suddenly, I heard the landlord shout out:—'The Woman!' But I saw nothing. I had a disagreeable sense that something repugnant was near to me, and I was aware in the same moment that the landlord was gripping my arm in a hard, frightened grip. Then I was looking back to where the Child had hidden. I saw the Child peeping out from behind its hiding place, seeming to be looking up the passage; but whether in fear I could not tell. Then it came out, and ran headlong away, through the place where should have been the wall of my mother's bedroom; but the Sense with which I was seeing these things, showed me the wall only as a vague, upright shadow, unsubstantial. And immediately the child was lost to me, in the dull violet gloom. At the same time, I felt the landlord press back against me, as if something had passed close to him; and he called out again, a hoarse sort of cry:—'The Woman! The Woman!' and turned the shade clumsily from off his lantern. But I had seen no Woman; and the passage showed empty, as he shone the beam of his light jerkily to and fro; but chiefly in the direction of the doorway of my mother's room.

"He was still clutching my arm, and had risen to his feet; and now, mechanically and almost slowly, I picked up my lantern and turned on the light. I shone it, a little dazedly, at the seals upon the doors; but none were broken; then I sent the light to and fro, up and down the passage; but there was nothing; and I turned to the landlord, who was saying something in a rather incoherent fashion.

As my light passed over his face, I noted, in a dull sort of way, that he was drenched with sweat.

"Then my wits became more handleable, and I began to catch the drift of his words:—'Did you see her? Did you see her?' he was saying, over and over again; and then I found myself telling him, in quite a level voice, that I had not seen any Woman. He became more coherent then, and I found that he had seen a Woman come from the end of the passage, and go past us; but he could not describe her, except that she kept stopping and looking about her, and had even peered at the wall, close beside him, as if looking for something. But what seemed to trouble him most, was that she had not seemed to see him at all. He repeated this so often, that in the end I told him, in an absurd sort of way, that he ought to be very glad she had not. What did it all mean? was the question; somehow I was not so frightened, as utterly bewildered. I had seen less then, than since; but what I had seen, had made me feel adrift from my anchorage of Reason.

"What did it mean? He had seen a Woman, searching for something. *I* had not seen this Woman. *I* had seen a Child, running away, and hiding from Something or Someone. *He* had not seen the Child, or the other things—only the Woman. And *I* had not seen her. What did it all mean?

"I had said nothing to the landlord about the Child. I had been too bewildered, and I realised that it would be futile to attempt an explanation. He was already stupid with the thing he had seen; and not the kind of man to understand. All this went through my mind as we stood there, shining the lanterns to and fro. All the time, intermingled with a streak of practical reasoning, I was questioning myself, what did it all mean? What was the Woman searching for; what was the Child running from?

"Suddenly, as I stood there, bewildered and nervous, making random answers to the landlord, a door below was violently slammed, and directly I caught the horrible reek of which I have told you.

"'There!' I said to the landlord, and caught his arm, in my turn. 'The Smell! Do *you* smell it?'

"He looked at me so stupidly that in a sort of nervous anger, I shook him.

"'Yes,' he said, in a queer voice, trying to shine the light from his shaking lantern at the stair head.

"'Come on!' I said, and picked up my bayonet; and he came, carrying his gun awkwardly. I think he came, more because he was afraid to be left alone, than because he had any pluck left, poor beggar. I never sneer at that kind of funk, at least very seldom; for when it takes hold of you, it makes rags of your courage.

"I led the way downstairs, shining my light into the lower passage, and afterwards at the doors to see whether they were shut; for I had closed and latched them, placing a corner of a mat against each door, so I should know which had been opened.

"I saw at once that none of the doors had been opened; then I threw the beam of my light down alongside the stairway, in order to see the mat I had placed against the door at the top of the cellar stairs. I got a horrid thrill; for the mat was flat! I paused a couple of seconds, shining my light to and fro in the passage, and holding fast to my courage, I went down the stairs.

"As I came to the bottom step, I saw patches of wet all up and down the passage. I shone my lantern on them. It was the imprint of a wet foot on the oilcloth of the passage; not an ordinary footprint, but a queer, soft, flabby, spreading imprint, that gave me a feeling of extraordinary horror.

"Backward and forward I flashed the light over the impossible marks and saw them everywhere. Suddenly I noticed that they led to each of the closed doors. I felt something touch my back, and glanced 'round swiftly, to find the landlord had come close to me, almost pressing against me, in his fear.

"'It's all right,' I said, but in a rather breathless whisper, meaning to put a little courage into him; for I could feel that he was shaking through all his body. Even then as I tried to get him steadied enough to be of some use, his gun went off with a tremendous bang. He jumped, and yelled with sheer terror; and I swore because of the shock.

"'Give it to me, for God's sake!' I said, and slipped the gun from his hand; and in the same instant there was a sound of running steps up the garden path, and immediately the flash of a bull's-eye lantern upon the fan light over the front door. Then the door was tried, and directly afterwards there came a thunderous knocking, which told me a policeman had heard the shot.

"I went to the door, and opened it. Fortunately the constable knew me, and when I had beckoned him in, I was able to explain matters in a very short time. While doing this, Inspector Johnstone came up the path, having missed the officer, and seeing lights and the open door. I told him as briefly as possible what had occurred, and did not mention the Child or the Woman; for it would have seemed too fantastic for him to notice. I showed him the queer, wet footprints and how they went toward the closed doors. I explained quickly about the mats, and how that the one against the cellar door was flat, which showed the door had been opened.

"The inspector nodded, and told the constable to guard the door at the top of the cellar stairs. He then asked the hall lamp to be lit, after which he took the policeman's lantern, and led the way into the front room. He paused with the door wide open, and threw the light all 'round; then he jumped into the room, and looked behind the door; there was no one there; but all over the polished oak floor, between the scattered rugs, went the marks of those horrible spreading footprints; and the room permeated with the horrible odour.

"The inspector searched the room carefully, and then went into the middle room, using the same precautions. There was nothing in the middle room, or in the kitchen or pantry; but everywhere went the wet footmarks through all the rooms, showing plainly wherever there were woodwork or oilcloth; and always there was the smell.

"The inspector ceased from his search of the rooms, and spent a minute in trying whether the mats would really fall flat when the doors were open, or merely ruckle up in a way as to appear they had been untouched; but in each case, the mats fell flat, and remained so.

"'Extraordinary!' I heard Johnstone mutter to himself. And then he went toward the cellar door. He had inquired at first whether there were windows to the cellar, and when he learned there was no way out, except by the door, he had left this part of the search to the last.

"As Johnstone came up to the door, the policeman made a motion of salute, and said something in a low voice; and something in the tone made me flick my light across him. I saw then that the man was very white, and he looked strange and bewildered.

"'What?' said Johnstone impatiently. 'Speak up!'

"'A woman come along 'ere, sir, and went through this 'ere door,' said the constable, clearly, but with a curious monotonous intonation that is sometimes heard from an unintelligent man.

"'Speak up!' shouted the inspector.

"'A woman come along and went through this 'ere door,' repeated the man, monotonously.

"The inspector caught the man by the shoulder, and deliberately sniffed his breath.

"'No!' he said. And then sarcastically:—'I hope you held the door open politely for the lady.'

"'The door weren't opened, sir,' said the man, simply.

"'Are you mad—' began Johnstone.

"'No,' broke in the landlord's voice from the back. Speaking steadily enough. 'I saw the Woman upstairs.' It was evident that he had got back his control again.

"'I'm afraid, Inspector Johnstone,' I said, 'that there's more in this than you think. I certainly saw some very extraordinary things upstairs.'

"The inspector seemed about to say something; but instead, he turned again to the door, and flashed his light down and 'round about the mat. I saw then that the strange, horrible footmarks came straight up to the cellar door; and the last print showed *under* the door; yet the policeman said the door had not been opened.

"And suddenly, without any intention, or realisation of what I was saying, I asked the landlord:—

"'What were the feet like?'

"I received no answer; for the inspector was ordering the constable to open the cellar door, and the man was not obeying. Johnstone repeated the order, and at last, in a queer automatic way, the man obeyed, and pushed the door open. The loathsome smell beat up at us, in a great wave of horror, and the inspector came backward a step.

"'My God!' he said, and went forward again, and shone his light down the steps; but there was nothing visible, only that on each step showed the unnatural footprints.

"The inspector brought the beam of the light vividly on the top step; and there, clear in the light, there was something small, moving.

The inspector bent to look, and the policeman and I with him. I don't want to disgust you; but the thing we looked at was a maggot. The policeman backed suddenly out of the doorway:

"'The churchyard,' he said, '... at the back of the 'ouse.'

"'Silence!' said Johnstone, with a queer break in the word, and I knew that at last he was frightened. He put his lantern into the doorway, and shone it from step to step, following the footprints down into the darkness; then he stepped back from the open doorway, and we all gave back with him. He looked 'round, and I had a feeling that he was looking for a weapon of some kind.

"'Your gun,' I said to the landlord, and he brought it from the front hall, and passed it over to the inspector, who took it and ejected the empty shell from the right barrel. He held out his hand for a live cartridge, which the landlord brought from his pocket. He loaded the gun and snapped the breech. He turned to the constable:—

"'Come on,' he said, and moved toward the cellar doorway.

"'I ain't comin', sir,' said the policeman, very white in the face.

"With a sudden blaze of passion, the inspector took the man by the scruff and hove him bodily down into the darkness, and he went downward, screaming. The inspector followed him instantly, with his lantern and the gun; and I after the inspector, with the bayonet ready. Behind me, I heard the landlord.

"At the bottom of the stairs, the inspector was helping the policeman to his feet, where he stood swaying a moment, in a bewildered fashion; then the inspector went into the front cellar, and his man followed him in stupid fashion; but evidently no longer with any thought of running away from the horror.

"We all crowded into the front cellar, flashing our lights to and fro. Inspector Johnstone was examining the floor, and I saw that the footmarks went all 'round the cellar, into all the corners, and across the floor. I thought suddenly of the Child that was running away from Something. Do you see the thing that I was seeing vaguely?

"We went out of the cellar in a body, for there was nothing to be found. In the next cellar, the footprints went everywhere in that queer erratic fashion, as of someone searching for something, or following some blind scent.

"In the third cellar the prints ended at the shallow well that had been the old water supply of the house. The well was full to the brim, and the water so clear that the pebbly bottom was plainly to be seen, as we shone the lights into the water. The search came to an abrupt end, and we stood about the well, looking at one another, in an absolute, horrible silence.

"Johnstone made another examination of the footprints; then he shone his light again into the clear shallow water, searching each inch of the plainly seen bottom; but there was nothing there. The cellar was full of the dreadful smell; and everyone stood silent, except for the constant turning of the lamps to and fro around the cellar.

"The inspector looked up from his search of the well, and nodded quietly across at me, with his sudden acknowledgement that our belief was now his belief, the smell in the cellar seemed to grow more dreadful, and to be, as it were, a menace—the material expression that some monstrous thing was there with us, invisible.

"'I think—' began the inspector, and shone his light toward the stairway; and at this the constable's restraint went utterly, and he ran for the stairs, making a queer sound in his throat.

"The landlord followed, at a quick walk, and then the inspector and I. He waited a single instant for me, and we went up together, treading on the same steps, and with our lights held backward. At the top, I slammed and locked the stair door, and wiped my forehead, and my hands were shaking.

"The inspector asked me to give his man a glass of whisky, and then he sent him on his beat. He stayed a short while with the landlord and me, and it was arranged that he would join us again the following night and watch the Well with us from midnight until daylight. Then he left us, just as the dawn was coming in. The landlord and I locked up the house, and went over to his place for a sleep.

"In the afternoon, the landlord and I returned to the house, to make arrangements for the night. He was very quiet, and I felt he was to be relied on, now that he had been 'salted,' as it were, with his fright of the previous night.

"We opened all the doors and windows, and blew the house through very thoroughly; and in the meanwhile, we lit the lamps in the house, and took them into the cellars, where we set them all about, so as to have light everywhere. Then we carried down three chairs and a table, and set them in the cellar where the well was sunk. After that, we stretched thin piano wire across the cellar, about nine inches from the floor, at such a height that it should catch anything moving about in the dark.

"When this was done, I went through the house with the landlord, and sealed every window and door in the place, excepting only the front door and the door at the top of the cellar stairs.

"Meanwhile, a local wire-smith was making something to my order; and when the landlord and I had finished tea at his house, we went down to see how the smith was getting on. We found the thing complete. It looked rather like a huge parrot's cage, without any bottom, of very heavy gage wire, and stood about seven feet high and was four feet in diameter. Fortunately, I remembered to have it made longitudinally in two halves, or else we should never have got it through the doorways and down the cellar stairs.

"I told the wire-smith to bring the cage up to the house so he could fit the two halves rigidly together. As we returned, I called in at an ironmonger's, where I bought some thin hemp rope and an iron rack pulley, like those used in Lancashire for hauling up the ceiling clothes racks, which you will find in every cottage. I bought also a couple of pitchforks.

"'We shan't want to touch it,' I said to the landlord; and he nodded, rather white all at once.

"As soon as the cage arrived and had been fitted together in the cellar, I sent away the smith; and the landlord and I suspended it over the well, into which it fitted easily. After a lot of trouble, we managed to hang it so perfectly central from the rope over the iron pulley, that when hoisted to the ceiling and dropped, it went every time plunk into the well, like a candle-extinguisher. When we had it finally arranged, I hoisted it up once more, to the ready position, and made the rope fast to a heavy wooden pillar, which stood in the middle of the cellar.

"By ten o'clock, I had everything arranged, with the two pitch-forks and the two police lanterns; also some whisky and sandwiches. Underneath the table I had several buckets full of disinfectant.

"A little after eleven o'clock, there was a knock at the front door, and when I went, I found Inspector Johnstone had arrived, and brought with him one of his plainclothes men. You will understand how pleased I was to see there would be this addition to our watch; for he looked a tough, nerveless man, brainy and collected; and one I should have picked to help us with the horrible job I felt pretty sure we should have to do that night.

"When the inspector and the detective had entered, I shut and locked the front door; then, while the inspector held the light, I sealed the door carefully, with tape and wax. At the head of the cellar stairs, I shut and locked that door also, and sealed it in the same way.

"As we entered the cellar, I warned Johnstone and his man to be careful not to fall over the wires; and then, as I saw his surprise at my arrangements, I began to explain my ideas and intentions, to all of which he listened with strong approval. I was pleased to see also that the detective was nodding his head, as I talked, in a way that showed he appreciated all my precautions.

"As he put his lantern down, the inspector picked up one of the pitchforks, and balanced it in his hand; he looked at me, and nodded.

"'The best thing,' he said. 'I only wish you'd got two more.'

"Then we all took our seats, the detective getting a washing stool from the corner of the cellar. From then, until a quarter to twelve, we talked quietly, whilst we made a light supper of whisky and sandwiches; after which, we cleared everything off the table, excepting the lanterns and the pitchforks. One of the latter, I handed to the inspector; the other I took myself, and then, having set my chair so as to be handy to the rope which lowered the cage into the well, I went 'round the cellar and put out every lamp.

"I groped my way to my chair, and arranged the pitchfork and the dark lantern ready to my hand; after which I suggested that everyone should keep an absolute silence throughout the watch. I asked, also, that no lantern should be turned on, until I gave the word.

"I put my watch on the table, where a faint glow from my lantern made me able to see the time. For an hour nothing happened, and everyone kept an absolute silence, except for an occasional uneasy movement.

"About half-past one, however, I was conscious again of the same extraordinary and peculiar nervousness, which I had felt on the previous night. I put my hand out quickly, and eased the hitched rope from around the pillar. The inspector seemed aware of the movement; for I saw the faint light from his lantern, move a little, as if he had suddenly taken hold of it, in readiness.

"A minute later, I noticed there was a change in the colour of the night in the cellar, and it grew slowly violet tinted upon my eyes. I glanced to and fro, quickly, in the new darkness, and even as I looked, I was conscious that the violet colour deepened. In the direction of the well, but seeming to be at a great distance, there was, as it were, a nucleus to the change; and the nucleus came swiftly toward us, appearing to come from a great space, almost in a single moment. It came near, and I saw again that it was a little naked Child, running, and seeming to be of the violet night in which it ran.

"The Child came with a natural running movement, exactly as I described it before; but in a silence so peculiarly intense, that it was as if it brought the silence with it. About halfway between the well and the table, the Child turned swiftly, and looked back at something invisible to me; and suddenly it went down into a crouching attitude, and seemed to be hiding behind something that showed vaguely; but there was nothing there, except the bare floor of the cellar; nothing, I mean, of our world.

"I could hear the breathing of the three other men, with a wonderful distinctness; and also the tick of my watch upon the table seemed to sound as loud and as slow as the tick of an old grandfather's clock. Someway I knew that none of the others saw what I was seeing.

"Abruptly, the landlord, who was next to me, let out his breath with a little hissing sound; I knew then that something was visible to him. There came a creak from the table, and I had a feeling that the inspector was leaning forward, looking at something that I could not see. The landlord reached out his hand through the darkness, and fumbled a moment to catch my arm:—

"'The Woman!' he whispered, close to my ear. 'Over by the well.'

"I stared hard in that direction; but saw nothing, except that the violet colour of the cellar seemed a little duller just there.

"I looked back quickly to the vague place where the Child was hiding. I saw it was peering back from its hiding place. Suddenly it rose and ran straight for the middle of the table, which showed only as vague shadow halfway between my eyes and the unseen floor. As the Child ran under the table, the steel prongs of my pitchfork glimmered with a violet, fluctuating light. A little way off, there showed high up in the gloom, the vaguely shining outline of the other fork, so I knew the inspector had it raised in his hand, ready. There was no doubt but that he saw something. On the table, the metal of the five lanterns shone with the same strange glow; and about each lantern there was a little cloud of absolute blackness, where the phenomenon that is light to our natural eyes, came through the fittings; and in this complete darkness, the metal of each lantern showed plain, as might a cat's-eye in a nest of black cotton wool.

"Just beyond the table, the Child paused again, and stood, seeming to oscillate a little upon its feet, which gave the impression that it was lighter and vaguer than a thistle-down; and yet, in the same moment, another part of me seemed to know that it was to me, as something that might be beyond thick, invisible glass, and subject to conditions and forces that I was unable to comprehend.

"The Child was looking back again, and my gaze went the same way. I stared across the cellar, and saw the cage hanging clear in the violet light, every wire and tie outlined with its glimmering; above it there was a little space of gloom, and then the dull shining of the iron pulley which I had screwed into the ceiling.

"I stared in a bewildered way 'round the cellar; there were thin lines of vague fire crossing the floor in all directions; and suddenly I remembered the piano wire that the landlord and I had stretched. But there was nothing else to be seen, except that near the table there were indistinct glimmerings of light, and at the far end the outline of a dull glowing revolver, evidently in the detective's pocket. I remember a sort of subconscious satisfaction, as I settled the point in a queer automatic fashion. On the table, near to me, there was a little shapeless collection of the light; and this I knew, after an instant's consideration, to be the steel portions of my watch.

"I had looked several times at the Child, and 'round at the cellar, whilst I was decided these trifles; and had found it still in that attitude of hiding from something. But now, suddenly, it ran clear away into the distance, and was nothing more than a slightly deeper coloured nucleus far away in the strange coloured atmosphere.

"The landlord gave out a queer little cry, and twisted over against me, as if to avoid something. From the inspector there came a sharp breathing sound, as if he had been suddenly drenched with cold water. Then suddenly the violet colour went out of the night, and I was conscious of the nearness of something monstrous and repugnant.

"There was a tense silence, and the blackness of the cellar seemed absolute, with only the faint glow about each of the lanterns on the table. Then, in the darkness and the silence, there came a faint tinkle of water from the well, as if something were rising noiselessly out of it, and the water running back with a gentle tinkling. In the same instant, there came to me a sudden waft of the awful smell.

"I gave a sharp cry of warning to the inspector, and loosed the rope. There came instantly the sharp splash of the cage entering the water; and then, with a stiff, frightened movement, I opened the shutter of my lantern, and shone the light at the cage, shouting to the others to do the same.

"As my light struck the cage, I saw that about two feet of it projected from the top of the well, and there was something protruding up out of the water, into the cage. I stared, with a feeling that I recognised the thing; and then, as the other lanterns were opened, I saw that it was a leg of mutton. The thing was held by a brawny fist and arm, that rose out of the water. I stood utterly bewildered, watching to see what was coming. In a moment there rose into view a great bearded face, that I felt for one quick instant was the face of a drowned man, long dead. Then the face opened at the mouth part, and spluttered and coughed. Another big hand came into view, and wiped the water from the eyes, which blinked rapidly, and then fixed themselves into a stare at the lights.

"From the detective there came a sudden shout:—

"'Captain Tobias!' he shouted, and the inspector echoed him; and instantly burst into loud roars of laughter.

"The inspector and the detective ran across the cellar to the cage; and I followed, still bewildered. The man in the cage was holding the leg of mutton as far away from him, as possible, and holding his nose.

"'Lift thig dam trap, quig!' he shouted in a stifled voice; but the inspector and the detective simply doubled before him, and tried to hold their noses, whilst they laughed, and the light from their lanterns went dancing all over the place.

"'Quig! quig!' said the man in the cage, still holding his nose, and trying to speak plainly.

"Then Johnstone and the detective stopped laughing, and lifted the cage. The man in the well threw the leg across the cellar, and turned swiftly to go down into the well; but the officers were too quick for him, and had him out in a twinkling. Whilst they held him, dripping upon the floor, the inspector jerked his thumb in the direction of the offending leg, and the landlord, having harpooned it with one of the pitchforks, ran with it upstairs and so into the open air.

"Meanwhile, I had given the man from the well a stiff tot of whisky; for which he thanked me with a cheerful nod, and having emptied the glass at a draft, held his hand for the bottle, which he finished, as if it had been so much water.

"As you will remember, it was a Captain Tobias who had been the previous tenant; and this was the very man, who had appeared from the well. In the course of the talk that followed, I learned the reason for Captain Tobias leaving the house; he had been wanted by the police for smuggling. He had undergone imprisonment; and had been released only a couple of weeks earlier.

"He had returned to find new tenants in his old home. He had entered the house through the well, the walls of which were not continued to the bottom (this I will deal with later); and gone up by a little stairway in the cellar wall, which opened at the top through a panel beside my mother's bedroom. This panel was opened, by revolving the left doorpost of the bedroom door, with the result that the bedroom door always became unlatched, in the process of opening the panel.

"The captain complained, without any bitterness, that the panel had warped, and that each time he opened it, it made a cracking noise. This had been evidently what I mistook for raps. He would not give his reason for entering the house; but it was pretty obvious that he had hidden something, which he wanted to get. However, as he found it impossible to get into the house without the risk of being caught, he decided to try to drive us out, relying on the bad reputation of the house, and his own artistic efforts as a ghost. I must say he succeeded. He intended then to rent the house again, as before; and would then, of course have plenty of time to get whatever he had hidden. The house suited him admirably; for there was a passage—as he showed me afterwards—connecting the dummy well with the crypt of the church beyond the garden wall; and these, in turn, were connected with certain caves in the cliffs, which went down to the beach beyond the church.

"In the course of his talk, Captain Tobias offered to take the house off my hands; and as this suited me perfectly, for I was about stalled with it, and the plan also suited the landlord, it was decided that no steps should be taken against him; and that the whole business should be hushed up.

"I asked the captain whether there was really anything queer about the house; whether he had ever seen anything. He said yes, that he had twice seen a Woman going about the house. We all looked at one another, when the captain said that. He told us she never bothered him, and that he had only seen her twice, and on each occasion it had followed a narrow escape from the Revenue people.

"Captain Tobias was an observant man; he had seen how I had placed the mats against the doors; and after entering the rooms, and walking all about them, so as to leave the footmarks of an old pair of wet woollen slippers everywhere, he had deliberately put the mats back as he found them.

"The maggot which had dropped from his disgusting leg of mutton had been an accident, and beyond even his horrible planning. He was hugely delighted to learn how it had affected us.

"The mouldy smell I had noticed was from the little closed stairway, when the captain opened the panel. The door slamming was also another of his contributions.

"I come now to the end of the captain's ghost play; and to the difficulty of trying to explain the other peculiar things. In the first place, it was obvious there was something genuinely strange in the house; which made itself manifest as a Woman. Many different people had seen this Woman, under differing circumstances, so it is impossible to put the thing down to fancy; at the same time it must seem extraordinary that I should have lived two years in the house, and seen nothing; whilst the policeman saw the Woman, before he had been there twenty minutes; the landlord, the detective, and the inspector all saw her.

"I can only surmise that *fear* was in every case the key, as I might say, which opened the senses to the presence of the Woman. The policeman was a highly-strung man, and when he became frightened, was able to see the Woman. The same reasoning applies all 'round. *I* saw nothing, until I became really frightened; then I saw, not the Woman; but a Child, running away from Something or Someone. However, I will touch on that later. In short, until a very strong degree of fear was present, no one was affected by the Force which made Itself evident, as a Woman. My theory explains why some tenants were never aware of anything strange in the house, whilst others left immediately. The more sensitive they were, the less would be the degree of fear necessary to make them aware of the Force present in the house.

"The peculiar shining of all the metal objects in the cellar, had been visible only to me. The cause, naturally I do not know; neither do I know why I, alone, was able to see the shining."

"The Child," I asked. "Can you explain that part at all? Why *you* didn't see the Woman, and why *they* didn't see the Child. Was it merely the same Force, appearing differently to different people?"

"No," said Carnacki, "I can't explain that. But I am quite sure that the Woman and the Child were not only two complete and different entities; but even they were each not in quite the same planes of existence.

"To give you a root idea, however, it is held in the Sigsand MS. that a child '*still*born' is 'Snatyched back bye thee Haggs.' This is crude; but may yet contain an elemental truth. Yet, before I make this clearer, let me tell you a thought that has often been made. It may be that physical birth is but a secondary process; and that prior to the possibility, the Mother Spirit searches for, until it finds, the small Element—the primal Ego or child's soul. It may be that a certain waywardness would cause such to strive to evade capture by the Mother Spirit. It may have been such a thing as this, that I saw. I have always tried to think so; but it is impossible to ignore the sense of repulsion that I felt when the unseen Woman went past me. This repulsion carries forward the idea suggested in the Sigsand MS., that a stillborn child is thus, because its ego or spirit has been snatched back by the 'Hags.' In other words, by certain of the Monstrosities of the Outer Circle. The thought is inconceivably terrible, and probably the more so because it is so fragmentary. It leaves us with the conception of a child's soul adrift halfway between two lives, and running through Eternity from Something incredible and inconceivable (because not understood) to our senses.

"The thing is beyond further discussion; for it is futile to attempt to discuss a thing, to any purpose, of which one has a knowledge so fragmentary as this. There is one thought, which is often mine. Perhaps there is a Mother Spirit—"

"And the well?" said Arkright. "How did the captain get in from the other side?"

"As I said before," answered Carnacki. "The side walls of the well did not reach to the bottom; so that you had only to dip down into the water, and come up again on the other side of the wall, under the cellar floor, and so climb into the passage. Of course, the water was the same height on both sides of the walls. Don't ask me who made the well entrance or the little stairway; for I don't know. The house was very old, as I have told you; and that sort of thing was useful in the old days."

"And the Child," I said, coming back to the thing which chiefly interested me. "You would say that the birth must have occurred in that house; and in this way, one might suppose that the house to have become *en rapport*, if I can use the word in that way, with the Forces that produced the tragedy?"

"Yes," replied Carnacki. "This is, supposing we take the suggestion of the Sigsand MS., to account for the phenomenon."

"There may be other houses——" I began.

"There are," said Carnacki; and stood up.

"Out you go," he said, genially, using the recognised formula. And in five minutes we were on the Embankment, going thoughtfully to our various homes.

AYLMER VANCE

in

THE FEAR

Claude and Alice Askew

As with Hodgson, both Claude Askew (1865–1917) and his wife Alice (1874–1917), fell victims to the Great War. While helping Serbian refugees in the Balkans their hospital ship was torpedoed. Alice's body was washed up on the shores of Corfu, but Claude's was never recovered.

The couple had written many popular books and stories after their marriage in 1900, but they rarely wrote works of the supernatural. Aside from the novel The Devil and the Crusader *(1909), in which London faces horrors after a man summons Satan, their other significant work of the paranormal was the series featuring Aylmer Vance, who seems to have a past he is reluctant to reveal though his colleague, Mr. Dexter, continues to pry. Vance calls himself a Ghost-Seer because he is highly sensitive to spirits whilst Dexter himself is also somewhat clairvoyant.*

One morning in late summer Aylmer Vance, after glancing through his correspondence, remarked that there was a gentleman coming to see us that day who would probably have something interesting to communicate.

"His name is Robert Balliston, and he's by way of being a millionaire," explained Vance. "A self-made man, so I understand. He's had a letter of introduction to me through some mutual friends, and he appears to be in great trouble about a house which he has recently taken on a long lease."

"Have you any idea what form the trouble takes?" I inquired.

Vance shook his head. "No," he responded, "I haven't been told anything about it yet. But I understand it's so serious that Mr. Balliston and his family have had to turn out after being in residence barely a month. No doubt we shall hear all about it when he comes."

In the course of the morning Mr. Balliston put in his appearance. Somehow I think I could have guessed at once that he was a man who had made a lot of money by his own endeavours—he was so exactly the type one would expect. Coarse, but withal kindly-faced; thin hair—still dark—that scarcely hid his shining scalp; overdressed; rotund of figure as of pocket-book—we have all met his like many a time. His loud voice filled the room.

"Mr. Vance," he said, "you are a man whose name is well known to me, though, upon my word, I never expected to meet you in your professional capacity."

Vance and I exchanged a glance, for there is nothing that my friend dislikes more than to be described as a "professional". He is a dilettante in every sense of the word, and has never in his life undertaken a research except for the sheer love of the thing. But it was impossible to be in the least offended with Mr. Balliston.

"You are, sir, I believe, an authority on ghosts," resumed the latter. He spoke the last word in a tone of depreciation almost comic. Level-headed Robert Balliston and ghosts!—the conjunction of ideas seemed quite ridiculous.

"On what you call ghosts," corrected Vance gently, "perhaps I am."

"I don't call 'em anything, sir," snapped the millionaire. "I don't believe in 'em, there aren't any such things. I've been told so all my life, and my father was a business man like myself. Yet a funny thing has happened to me, and as it seems to be in your line I got my friends, the Whittakers, to give me an introduction. And I needn't say that I'm pleased to make your acquaintance as well as that of Mr. Dexter."

Of course we acknowledged the compliment, and then Aylmer Vance proceeded to inquire the source of the trouble.

"Well, it's this," was the reply. "How would you like it, Mr. Vance, if you had leased a house—spent a great deal of money on it, too—and then had to leave it in a hurry, without any particular prospects of going back? Pleasant, isn't it? One may be well off, but there are limits."

"Was it a new house?"

"New? No, old as they make 'em. Dates back to I don't know what period. Never was good at that sort of thing myself. Moated grange kind of place, you know. It was my wife's idea. She said when we had made enough we should take a big house and become county people. I heard of Camplin Castle from an agent, who said that it was just what we wanted—Lord of the Manor, good style of neighbour, and the rest of it. It's in Hampshire, near the borders of the Forest, not far from the sea. A fine, imposing place I found it, but out of repair. It hadn't been occupied for quite a time, as the price was so stiff. That put me on my mettle, I suppose, and I closed the bargain. Well, it took more repairing than I thought, and I spent quite a lot of money on it before we moved in. That's not a month ago, and here we are." He spread out his hands with a despondent gesture.

Vance regarded our visitor critically.

"A man like you wouldn't give in easily," he observed. "Now what was it that drove you away, Mr. Balliston?"

"That's just what beats me," cried the other. "I don't know. We've seen nothing, heard nothing—at least, not in the ordinary sense of the word. Every room is as comfortable as money can make it. But we couldn't stay in the castle, and the only explanation I can give is that we were frightened away."

"And what frightened you?"

"Don't I say I haven't an idea? Every one of us in turn got seized with an unaccountable sense of fear. It's very difficult to explain, and all I know is that it's there, and that you can't fight against it. The feeling you get is of an invisible presence that is itself suffering from fear, a fear that is imparted to you. The thing, whatever it may be, radiates fear, if I may put it so."

"And is this fear confined to one place, or to any particular time?"

"No, that's just the worst of it. If it were, we could avoid the place, for the castle's so big that I shouldn't in the least mind shutting up any particular room. But it happens at all manner of times and anywhere."

"You say that you have all felt it. How many are you in family, Mr. Balliston?"

"My wife and myself and our four children, two girls and two boys, ranging in age from twelve to eighteen. Our youngest child got it first—she's a girl of twelve, and we put her and her sister into two rooms communicating with each other. It was the very first night after we moved in. Gertrude—that's the eldest girl—heard her little sister sobbing, and when she went to find out what was the matter the child told her that she couldn't sleep, she was too frightened. She couldn't say what she was frightened of, and Gertrude laughed at her and told her not to be a little goose. But the child wouldn't stop crying, and so, to soothe her, Gertrude got into bed with her. And then she felt it too. She said it was awful. She snatched up little Myra and carried her to the other room, and there they both lay, shivering and trembling with the recollection of it, till the morning, when they told us what had happened."

"And did anyone else ever sleep in that room?"

"Yes, we tried it one after another, at least, my two sons and I did, and we found it just as they had said. So we decided not to occupy that room any more, as there seemed to be something queer about it, and it would have been all right if things had not developed in another direction."

"You got the same impression in other parts of the house?"

"Yes. A day or two later my wife had hysterics in the drawing-room; she said that she felt certain there was something going to happen to her, and it was a long time before she came round. Then one of the servants pitched down the stairs and hurt herself badly. It was rather late, and she was going up to bed. She said that there was something following her, and she knew it meant mischief. And so it went on, everybody was affected, and sometimes it caught several of us together. The sensation never lasted long, but it always made one feel as if one couldn't get through it alive. And so that's why we've left Camplin Castle, Mr. Vance, and that's why I've come to consult you."

Vance reflected for a few moments, then he inquired:

"Do you know anything of the history of Camplin Castle, Mr. Balliston?"

"Very little. It didn't interest me you understand. And we hadn't time to get to know any of the neighbours."

"But you must, of course, be acquainted with the name of the owner?"

"Yes. Camplin has belonged for hundreds of years to the Oswald family—the last of them died about a dozen years ago. He was never married, and there is no heir in the direct line. The present owner is a nephew and he is too poor to live in the place himself—at least, that's what the agent told me."

"And didn't you try to get any more information from the agent?"

"Catch him giving me any!" was the somewhat scornful response. "The man had done his deal and pocketed his commission. He wasn't likely to tell me anything against the place, and quite right, too, from a business point of view."

Vance put a few more leading questions, and then informed Mr. Balliston that he and I would go down to Camplin Castle the next day.

"I suppose there is someone on the premises to look after us?" he inquired.

"Yes, there's the lodge-keeper and his wife. I couldn't get any of the other servants to remain. I'll wire to Smith to expect you." With a sudden burst of confidence Mr. Balliston added: "For heaven's sake, Mr. Vance, find out the cause of the mystery. I tell you I was so frightened that the hair stood up on my head!"

I was trying to picture Mr. Balliston's thin hair taking on this peculiar disposition as he took his leave.

The next day we travelled down to Camplin Castle, which we found to be situated several miles from the nearest station.

Mr. Balliston had arranged for a motor-car to be placed at our disposal for as long as we cared to stay. It was to be garaged at the village close by.

The sun was setting when we reached the gates of the park, which were opened for us by a somewhat surly and reticent lodge-keeper. He mounted the box by the side of our chauffeur, after informing us that his wife was at the castle making preparations for our reception.

Neither of them slept at the house, which we were to have quite to ourselves.

We passed down a fine avenue of elms, and presently, on either side, appeared great stretches of well-kept lawns and carefully-planted flower beds—every indication of the expenditure of much money.

A sweep of the road brought us to the house, which was a huge grey pile of varied architecture. Yet the whole effect was one of symmetry. In the centre appeared a time-worn, ivy-covered tower, round which the rest of the edifice had sprung up.

A neat, comfortable-looking woman admitted us to a vast hall, and thence to a dining-room, where the table was laid for dinner.

Vance spoke a few words of compliment on the arrangements that had been made for our comfort.

"You will look after us, I suppose, during our stay?" he remarked to Mrs. Smith.

"Oh, yes, sir, as long as I don't have to remain at night," was the response. "I don't mind it so much otherwise."

"It?" queried Vance, looking at her keenly.

"Yes, sir, the Fear. One never knows when it may come. I felt it this afternoon, but it passed quickly. At night, oh, it's terrible at night. I think Smith has taken your bags to your rooms," she added hurriedly, as if to change the subject.

At this moment Smith reappeared, evidently anxious to take his departure. His more self-possessed wife conducted us upstairs to two large adjoining rooms on the first floor.

"It was Mr. Balliston's instructions, gentlemen, that these rooms should be prepared for you tonight. This one that we are now in"— she seemed to be looking over her shoulder with an expression of tremulous nervousness—"is the one in which nobody has been able to sleep. It's a long time now since it has been occupied at all."

"Do you know anything of the story of this house, Mrs. Smith?" inquired Vance.

"No, sir. We are London people. Mr. Balliston brought us down."

"But the village folk, don't they talk?"

"Well, sir," was the answer, given in a faltering tone, "of course we have heard all manner of stories, Smith and I, but there isn't one of them that really explains the Fear. You see, nobody had ever heard of it before Mr. Balliston took the Castle. The house had stood empty ever since old Mr. Luke Oswald died, and he only used to occupy a few rooms in the south wing. He was a queer old gentleman, they say, and lived quite by himself except for one servant, and he wouldn't ever see any company, so that people got calling him a miser and whatnot. The old servant, whose name was Somers—John Somers—died soon after his master, but his grandson is living in the village—he is a builder by trade, and I should think he could tell you more than anyone else about the Oswald family, if you cared to go and have a chat with him."

"I certainly shall make a point of doing so," replied Vance, "and thank you very much, Mrs. Smith, for the information."

With which he dismissed the good woman, who bustled away evidently pleased at being able to take her departure from the dreaded room.

I think I have said that our rooms had a communicating door between them—they were the ones originally occupied by Robert Balliston's two daughters.

The "haunted room"—I will define it as such—was the smaller, and I imagine that the larger one—which I was to occupy—may have once been a boudoir. It was a bright, cheerful room, with windows looking out upon the front. Both apartments were quite modern in appearance, and had no suggestion of ghostly influence about them. They had evidently been quite recently furnished and decorated with good taste and the expenditure of plenty of money.

It struck me that the only antique piece of furniture was the bed in the smaller room, and this was of handsomely carved oak, surmounted by a high canopy.

I commenced unpacking my portmanteau, talking to Vance all the time through the open door. I could not see him, but could hear him moving about.

"We must certainly go to the village tomorrow and make some inquiries of this man Somers," he was saying. "I want to know—"

Suddenly he ceased speaking, and I thought I heard a sound like a stifled gasp, and then there came a deep silence.

I was seated by my dressing-table. I was about to turn and ask what was the matter when suddenly a cold breath seemed to pass across my face and I became riveted where I sat; I could not have looked round to save my life, though I felt that there was something there just behind me.

I could not utter a sound, my tongue seemed to cleave to a dry palate. I knew that I was trembling, filled with a sensation, a terrible pervading fear of impending death, a feeling that long fingers were about to grip me by the neck from behind and squeeze the life out of me. If not now, immediately, I knew that it must come soon, that a death, swift and cruel and terrible, awaited me.

I grasped the arms of the chair, and during that ghastly second a very eternity seemed to pass over me.

At last relief came. I felt the cold breath upon my face once more, and the next moment I was able to turn my head. Aylmer Vance stood in the doorway between our rooms.

I put my hand to my forehead and found the hair wringing wet.

"So you've had a turn, too?" asked Vance with a quiet smile. "It isn't pleasant, is it?"

I vowed that it was anything but pleasant. I think I swore lustily.

"What does it mean?" I inquired.

"That's what we've got to find out," he replied, looking at me with some anxiety. "Whatever it is it seems to have passed from my room to yours—as if it follows the course of some invisible being—a being that is afraid, horribly afraid, and that is able to impart its fear to anyone who comes in its way. It's a ghastly kind of experience, Dexter, and it will no doubt be worse at night. Are you prepared to go through with it?"

I grasped his hand and said I was. But I must admit that I was anything but happy in my mind.

Mrs. Smith looked at us curiously when we appeared for dinner, but made no remark. The meal over she took her departure, promising to be round early in the morning to give us our breakfast.

After dinner we sat and smoked for a while, and then, as the night was oppressively hot, we made our way to the garden.

It was really delightful to escape for a short time from the evil influence which seemed to pervade the house—even in the absence of the actual overwhelming terror. One felt—one knew—that something horribly, abominably cruel must have been enacted within the walls of the Castle, and that, however long ago it may have been, the impression had never been eradicated.

The night air was deliciously cool and balmy with scented air. It was rather dark, though the sky was rich with stars. Our walk was not objectless. Vance wanted to explore the house on the outside and at night.

Twice we made the circle of it. There were broad terraces to most of the wings, but at the back, beneath the tower, there was only a narrow strip of lawn flanked by a shrubbery.

There were a few windows in the tower, but quite high up there seemed to be a circular apartment with several windows, and one of these stood wide open. And while we were looking up at it the Fear overtook us once more, although, on this occasion, it was only of a very transitory nature and disappeared altogether as soon as we were able to leave the spot.

When, a few minutes later, we mustered up courage to return, there was no recurrence of the ghastly feeling, but as we stood there, waiting for it, Vance suddenly placed his hand upon my shoulder, and pointing up to the tower exclaimed:

"Look there, Dexter. Do you notice anything strange?"

I looked and realised at once that the window, which had stood open only a few minutes ago, was now closed—yet, as we knew, the house was absolutely untenanted.

"What is the time, Dexter?" asked Vance in a tone that, for him, was almost excited. "I think it is of importance."

I struck a match and looked at my watch. It was then half-past eleven.

We returned to the house after this experience, and I knew that I was glad of a stiff peg of whisky and soda—for it wasn't as if the terrors of the night were at an end.

There was still the haunted room to be faced.

But Vance would not allow me to share this room with him as I offered to do. My nerves were already sufficiently on edge, he declared, and though I protested, I must admit that I allowed myself to be easily persuaded. I insisted, however, that the communicating door between the two rooms should be left open so that I might be summoned, if necessary, at any moment.

And so we retired for the night, though, as far as I was concerned, it was not to sleep. I lay tossing about in my bed, expecting at every moment to hear Vance's call, and at last, unable to bear the strain any longer, I got up and went into his room to see how he was faring.

To my surprise, I found him sleeping calmly and peacefully. He had a shaded light burning beside the bed, and he did not stir when I approached. It was evident that the Fear had not assailed him, for I was quite sure he could not have slept through it if he had.

I tip-toed back to my room, and laid down again, and soon afterwards, my mind relieved, I got off to sleep, and did not open my eyes until I was aroused by the sun shining in at the window.

Vance was already up and dressing, and when he heard me astir he called out to know how I had slept.

"I've had a remarkably good night myself," he said cheerfully. "Not a sign of the Fear or of anything else."

"And yet other people have been unable to sleep in that room!" I exclaimed wonderingly. "How do you account for that, Vance?"

He shrugged his shoulders.

"I can't account for it—yet," he replied. "We must wait and see what happens tonight. I've got a theory, but I'll keep it to myself at present."

"Well, I claim my turn to sleep there tonight," I declared, for in the sunlight my courage was completely restored. "Perhaps my faculty of seeing visions may be of service in solving the mystery."

We found that Mrs. Smith had provided us with an excellent breakfast, and though I am sure she wanted to question us, she did not venture to do so directly, nor did Vance or I show ourselves responsive to her hints.

We spent the morning exploring the Castle, and, as may be expected, it was to the tower that we first turned our attention.

We mounted to the circular room near the summit by means of a winding staircase to which access was obtained from the portrait gallery.

The room had been furnished, evidently by Mr. Balliston, in semi-oriental fashion, and the walls of great age, were hung with tapestry. Somehow the impression of modernity jarred. We soon localised the window which we had seen open the night before. It was now closely shut. It was large and heavy, and we found that it was only with difficulty and by our united efforts, that we could raise the sash. Looking out, we saw beneath the little shrubbery where we had received the impression of fear.

There was nothing, however, by which the mystery might be elucidated, and we could only decide to make a further investigation when night came on.

In the afternoon we made our way to the village and inquired for Mr. Somers, the builder.

Unfortunately, he was absent for the day, so all we could do was to leave a message making an appointment for the next morning.

We made certain other inquiries, but learnt little more than we already knew.

With the exception of Mr. Somers, no one in the village—at least no one that we could find—had been inside the Castle while it stood empty. Stories had, of course, got abroad, but they were indefinite, and did not touch upon the Fear. Mr. Somers's father and grandfather had both been reticent men, while the builder himself was apparently loath to admit that there was anything wrong. In fact, he made light of what had become common talk.

We returned to the Castle towards six o'clock, and were again caught by the Fear in our rooms at the same time as the night before. All that we could determine was that it certainly passed from the smaller to the larger room and then went out to the passage. We felt it quite distinctly just outside the door.

After that we proceeded to the tower room and made sure that all the windows were firmly closed.

We dined, attended by Mrs. Smith, as on the night before, but we retired early to our bedrooms, for Vance wished to put his theory to the test. He explained his undisturbed sleep of last night by the possibility that the Fear, which everyone had experienced who slept in that room, came on earlier—before he went to bed—and that consequently he had missed it.

"Mr. Balliston did not say that anyone spent the whole night in that room," he remarked.

It was decided that I should occupy the "haunted room". I lay down accordingly, practically fully dressed, on the outside of the bed, and Vance sat up in the other room, with the light full on, reading a book. It was then about half-past ten.

And half an hour later the Fear assailed me.

I have already described the sensation, so I need not repeat it, except to say that tonight it seemed increased a hundredfold.

I lay perfectly rigid, fully conscious of Vance's propinquity in the next room, but voiceless, absolutely unable to call out to him for assistance. My forehead was wringing wet with perspiration, and all my being was strung up with expectation—the expectation of something imminent, something ghastly, something inevitable.

And then, of a sudden, though there was nothing to be seen, absolutely nothing, I received the impression that the bed upon which I lay was already occupied—that someone else was lying there, someone who trembled and shook and sobbed so that the whole structure seemed to quiver beneath me.

I reached out my hand, but it encountered nothing, and yet I knew—I knew.

I cannot say how long I lay thus. It seemed to me an eternity—it may in reality have been a quarter of an hour. And the most awful part of it was the sense of helplessness, and the fact that instead of passing off as it had done on the other occasions, the Fear seemed to be increasing, to be growing momentarily more intense. Every successive moment was charged with acuter agony. Something was going to happen, and it was going to be now—now, at once.

I found myself sitting up upon the bed, straining my ears to listen for the approach of the danger. Perhaps my power of visualising things added to the intensity of the emotion, for I knew that I myself underwent every tiny detail of the agony that was endured by someone who had occupied that bed in years long gone by, and whose presence I vaguely felt by my side.

And as I sat thus it seemed to me that certain sounds fell upon my ears, and yet I cannot assert that they existed except through some impression mysteriously imparted to my brain.

Had there been any reality about them they were certainly loud enough to have disturbed Vance, who sat in his room quietly reading on, totally unconscious of the torture that I was enduring.

I thought I heard the furtive opening and closing of a door below and then a stealthy step upon the stair drawing nearer and nearer, and it seemed to me, as I listened, that I gave vent to a wild scream of terror—and yet I know now that not a sound escaped my lips.

Like all other impressions of those ghastly moments, the scream was a suggested product of my own brain—just as was the feeble crying of a child that I heard at the same moment, the frightened wail of an infant disturbed in its sleep.

And now I could hear laboured breathing in the passage outside, and the next moment it was at the door.

I felt a strange tingling at the roots of my hair, and the sudden recollection flashed through my brain of what Mr. Balliston had said: "I assure you it made my hair stand on end!"

A suggestion that had amused me at the moment, but now I understood it—if Mr. Balliston had gone through one tithe of what I was enduring.

I gazed with horror-riveted eyes at the door, and presently it seemed that the handle moved as if it were being slowly turned; then I was vaguely conscious of another shriek, louder by far than the first, and this was followed, to my acutely sharpened perception, by a sound as if someone had sprung from the bed by my side and was pattering across the floor with bare feet in the direction of the room occupied by Vance.

And all the while I could hear the whimpering of the child, carried, as it seemed, by the owner of the running feet, into the adjoining room.

The next moment the spell was broken—the terror had passed from me, and I lay there, panting and gasping, struggling to recover my shattered senses.

I had regained the use of my limbs, and blindly, wildly, following some impulse which I could not for the moment account for, I sprang from the bed and rushed into my friend's room.

Vance was sitting immobile in his chair, and the book which he had been reading had dropped to the floor. His face was drawn and troubled, and his eyes were intently fixed upon the door leading into the passage.

And I knew that the Fear was upon him, that it had passed from my room to his.

"It's there at the door," he whispered. "Do you feel it too, Dexter? It's there at the door."

I felt it afresh. I knew that someone was struggling to open the door from the inside, to turn a key which appeared to resist the nerveless, frightened fingers.

And there was the whimpering of the child too.

And then it passed away. Vance sprang to his feet, and we stood gazing at each other for one distracted moment.

Then, like myself, a few moments before, he seemed to pull himself together.

"Dexter," he muttered hoarsely, "we must follow."

Without pausing for my reply he made for the door, tore it open, and together we rushed out into the darkness of the passage.

Luckily he had his electric lamp with him, otherwise we should never have found our way along those little-known corridors and staircases, enveloped as they were in complete obscurity.

And it must be remembered that we were not following anything that we could actually see or hear—we were following the thread of terror that by some inconceivable means was imparted to our brains.

On we went, and we knew that we were following something that was following something else—a wild, cruel chase in which the pursued, in a very agony of terror, sought vainly for some means of escape.

And so, across the picture gallery, we came to the tower, and eventually to the room at its summit.

A breath of night air blew in upon my forehead. The window stood wide open, and it was there that the Fear reached its climax, though to the normal sense perfect stillness reigned—the whole room seemed to me full of horrid sound.

Vance and I were rooted to the spot where we stood while some abominable tragedy, only dimly guessed at, was played out to its culmination.

And then the window slid softly down, and all was over.

And it was well that it was so, for it seemed to me that another moment of such strain would have sent me mad. I looked at Vance and noticed the great beads of perspiration upon his forehead, the ghastly pallor of his face, the quivering of his hands and his shoulders—he had felt the terror no less than I.

"It's all over," he muttered; "it's gone!"

"Thank God for that!" I panted in reply. "Let's get away, Vance, for fear that it may recur. I—I couldn't stand it any more."

"It won't recur tonight," he replied, trying to force a smile. "But let's go down to the dining-room, Dexter, and have some brandy and a smoke. That will steady our nerves."

I was very glad to act upon this suggestion, and a stiff dose of brandy soon put me to rights again.

And then I told Vance of all I had gone through in the earlier part of the night; how I had lain there upon the bed, unable to call out to him, while the Fear gradually possessed me.

"What do you make of it?" I inquired.

He shrugged his shoulders and remarked that at present we could do little but conjecture.

"It's to be hoped that tomorrow may bring light," he continued; "that is, if we can persuade Mr. Somers to speak."

We spent an hour, however, discussing our own theories, which, as it turned out, were not very far from the truth, and eventually we went back to bed, where our sleep was undisturbed for the rest of the night.

The next day we sought out Mr. Somers, whom we found to be a young man of rather taciturn disposition; nevertheless, he eventually yielded to the charm of Aylmer Vance's manner, and consented to tell us all he knew, after exacting a promise that, for his own family reputation, the story should not be published abroad.

"But, indeed, gentlemen," he said, "if you can do anything to stop the horror—to clear Camplin Castle of its ghosts—I shall be grateful to you, and glad I have spoken. You see, my grandfather— but I'd better tell you the story."

And so, sitting there in the little shop parlour to which he had led us, we listened to the story of Camplin Castle, or, rather, to the portion of it that was of interest to us at that moment.

Camplin Castle had belonged to the Oswald family for centuries. For years and years it was handed down to father and son, and nothing had occurred to break the succession till about the middle of the nineteenth century, and the then owner of the estate, Jasper Oswald, quarrelled with his eldest son, Luke, who was a wild young fellow, and had contrived to offend his father deeply. Luke ran away from home before he was twenty-one, and at last a report was received that he was dead.

So, on the death of Jasper, the younger brother, Philip succeeded to the estate.

Philip had a beautiful wife, whose name was Elen, and a child, of whom they were both inordinately fond—a little boy of two. He was a passionate, ambitious man, was Philip, imbued with the violent temper that was characteristic of the Oswalds.

But Luke, the elder son, was not really dead, and soon after Philip and his family were installed at the castle he returned to claim his own from his brother. They would not recognise him, said that he was an impostor, and when he took his case to the Law Courts he lost it. He could not wholly prove his identity at the time, and it was suggested that Philip was able to suborn evidence against him.

Well, Luke came up to the house and saw his brother after the case was over. Philip sat in the dining-room with his wife and child, and made the servants throw Luke out.

Then Luke turned and cursed him, swore that he would kill them all, and that he would not do it at once, but, as they had made him suffer, so should they suffer, too. The torture of Fear, fear of impending death, the knowledge that it might fall upon them at any moment, was to be their fate.

And they read in his face that he meant what he said.

From that day they knew no rest; the fear of death was constantly upon them. And so it was that fear, a fear which was drawn out for the best part of twelve months or more, that impregnated the walls of Camplin Castle, and had reigned there ever since.

"And did Luke Oswald kill his brother?" inquired Vance.

The builder shrugged his shoulders.

"Philip Oswald died mysteriously about six months after the termination of the law case. He was found drowned in a pond, and it was assumed that he was killed by poachers, with whom he was constantly coming into conflict. But the murderer was never found."

"And the wife and child?"

"Luke did not spare them, either. You see, it was not only revenge that he wanted. He wished to recover the estate for himself and his possible heirs. But nobody knows exactly what happened. Another six months went by, and then it was reported that Elen Oswald had gone mad, and that, in a fit of frenzy, she had thrown her child from a window in the tower, killing it at once. She was carried off to an asylum, where she died soon after. And then, some years later, Luke Oswald was able to bring evidence to show that he was indeed the rightful heir to Camplin Castle, and so he took possession and moved in, and it seemed at first as if he was going to live in luxury and in great style.

"But everything went wrong with him. He got engaged to a beautiful girl, but she died a few days before the wedding. And so he never married, and there was no child to succeed him, no Oswald to be lord of the manor after his death. And then, no one could say why, but people shunned him; there was something in his appearance that set them against him—he was hard and cruel to his tenants, who loathed him, and would not work for him, so that his land went to waste. And by degrees health forsook him, too, and he would go about, worn and old before his time, with the appearance of a haunted man.

"No servants would stay with him at the castle—none, at least, except my old grandfather, who had been there in Philip's time, too, and who was a queer type of man, sullen and morose, and who was not afraid of God or devil. They shut up the best part of the castle, and lived in a few rooms only, seeing no one, and wanting to see no one—a pair of recluses.

"And so, twelve years ago, Luke Oswald died, and the mystery of his life remained a mystery to the world outside. Camplin Castle passed into the hands of the next-of-kin, who was a distant cousin, a man who had no interests in the estate, and who bore another name. He came to Hampshire to view his new property, stayed there a few days, and then placed it in the hands of the house agents, took his departure, and has not been seen again in the neighbourhood."

"You think that he had his experience of the Fear," suggested Vance, "and made the best of a bad bargain by attempting to let his property?"

"He gave out that he was too poor a man to live at the castle," was the guarded reply, "and I know nothing of what happened while he was actually in possession. My grandfather remained as caretaker until his death the following year, and it was upon his death-bed that he told my father things that my father only told me when he, in turn, was dying, begging me to keep the secret for our honour's sake."

"And you can tell us this secret?" asked Vance gently.

The young man flushed.

"Let it be a hint," he said. "My grandfather, while in Mr. Philip's service—and after his death, too—was in the pay of Mr. Luke. He connived at that year of terror. It was with his help that Luke obtained access to the castle whenever he wished. And"—he lowered his eyes—"I do not think that the unfortunate woman threw her child from the window. Oh! do you wonder," he added, with some display of emotion, "that Camplin Castle is not habitable today, that it reeks with horror from cellar to attic?

"My advice to Mr. Balliston," he concluded, "would be to raze the whole place to the ground, and to build a new house upon the site. Short of that, I don't see what he can do."

"I'm inclined to think that our friend, the builder's, advice is good," remarked Vance to me, after this interesting interview. "So long as bricks and mortar, and the atmosphere itself, are retentive, as we know them to be, there is little, Dexter, that you or I, or anyone else, can do to be of assistance.

"And that's the worst of this hobby of ours," he added, with a suggestion of sadness in his voice; "for people come to us, as Mr. Balliston did, begging for our assistance, and thinking that by some strange mysterious power we can lay the ghosts, or what they are pleased to call the ghosts. But that's just what we can't do; we can only prove what has been proved hundreds of times before, that there are more things in heaven and earth than the human philosophy of the present day can understand.

"And again and again I find the same advice recurring—the advice which Somers has given us—the advice of one who has not had the experience of years such as I have had, but which is quite as good as any that I can give—destroy. And that, too, is the advice that applies to Camplin Castle."

MESMER MILANN

in

THE VALLEY OF THE
VEILS OF DEATH

Bertram Atkey

*Bertram Atkey (1879–1952) was a prolific and popular contributor to the
fiction magazines of the early twentieth century often with light-hearted
stories of crime and fantasy. His best-known character was Smiler Bunn,
a mischievous crook who develops a skill for solving crimes much in the
vein of E. W. Hornung's Raffles. Atkey created many series characters
including Prosper Fair, really a member of the aristocracy who disguises
himself as a traveller doing good deeds and solving crimes, and Winnie
O'Wynn, a charming female "con man". Amongst his characters were
several of fantasy interest such as Hobart Honey whose mind travels back
and experiences his past lives, and a modern-day version of Hercules—an
early super-hero. Surprisingly overlooked was his series featuring Mesmer
Milann, who calls himself a "mediator" between the living and the beyond.
He has the ability of placing himself in a trance whilst his astral body
investigates problems. Unlike many of Atkey's stories these were not light-
hearted but serious explorations of the paranormal. The series, of which
the following was the first story, has never been reprinted.*

*With part of the story recalling an expedition through the Australian
desert, some of the language relating to the guides and indigenous peoples may
be jarring, though it is typical of the time of the story's first publication in 1914.*

I

The Place of Skeletons

Mesmer Milann, Mediator, pressed a bell-button upon the massive ebony table at which he sat and leaned forward in his great chair, awaiting the entrance of the client whose card had borne the name Tarronhall—Mr. George Tarronhall.

Save for the deep purple curtains which were hung round the room so that they shrouded the walls and windows completely, the number and odd placing of the electric bulbs—only one of which was burning—and a huge centaur, savagely sculptured in shining, slate-hued marble, there was nothing in the room to suggest that this was a temple of the occult. Nor was there in the appearance of Milann any studied effect to hint that he dealt in mystery and—many said and believed—magic. He wore a well-fitting black frock-coat which served better than any "robes" to intensify the extraordinary pallor of his square, powerful, hard-chiselled face, and yet did not lessen the strange fire that glowed steadily in his eyes—eyes so intensely dark that no iris was visible. His head was bare, and there was a singular quality of immobility pervading the man, so that he looked as though he had been sitting there precisely in that attitude, without any movement whatever, for many years—frozen into everlasting stillness—a carven man, with eyes that burned. It was impossible to tell from that marble mask the age of the man. He may have been thirty—forty—fifty—anything; there was nothing to be gleaned from the cold, unsmiling face but the evident fact that here was a man possessing extraordinary power of will, and probably profound knowledge of strange and terrifying and secret things.

Indeed, it is certain that he knew many secret things, for he had been recipient of the more weighty secrets of thousands of the class of people likely to possess secrets. And as to his knowledge of strange lore, there are in London at this moment hundreds of educated people, both hard-headed men and highly intelligent women, who are unalterably convinced that Mesmer Milann is, seriously, one of those extraordinary men who have been favoured or cursed by the gods with knowledge that is granted to few.

This was the man from whom George Tarronhall, newly returned from his successful crossing of the great Australian desert (world famous for that alone, even if he had not been one of the most famous of English explorers before), had requested and received an appointment almost before he was comfortably settled in town again.

Tarronhall had never seen Mesmer Milann until now, and strong, rigidly calm, iron-nerved as he was and an explorer needs to be, he was conscious at the instant of his entry, at the first meeting of their glances, that here was a man awaiting him whom, whether he was a charlatan or not, it would be wise to approach seriously— a man who was competent to deal quickly and effectively with those who came for merely frivolous reasons, expecting to amuse themselves for a few moments at the cost of a piece of gold, or those who came with any intention of "exposing" him. Here at any rate was no police-hounded, semi-illiterate palmist. If it were possible for any man to "mediate" between human, living people and those that were neither human nor living, it occurred instantly to Tarronhall that here, indeed, was such a man... even as he claimed to be...

Tarronhall realised before he was seated that he was to traffic with no small man. "If I am to be swindled," he thought, dryly whimsical, "I shall be thoroughly swindled. This man is no—piker, as the Americans say."

His deep, far-seeing eyes—sailors' eyes—took in every detail of the big, smooth, dead-white face that jutted, hung forward, as it were out of the purple-black background as he advanced to the chair facing the mediator's table.

Tarronhall was a little man, slim, dried-up, grizzled, but under his short, close-clipped greyish-yellow beard, Mesmer Milann judged swiftly, was the right kind of chin and jaw.

"Be seated, Mr. Tarronhall," he said without moving.

A faintly perplexed look dulled the explorer's eyes for a moment. He was wondering exactly where he had heard just that deep, vibrant note in a voice before. Then his eyes cleared. He remembered it—but it was not in any human voice. He had heard it in the low, rolling, cavernous note of the growl of some of the big African and Asian carnivores he had shot—except that where the note of the lion or the tiger had hinted at harshness behind it, Milann's promised a sort of deep, organ-like harmony.

"Thank you," he said.

There was a momentary silence, then Tarronhall spoke—directly, to the point.

"I bring you a very strange story," he said. "Strange to me, though I understand that what may seem inexplicable to me may not appear so to you. I have just returned from Australia; but no doubt you know." He smiled faintly; for the newspapers had worn his exploit threadbare.

The mediator moved his hand in assent.

But Tarronhall hesitated a little, began to speak, stopped, and finally chose another opening.

"I am not an imaginative man, or, to make it perfectly clear, my imagination, such as it is, concerns itself more with areas, countries and peoples rather than with—fragments, shall I say? Perhaps that is not clear to you. I mean that I can imagine a country, a mountain range, a desert, and, in my mind's eye, even people it; but I cannot, or am not prone to, imagine incidents such as that about which I am anxious to consult you."

Mesmer Milann smiled gravely.

"That is hardly imagination, Mr. Tarronhall," he said in his strange vibrant voice. "You get your country, mountain range, desert, or your people by deduction; you base it, perhaps almost subconsciously, upon certain facts—for instance, points of longitude and latitude, climate, the course of rivers, the trend of forests in that direction, and such things. It is a sort of sketchy deduction rather than imagination!"

Tarronhall answered readily.

"You are right. I am glad you emphasise the distinction. Good. I am not an imaginative man in the ordinary sense, and that makes the affair I shall describe more puzzling than ever... I crossed the Australian desert from north to south. There is nothing much to say of the actual exploration work—nothing, I think, that would peculiarly interest you—until it was practically finished, when I was within three days' march of the southern edge of the desert.

"I had camped early in the afternoon by an unexpected water-hole. There were ten people, all but Rivers, the scientist of the expedition, and myself being blacks." The explorer's face grew bleak for a moment. "You will remember, probably, that we lost Kerman and De Vigne *en route*, both of snakebite.

"Towards evening Rivers and I strolled out from the camp, perhaps with no definite purpose in view, and almost immediately came upon the ravine or small valley, where the events I shall describe took place. It was a quite ordinary formation, a long narrow depression, through which on one side pierced a small outcrop of softish slaty rock, a sort of shale. It was as though the rock had grown up through the sand, and the action of the wind, checked by the rock, had scooped out the ravine in the course of years. There are thousands of such places. The floor of the valley was of the shale, lightly powdered with the coarser, heavier particles of sand. It was the sort of place that might appeal to a gem prospector as being worth examination.

"But it was not that aspect of the place which interested us. No doubt the newspapers will have told you that we made immense finds of minerals, precious metals and gems in the heart of the desert, and I may tell you that those finds had been huge enough to enable us both to feel that it was hardly worth our while to examine this little valley with any view to our own profit... And yet"—Tarronhall's voice became extraordinarily impressive, the more so because the explorer was plainly unconscious of any change of tone—"and yet of all the strange places I have passed through, of all the odd corners of the world I have seen, that little insignificant valley is the one place that remains, and will remain always, in my mind... *It was haunted*—if ever any place in the world is haunted."

The explorer glanced with a sort of deprecatory, half-apologetic smile at Milann, as though a little ashamed. But there was no answering smile on the white, carven face of the mediator.

"There was a sense of oppression weighing down upon the place?" he asked quietly. "In spite of the sunlight, you felt, perhaps, what you might feel when passing a jungle thicket at night, in which you could see nothing, but wherein, you felt quite sure, lurked some big dangerous beast watching you go by?"

"Exactly. You have described it exactly," said Tarronhall with a sort of relief. "It was... odd, you know. Rivers, my companion, felt it instantly.

"'What is wrong with this place?' he said, looking at me rather queerly.

"I was about to answer him when I saw the skeletons... At first I thought they were skulls only. There were two of them at the foot of the miniature cliff on which we stood. I leaned over to see them better, and found that they were skeletons, lying on their sides, with the skulls half turned upwards, so that we looked down straight into the empty eye-sockets. It may have been my fancy—probably it was—but it seemed to me that there was a queer *craning* look about the poise of the skulls, exactly as though they were watching us. Picture two people lying at the foot of a little, slightly overhung cliff, craning out from under to peer up at two people at the top. Well, that would be the effect. Only the hollowness of the eye-sockets gave to the skeletons a grotesque look of angry watchful alarm.

"Angry watchful alarm," repeated Mesmer Milann quietly, half to himself. "You choose your words well, Mr. Tarronhall. I understand perfectly."

"Well, that was the impression... But, of course, a man exploring in desert places becomes used to skeletons, and for a place to possess an atmosphere of oppression—to be forbidding—is to render it inviting to an explorer rather than otherwise. So Rivers and I went down into the valley.

"As I said, it was quite ordinary—to an explorer. The presence of the two skeletons, perhaps, would put it out of the common to the mind of the average Londoner, but—no, perhaps I shouldn't say that. The skeletons put the place out of the ordinary for us also. You see, they seemed to be *watching* us. It may have been the angle at which they lay—no?"

Milann had shaken his head.

"Well, at any rate we went over and examined them. As nearly as we could judge they were all that was left of two men; probably under middle-age, well built, one short with fair hair, the other unusually tall with darker hair. The left shoulder-blade of the dark-haired one was shattered, as though by a bullet passing through the left breast. There was no sign of any belongings, no scraps of clothing, weapons, utensils, or tent. Nothing but the bones, with the dry ligaments still holding them together.

"Rivers, guided by the different height of the men and the probable upward flight of the bullet through the broken shoulder-blade, suggested that the short, fair-haired one had shot the other; but beyond that it was difficult to form any conclusion as to how they had come to their end there. It was not thirst—the usual cause—for, as I said, there was a waterhole not more than five hundred yards away.

"No doubt they came there with stores; it would be impossible without them, for that is a barren country—not even rabbits. Blacks may have taken away the stores. It's possible; really, it's the only conceivable explanation. However, that hardly matters. We will for the moment, if you like, leave it at that; these were two prospectors who quarrelled, fought, killed each other, and whose stores, weapons, and so on were taken away later by a party of blacks.

"The first point I want to emphasise to you is the extraordinary sensation of menace that pervaded the place. I—we were acutely uncomfortable, uneasy there. Within sight of our own camp, and in broad daylight! I do not claim to be a brave man, but nevertheless I may say, I think, that I should have the right to protest against any imputation of cowardice or even timidity. Indeed, at the risk of being considered boastful, I will say that I am not afraid of death, and that I could face without terror any physical pain I know of; but"—the little explorer's face was suddenly pale and hard and grim—"but I confess that I could not have camped alone in that place. It weighed me down, chilled me... It was eerie. And yet, save for those two poor bleached skeletons, there was nothing there, nor even a cranny where anything could hide. Remember that I was, as I am now in perfect health, fit to retrace my steps back across that desert if necessary... Perhaps I repeat myself; if so let me explain that I am very anxious to make you see quite clearly that there *was* distinctly a—what shall I say?—a *quality* of malignity in the atmosphere of that place. Do I convey it to you?"

The mediator nodded slowly.

"Perfectly," he said. "It was your first encounter with the Unseen, and your spiritual rather than your physical side was perturbed—distressed."

Tarronhall thought for a moment, then nodded.

"That was it precisely," he agreed.

"Then we turned to leave the ravine, and as I turned I kicked against a bag, the corner of a small canvas bag that protruded from a litter of broken, crumbling shale at my feet.

"I bent, cleared away the rubbish, and took out the bag—a sort of little sack—very well made, it proved, with a soft, thick chamois leather lining.

"Rivers bent over curiously as I cut the thong that bound the mouth of the sack. I noticed him glance over his shoulder furtively at the skeletons as he bent, and he is not a man who ordinarily is furtive. And, for myself, I was conscious, even as I drew my knife across the leather, that the oppression had redoubled. It weighed upon my shoulders, enveloped me like tangible stuff—horrible. Like a huge, choking mass of wool—damp, poisonous stuff. I felt a sensation of cold. But when instinctively I looked up the sunlight was there, and I could see the heat waves quivering low down on the sand.

"I heard Rivers say, to himself rather than to me, 'I could have sworn the thing moved.' And he was looking at one of the skeletons behind him.

"I affected not to hear, and turned up the bag, pouring out on the sand such a collection of precious stones as Australia, or any other country, has never before produced. Sapphires, emeralds and rubies, for the most part, with a slab of wonderful opal, dirty and uncut, of course, but magnificent. We have brought home some remarkable gems, some of them we had believed unique until then. But the stones in the sack surpassed ours to an extent that made comparisons ludicrous. The worst of these outrivalled the best of ours... Well, they were of no use to the skeletons, and so we took them back with us to the camp. You understand that? It may be a hundred years before anyone sets foot in that particular valley again—we were entitled to take them."

Mesmer Milann nodded again.

"Yes, of course," he said. "And where are they now?"

There was a sort of restrained expectancy in his voice.

Tarronhall looked at him curiously.

"They are still in the sack, and the sack is lying half buried in the loose litter of shale in the valley—exactly as we found it," he answered slowly, looking for the mediator's surprise.

But Mesmer Milann gave no sign of surprise at all. It was almost as though he had expected the answer. Yet he had one other question, but he asked it in the tone which a teacher may use when leading a child to the answer of its first sum.

"And who put the gems back in the place where they were found?" he said.

Tarronhall half rose, a little excited.

"A—ah! That is the question I have come to ask *you*!" he said.

The mediator nodded.

"I imagined so," he replied. "When you have finished your story I may be able to tell you," and leaned forward, waiting for the explorer to continue his narrative.

II

The Things in the Tent

"We took the bag of gems back to our camp, and I was glad to get out of that valley. That evening we looked them over carefully. They were priceless, unique; but there is no necessity to go into that now. In view of a long march on the following day, Rivers and I turned in early. We shared a tent, and the jewels we left in the bag under a rug between us. Once free from the valley the sense of oppression had left us, and we slept quickly enough.

"There had been a moon when we turned in. It was midnight when I woke, suddenly, sharply, with a sort of shock; and the moon was gone, and it was extraordinarily dark.

"I am as quick to sense danger as most men who have lived in the wilds; one learns the knack of it there, or dies for his ignorance, and before my lids were fully opened I was aware that something was wrong—dangerously wrong... At these moments it is not always wise to make haste in the darkness. It is better to lie very still, to keep breathing steadily, and to listen—to listen, and while you are listening to run over in your mind quickly just exactly the things you must remember; for instance, to recall the exact spot at which your revolver should be lying, so that at the first thrust in the dark your hand will seize it; to re-locate in your mind precisely where the entrance to the tent door is. Also one must remember the sense of smell, and use it, silently, stealthily, slowly. If it is a snake or a beast, one will smell it, even though one may not see it. Things like that...

"I listened, but I heard nothing. I smelt nothing. I lay there for a long time—a long time—tense, strung like a banjo-wire. Nothing happened. I was like a mechanical thing that was being tuned up, screwed up, to an impossible pitch. Audible things, of course, became magnified; the sound of Rivers' breathing was like a regular succession of long, slow waves breaking on sand; my heart-beats were like a series of immensely muffled explosions; the blood traversing its regular round of my veins was like the everlasting roar of a waterfall. But that was all I heard.

"Well, I couldn't stand it. I began to edge my hand up and out towards my automatic pistol. I *knew* that there was something, somebody, in the tent watching us. Something strange, malevolent. And at the first fractional movement of my hand it acted.

"Something clashed—*clashed*—a dull, dry, rattling sort of sound. Understand me, please, Mr. Milann. I have thought of the word carefully; it was a clashing sound, exactly as though someone had clashed two or more bones together. (I have since tested *that* sound for myself.) At the same instant something flat and knotted and hard pressed for an instant on my neck. It was cold but dry, and hurt. And it was removed at once. And, if you can imagine it, the darkness became *charged* as it were with warning—most horrible. Warning; it poured down on me, into me, like an electric current, enveloped me like water, paralysed me momentarily. I was frightened too—terror-stricken. You have heard how a serpent is supposed to fascinate a squirrel? Well, there was something Unseen, some Force, in the darkness that fascinated me then. I lay still, every nerve in my body wrung and vibrating and excruciated. And, save for that one clashing noise, not a sound... God knows how long I lay there—quite helpless. But it was Rivers' voice that galvanised me into life. It came across the darkness like a man calling in a tiny voice, across a great abyss, and it quivered in a sort of tremulous falsetto.

"Tarronhall—Tarronhall—Tarronhall," said Rivers, three times. It sounded exactly as though he was about to start crying. But it unlocked me, as it were. He went on:

"Get a light, Tarronhall—get a *light*, for God's sake!"

"I picked up the matches near my pistol and we lit a lamp. Rivers' face was greyish white; he says mine was, too. No doubt it was.

"The tent was exactly as we had seen it last, except for two things. The bag of gems was gone, and the rug which had covered it was at the other side of the tent. We sat staring at the place where the bag had lain; it had made a little depression in the sand...

"We spent the hour remaining before the dawn talking it over; talking rather at random, carefully avoiding any mention of what was in our minds. We were extraordinarily careful to suggest common-place reasons for the disappearance of the bag. We pretended to believe that the clashing sound had been caused by two spears coming in contact—black fellows' spears, or, possibly, boomerangs. It was absurd, but no doubt you will understand better than I do the sort of 'shyness,' the hesitancy to countenance any acceptance of the occult that sometimes obtains between men. Why, it needed quite an effort on my part to come here to you with this story.

"So we talked about black fellows' spears—boomerangs—anything plausible—until the dawn, when I called in one of the black trackers, and told him to pick up any strange trail in the sand. You have heard of these bush-trackers, of course? They are really wonderful, you know—better than blood-hounds.

"It was loose, dry sand that would not take any definite footprint—the fine dry stuff you can pour like water. But the tracker found some trail that interested him and seemed to puzzle him. He followed it out of the tent. It always seems a little uncanny—to me, at any rate—to watch a black tracker at work. They seem to read the desert as easily as you would read a book. But there is effort there, in reality a sort of exalted concentration. I have seen a tracker sweat over his work like a coalheaver. White men can't do it, you know. And a black tracker can't teach a white man to do it as *he* can do it. It's a little eerie, *I* think—like someone reading aloud from a blank page... However, our man followed the tracks, or whatever he saw, from the tent to the edge of the valley of the skeletons. He stopped on the cliff edge and looked down, muttering to himself. He saw the skeletons, and the man went grey with fear. Grey... I urged him on, but he wouldn't stir a foot. He grinned in a nerveless sort of way, like a frightened dog, but he wouldn't move. What he had read on the unreadable—to us—sand I don't know, and what he feared in the valley I don't know; but I *do* know that that black tracker would not have set a foot in the valley, even though I had jammed the muzzle of my automatic between his shoulder blades and ordered him to move on or die.

"So we sent him back to the camp, and when he was gone Rivers pointed out something to me that sent a chill down my spine.

"It was one corner of a little sack sticking out from a litter of loose, crumbly shale on the floor of the valley. *The* sack, Mr. Milann, in exactly the place where we had found it and from which we had taken it!..."

He paused for an impressive moment.

"We spoke with the tracker later, took him back to the valley edge, and he searched the cliff-top—quartered it like a hound—but he would not go down into the valley. But he swore that no men except ourselves had approached the valley for many days. We asked *whom* it was he had tracked from the tent to the valley-edge. He said it was no man, but something that was *not good*. And that was all we could get from him. The man was scared to the roots of his soul...

"We left the gems there—they are there to this day, for all I know. Frankly, I and Rivers were afraid to go in after them again... But that's all right. What I want you to tell me are three things. One is: Were we in any real danger in the tent that night? The second is: *Who* or *what* returned the gems to their place where we found them? And the last is the least important: a question of vanity, self-esteem. I don't like to feel conquered—routed. I feel as though I've left my reputation for courage behind in that infernal valley, and I'm thinking of going back to regain it. It's only hurt pride, I know; but it really hurts—galls. I want those gems, not for their intrinsic value, but as a trophy. Still, I hope I am not a fool, and while I don't understand these matters in the least, I am not prepared to deny that there may be in or *near* this life of ours things that are not to be dealt with by a rifle or pistol. That brings me to my last question. Have I, do you think, a sporting chance of retrieving my trophy from that valley?"

The little explorer's face was grim and his grey eyes were hot as he put his concluding question.

Mesmer Milann did not answer at once. He stared straight before him, apparently lost in thought. But when he spoke it was in a voice of extraordinary gravity.

"You ask me if you were in any real danger that night. I say to you, in the most solemn earnest, that you never have been before, and probably never will be again, in such a fearful peril as you were in the tent that night. I, too, am weighing my words with the utmost care. And I say to you now that you were beyond the reach of human aid had *that* which was in the tent with you cared to molest you."

There was something in the mediator's tone that drained the blood from Tarronhall's face and set his scalp pringling.

Milann continued.

"You ask: Who removed the gems? For the moment I will content myself with saying they were restored to their hiding-place by certain Forces, unseen but none the less existent and powerful to inflict harm upon humans. And, for your last question, if you return to that valley with the intention of 'tampering'—that is the right word, believe me—with these Forces, or that which they guard, then I"—the deep voice vibrated in that still room like a great quivering blade—"I, Mesmer Milann, say to you, God help you, for you are a doomed man!"

He ceased abruptly, and the purple room seemed of a sudden to be strangely quiet with a vast and tomb-like silence...

Tarronhall stared. He was so tremendously impressed as to appear almost horrified.

Then he recovered himself.

"You—gave me a shock—for a moment," he said. "Are there really these Forces? But, of course, there are. After what I felt out there I can readily believe it. But I don't quite see even now. Why, for instance, should Forces—spirits, or whatever they are—guard those gems? What good are sapphires and emeralds to spirits?"

The mediator stared at his client with thoughtful, sombre eyes. "That is what I shall discover," he said slowly.

Tarronhall looked a little uneasy, for there was that in Milann's voice which strangely discomposed him. He was a man of the open air, direct, simple, unimaginative, very wholesome, a man's man; but now, physically intrepid though he was, his spirit recoiled a little from the idea that he was involving himself in a matter that had to do with things not of this world—dark, dangerous, and unguessable things.

"May I ask how you hope to discover it?" he inquired uneasily.

Mesmer Milann spoke softly in a voice that, for all its softness, was vibrant with latent power.

"Tonight I shall be in the valley, and, later, in another and a more perilous place," he said.

Tarronhall felt a momentary relief. This was obviously impossible. This man *was* a swindler, then, for all his impressive personality.

"But that's impossible, of course," he said, his eyes hardening.

"For my body, yes," responded Mesmer Milann. "*But I shall not need my body. I shall go in the spirit!*" His voice was softer than ever. But Tarronhall shivered.

"I—I—you—that's impossible, too," he said.

The mediator smiled slowly.

"You think so?" he said in a voice so slow and cold that it seemed to drip upon the silence of the room, as water drips from a stalactite in the profound darkness of some great cavern. "Then come with me. You and your fellow-explorers have exhausted the globe; soon enough, now, the arc-lights of civilisation will illuminate the darkest corners of this world. Come with me tonight to another—to the

Sub-World. There are sights to test the courage of the bolder spirit. I will free you from the gross flesh, and we will traverse together the dim Tracts of the Elementals, enter the Red Fogs of the Tentacle-Spirits, pass over the Place of the Were-Wolves, look upon the Craters of the Unicorns, the Plains of the Centaurs, the Morass of Minotaurs!" His eyes glittered and flamed like jewels, and his voice rolled like distant thunder. "We will adventure through the Haunts of the Vampires together—"

But Tarronhall thrust out his hand. And it was trembling.

"No," he said, not without a certain dignity. "God knows whether you can do these things, whether you—your spirit—are familiar with these places. I do not deny it. I don't question it; but it sounds to me unholy. I am a plain man. Let me alone to deal with men."

The mediator nodded.

"You are wise. To you is your own channel in life; follow it. And to me is mine, and I follow it—*where few can follow me!*" he said. Then, "You used the word 'unholy' wrongly. You meant 'strange.' Yet the world of which I spoke *is* unholy, but I go there to war upon it." He rose suddenly to his full height, and with a dignity and simplicity which remained in Tarronhall's memory for his whole life, added, "To war upon it, unarmed, save only by the faith in holy things which is God's armour."

Tarronhall, feeling strangely humble in the presence of this man, rose after a moment.

"You have made me ashamed of the—yes—the curiosity that impelled me to consult you," he said. "Let us forget the matter."

But Mesmer Milann shook his head, smiling faintly.

"The matter has now fallen into the channel of *my* life," he said. "And I must investigate it."

He held out his hand.

"You shall hear from me again," he concluded.

Tarronhall gazed at him for a second, then shook hands, and quietly went out. Once in the busy, sunlit London street he turned and looked at the door from which he had come.

But he turned away with an air of uncertainty.

"I don't know—I *don't* know. I don't understand," he muttered to himself. "The man impressed me, if it's all *true*."

He stared blankly before him, then impatiently shrugged his shoulders and proceeded down the street. "If he is not an impostor... if all that is true..." he repeated, then started a little. "'The Faith in Holy Things which is God's Armour.' By Jove! *that's* true, at any rate..."

For he was a simple man and a brave man; his soul was a clean soul, and so he was able to recognise a great truth when he heard it.

He nodded vigorously, and his keen grey eyes began to clear from their perplexity as he nodded.

III

Pilar Steyne

Whether Mesmer Milann really possessed the well-nigh incredible power of projecting his soul into that boundless unknown which we call Space, I, who write, do not care to say with any pretence of authority. Personally, I believe that he *could* do the thing, but I cannot prove it in the least degree.

It is quite certain that in connection with this case of the haunted valley, on the evening of the day he interviewed Tarronhall his body lay upon a couch in his chambers from eight o'clock until past midnight, utterly unconscious, not asleep, but in a still trance too deathly for sleep. So much his valet has told—unwittingly, be it said, but, once told, not denied.

And it is equally certain that upon waking he wrote at once a letter to Miss Pilar Steyne, asking her to call upon him on the following morning.

It says something for the great influence of Mesmer Milann that Pilar Steyne went unhesitating to him, for at that time she was unquestionably the most famous, most spoiled and petulant "star" of musical comedy in London.

But she went, and broke three appointments to go.

The interview was not long. Miss Steyne, extremely pretty—though her prettiness, like her manner and her clothes, was a shade too pronounced—had visited Mesmer Milann before, and had learned to be serious in the purple room. Indeed, like most of the mediator's clients, she had no desire to be anything but serious. There was that about the man, as about the room, that quenched the frivolity of the most thoughtless.

"You came to me on the ninth of May last year, and described a very vivid dream which you had dreamed some two days before, Miss Steyne. Do you remember it?" asked Milann.

The musical comedy star frowned with an air of perplexity.

"Yes, I did, didn't I?" she said. "I always come to you when things like that happen. But I can't remember what the dream was. I have hundreds of dreams, and they get mixed up."

She stared at him with the wide blue eyes of a child. Clearly, she had forgotten; what happened a year before was ancient history, dim, vague, misty to a woman such as this, who lived only for the sensations and excitements of the moment, rarely thought seriously of anything for five consecutive minutes, and, beyond her knack of looking *chic* and pretty in all circumstances, possessed no real intelligence at all. One might as well have looked for sustained and useful thought, or even memory, in a marmoset as in this physically exquisite and hopelessly spoiled girl.

But Mesmer Milann had anticipated this.

"You have forgotten," he said gently. "Wasn't it a dream of two men fighting somewhere—one with a pistol and the other with a long knife? Trampling over sand, somewhere?"

Her face lighted up.

"Yes, yes," she said; "I remember telling you. Oh, yes, it was dreadful—horrible! There were two men struggling together. One had a pistol—it kept exploding. The smoke looked like a feather duster made of grey feathers. He shot the other man, the man with the knife, and they both fell down under a sort of cliff. I suppose the man with the pistol was stabbed. Then I woke up."

"You said at the time that you thought you 'recognised' one of the men. It was all dim and dream-like, but he reminded you of a Mr. James Westby whom you had known."

"Jimmy Westby. Yes, I remember Jimmy."

"And the other man—you did not know the other man, or, at any rate, you did not definitely recognise him in the dream as anyone you knew. He might have been—he rather resembled—a Sir Percy Talbot, with whom you had once been friends. But you were not sure."

"Yes, I think I said that."

Her eyes were doubtful again.

"I made notes of it, Miss Steyne," he reminded her. (He noted everything, and his collection of press-cuttings was unique.) "Nothing came of that interview; you were called away by telephone halfway through. You were very busy with a new comedy,

I think, and when, some months later, you came again it was in connection with another matter. The affair of the dream, or vision, was dropped."

"Yes," she agreed, without much interest.

She was not in the mood for difficult things this morning, and her thoughts were at her milliner's.

Mesmer Milann was patient with her.

"Can you tell me, Miss Steyne, where Mr. Westby and Sir Percy Talbot are now?"

She shook her head.

"They went broke, poor boys," she said, not without sympathy. "First Percy, and then Jimmy Westby. They went abroad, I think. I know Jimmy did. I had a letter from him—from Australia—and he said he was going to make another fortune and come home and marry me. He was very fond of me, I think. Both of them were. They were rather extravagant about me. I wasn't in love with either of them, of course, but they were nice boys, and we used to go about quite a lot."

"Were they friends?"

Her eyes opened again.

"Oh, no! I don't think they knew each other at all. Jimmy Westby came after Sir Percy, I think. Yes, I am sure."

"You never heard from Sir Percy Talbot after he went abroad?"

"Yes, two or three times. Just love-letters; nothing much. I get thousands of them. He went to New Zealand... Why, did my dream mean anything, Mr. Milann?" She began to get interested. "Was it a sort of vision? Or telepathy, don't they call it?"

Mesmer Milann smiled slightly at her, as he would have smiled at a butterfly that alighted on his hand. Indeed, that is what she was to him—a brightly-coloured, pretty, transient, empty-headed thing, floating easily and pleasantly along in her brief gleam of the sunshine of popularity, caring nothing for the past, thinking nothing of the future, as incapable of real grief as of real enjoyment. He realised that these two men—Westby and Talbot—who probably had ruined themselves for her, were only two out of scores who had sought, pursued, and possibly held her in a brief captivity. They meant nothing to her, and probably never had. No doubt they were two of those innumerable, young, pleasant-looking, well-groomed youths about town, as useless, thoughtless, and heedless as herself.

She spoke of a "vision" and "telepathy" as she would of a new conjuring trick...

"Yes," he said tolerantly, gently, "I think it did."

"Really! Oh, do tell me!"

His smile died out.

"In good time... Miss Steyne, are you fond of jewels?"

She laughed gaily.

"*Am* I? Try me Mr. Milann!"

"If I tell you that there is in a desolate but easily accessible place on the edge of the Australian desert a small sack of jewels, each one of which is *unique*—sapphires, emeralds, rubies—which belong to you, and only await your taking, would you go and get them?"

"I would send for them," she said promptly. "Somebody trust-worthy," she added.

"But if I say that those who are caring for the jewels will only give them up to you personally, what then?" asked Mesmer Milann.

She hesitated, and he saw that all her instincts were at war with each other. She hated the thought of leaving London and the frothy homage which a section of Londoners paid her; but she had a passion for jewels. She possessed a good many—very valuable, but by no means incomparable.

Her eyes gleamed.

"Oh, yes, I would go and get them myself! I could take a friend or two, I suppose? How did it all happen? I haven't got any rich relatives in Australia, Mr. Milann. Do tell me; it's exciting."

"I am not at liberty to tell you yet, Miss Steyne," replied the mediator. "Yes, you can have friends. It will be necessary, I think, for Mr. Tarronhall, the explorer, and myself to accompany you. When can you start for Australia?"

She rose. She knew it was useless to attempt to extract more from Milann than he was inclined to tell her.

"Oh, soon, I expect. I will let you know. I must go now."

She shook hands.

"I suppose these jewels really are all right?—unique, you know," she inquired.

"I have Mr. Tarronhall's word that they are," said Mesmer Milann gravely.

"That's all right, then. I like the sound of this Tarronhall man. Goodbye, Mr. Milann. I'll let you know."

And Miss Steyne hurried out to the immense car which was awaiting her. Mesmer Milann sat thinking for a moment, his eyes on the door through which she had gone. There was a smile on his lips, but it was a little sad and bitter. He was thinking of the hopeless folly of a world which permitted a girl like Pilar Steyne to sway, as she did, the destinies of so many men.

Then, slightly shrugging his shoulders, he rang for his secretary, instructing him to telephone to Tarronhall.

IV

The Valley of the Veils of Death

It was three months later, and another camp was pitched near the valley—a larger and altogether more imposing and extravagant camp than that to which George Tarronhall was accustomed.

It was like a little town of tents, with that of Pilar Steyne, fringed, tasselled, beflagged, with carpets and awnings, looming high in the midst of all. Round about the big tent were pitched others, many of them. For it was no part of the inclinations or customs of the actress to travel upon such a quest in any sort of discomfort, nor of the policy of her manager and press agent to allow her to engage in such an enterprise without extracting the last possible word of publicity and advertisement out of it. They had made the most of the affair from the moment the girl had left Mesmer Milann on the day he had told her of the jewels. They were men who knew their business, and so thoroughly had they engineered the thing that, when three months later the expedition camped near the valley, it was accompanied by an oddly assorted retinue that included several of Pilar Steyne's men friends, two other actresses, some maids, two newspaper men and a newspaper photographer, servants, cooks, camel-men (Miss Steyne had insisted upon the camels, though they were not essential), and an official-looking quiet man who had described himself rather vaguely as a representative of the Australian authorities, and had joined the expedition without showing any papers or being requested to produce them. He had given Tarronhall, who nominally was in charge, his name as Burroughs—*Inspector* Burroughs—but had asked the explorer to drop the "Inspector" in favour of plain "Mr."

Tarronhall, aware of the wide publicity which the affair had attracted, had readily agreed, and thereafter Mr. Burroughs had been an unobtrusive but ever present member of the party.

It was about an hour before full dawn on the day after the arrival of the company, and Mesmer Milann was sitting at the entrance to his tent, talking quietly with Tarronhall over a cigarette. Save for the servant who had just made them some coffee, none other of the camp was stirring.

Mesmer Milann, with his usual wide tolerance, had neither objected to nor encouraged the swelling of the party by Pilar Steyne, her friends and supporters, though during the journey he had kept somewhat aloof, conversing little with anyone except Tarronhall and the actress herself.

But, the evening before, he had agreed with Tarronhall's suggestion that they two should walk over to see the valley again; in the early dawn, before the little crowd of sightseers were awake, they were drinking a cup of coffee before going.

Milann's face was very serious, and Tarronhall was manifestly uneasy.

"But if your theories, your researches have been faulty, what then?" he was saying anxiously.

The mediator smiled slightly, a brief, evanescent smile that was gone in an instant.

"It would probably mean that the instant Miss Steyne sets foot in the valley she will be destroyed, annihilated. If I am wrong. But I am not. You will see presently. I fancy you will discover a difference in the valley already. And I am quite certain that, not even excepting myself, there is no person in all this party save Pilar Steyne who can enter that valley today and live five seconds after entering it!"

The explorer looked at him with a sort of awe in his keen, hard eyes, and shook his head slowly.

"You convince me against my will—against my experience, Mr. Milann. I thought I had courage—I believe I have—but it is only the courage of the gun-muzzle." He took out a heavy automatic pistol of unusually large calibre, well oiled, beautifully kept, and looked at it thoughtfully. "I have believed for so many years that these things"—he tapped the sinister-looking weapon gently—"represented the last word in matters of brute force, that it is difficult to readjust my ideas. There is practically nothing in life that this pistol cannot deal with effectively; at short range it would kill an elephant, skilfully used. That is definite, hard-and-fast knowledge. Mathematical, practically... And you tell me that the thing would be as useless and ineffective as a paper fan against the unseen perils that haunt that valley yonder. And I believe it implicitly. Yet you tell me that that child, that frail butterfly girl, can walk unarmed in that valley where she will and how she will! Incredible! It offends every instinct of self-protection, of enterprise, of logic, of common sense I possess. And the bewildering part of it all is that I believe you, and am afraid."

Mesmer Milann nodded.

"Don't worry, Mr. Tarronhall," he said. "You, like the vast majority of people, have dealt all your life with the physical side of life. This affair is not primarily concerned with the physical side at all; but you will see for yourself."

He drained his cup and rose.

"The dawn is at hand," he said. "Let us go."

They left the sleeping camp and moved silently through the dim light towards the valley. Before they had covered a third of the two hundred yards or so between the camps and the valley Tarronhall halted, turning troubled eyes upon his companion.

Mesmer Milann nodded.

"You feel it?" he asked.

"Yes. It is as though we were walking through the outer zone of some fever belt, where you can *feel* the danger as you walk. Only this is worse."

"The Forces within the valley are roused and watchful; the depression you feel emanates from them. It will be worse as we go on," said Mesmer Milann absently.

But they went on.

The air, the atmosphere, was dull and heavy, with a queer oppression that was not a result of climatic or weather conditions. It was full of a sense of menace—immense, all-pervading.

The explorer's eyes were very keen and quick, searching the dimness all about them. Once his hand dropped almost unconsciously to the pistol at his belt, and Milann, noting the instinctive movement, smiled slightly.

So, moving through the grim, clogged atmosphere, they came to the valley edge, and there paused, looking down. It was still dark down there, almost black, but from the darkness the sense of malignity came up to them in waves, as heat rolls up from a furnace.

Tarronhall's face showed whitely through the vague light of the coming dawn.

"It feels as though some monster, some giant alligator thing, were crouching down there watching us, waiting for us."

He peered down into the slowly paling, pit-like hollow.

"Good God!" he said suddenly under his breath. "There *is* something there. It moved—"

Milann was staring down with a little fixed smile.

"Keep well back from the edge," he told Tarronhall. "There is sometimes a—fascination... Beyond a certain point these things cease to exercise a repellent force, and lure instead. There is no hope for the man who leaves himself open to that spell... this fearful fascination is at the back of the mythology concerning the Sirens of old..." he added musingly. Then started to swift action.

"*Back*, man! Didn't you hear?"—he tore at Tarronhall's arm, jerking him back with a force that seemed almost savage—*for Tarronhall, his face set and his eyes blank and rapt, had moved swiftly forward as though to walk over the cliff edge.*

It was like waking a sleep-walker; a cold sweat burst on the explorer's forehead, and he looked dazedly at the mediator.

"I—I—felt a sudden impulse," he said weakly.

"Yes, I know. It is all right—" began Milann, but broke off sharply. "Listen!" he said.

They were silent.

Away to the right of them, in the shallow entrance to the valley, where the sides ran down like the ends of a railway cutting, and the valley floor and the desert merged on the same level, someone was moving over the sand. They could hear the soft, dull slither of his feet in the fine, dry stuff. He was muttering to himself, this one, as he came on into the denser shadows of the valley, just under the two men who were watching.

"This is a h—l of a place—a h—l of a place," he was muttering over and over again, with a sort of resentful anguish. "But I'll have the stones—I'll have the stones."

"Stop him—stop him!" said Tarronhall. But even as he opened his mouth to shout a wild warning, a sudden and appalling cry for help went up, followed instantly by the report, seeming curiously muffled, of a revolver.

Where the weapon had darted its pinkish-orange, snake-swift tongue of flame, the watchers saw a whirling blur. Then immediately there followed a low, wailing cry, the soft thud of an inert body falling on sand, and silence.

The deep shadows in the valley seemed to billow and eddy, strangely agitated. Tarronhall, staring down horrified, saw a transient, fugitive gleam, gone in an instant, as of dreadful eyes glancing up at him...

"Milann," he said, horribly shaken, "there is some poor devil down there. We must—do something."

But the mediator's fingers were clamped on his wrists like hooks of steel.

"We can do nothing," said Mesmer Milann. "That was Burroughs. He was an impostor—a thief. He came to steal the jewels. He is dead. *They* killed him even as he fired. We must wait."

Then the dawn broke swiftly, and all that waste and desolate region was flooded with sunlight as they watched.

But though they waited long no sunlight brightened the valley. The darkness down there cleared away, but left behind a blurred, intangible greyness, vaguely fog-like, as though the place was hung with filmy veils, or full of shapeless shadows. Through these strange veils the two men, peering over, saw the wreck-like ribs of the skeletons, bone-white. Tarronhall pointed out the dimly seen outline of the corner of the jewel sack where it protruded from its loose covering of shale; and further along the valley they saw the crumpled body of a man lying upon his face, curiously still.

And from the valley there arose that terrible emanation, that outpouring of Menace and of Warning.

"This—this is—shocking," said Tarronhall. It sounded queerly, that word "shocking" applied to the fearful place into which they were looking. "It—the sensation of threat and secret terror and peril—it grows worse. It's a thousand times worse than it was."

There was an odd, grim look on the pale face of the mediator as he replied:

"With the lapse of time the Forces grow stronger. But this is an unusual development. Already they are suggesting themselves to the human eye. As yet they are no more than faint, formless veils of shadow, but, left undisturbed for a space of years, it is probable that they would take shape and become material, solid things, infinitely dangerous, capable of being seen."

Tarronhall looked a little awed.

"But—what shapes? What would they be like?"

Milann shook his head.

"I cannot say. But try and imagine what mortal anger or jealousy or deadly hatred would look like if one of these suddenly took visible form..."

Then he turned.

"Let us get back to the camp," he said. "After breakfast Miss Steyne will take the jewels, and we can leave this place."

"But the body, man. That chap, Burroughs—we can't leave him lying there—" began Tarronhall.

"His body is beyond human aid until the jewels are moved by Pilar Steyne," said Mesmer Milann in a voice of singular authority. He stared at the pitiful heap where it lay under the veils of shadowy fog that hung about it. "It would be safer for an unarmed man to try to take the carcase of an antelope or a deer-calf from out of the paws of a hunger-mad tigress than for anyone in this world—except Pilar Steyne—to approach that man's body and live."

Tarronhall said no more, but turning his back on the valley set out with the mediator towards the camp.

Before they had gone twenty yards they stopped suddenly, for Pilar Steyne, her friends, and the newspaper men were coming towards them.

They waited for them to come up, and Tarronhall became suddenly uneasy again.

"Forgive me, Mr. Milann," he said half apologetically—and this was the man whose name was a byword for courage, and whose reputation was established from one pole to the other—"forgive me, but—you are sure that your calculations—theories—are right? It would be too appalling for that butterfly to meet with the same fate as Burroughs."

"There is no danger—to her, Mr. Tarronhall," said Milann. But the explorer had never seen his face so white and grim as now... The little party came up, laughing, eager, very curious.

"Good morning, Mr. Milann," said Pilar Steyne. "We have come to get the jewels—before breakfast. May we, please?"

The woman giggled slightly. But the newspaper men looked curiously at the white face of the mediator. The photographer was already at work, quickly, deftly.

Mesmer Milann bowed, without smiling.

"Yes," he said. "They are here," and led the way to the valley. The whole party ranged along the top of the little cliff, looking down.

And, suddenly, the laughter and chattering died—swiftly, instantly, as a candle-flame vanishes when blown out. The fell influence of the place gripped them at once, all except Pilar Steyne.

She glanced carelessly down into the valley, and then turned to her friends in amazement.

"Why, what is the matter with you all?" she cried, her astonishment evidently unfeigned. "Kitty, you're as white as paper! You, too, Jack. Why, you all are! What is the matter?"

"This—this *awful* place, Pilar dear," began one of the women, and stopped abruptly, shuddering.

"It's full of fog—poisonous-looking place," said the man called Jack. "Look! The stuff is moving—swirling."

And indeed the veils of greyness were swaying with a long, slow, sinuous, *deliberate* motion, with something in it vaguely suggestive of the muscular, rippling movements of a great cat stalking its prey.

And wave upon wave there poured up over the cliff edge that overwhelming, sinister sense of peril. The photographer, with a pale, rigid face, was already taking picture after picture of the valley.

One of the women shrieked that she could not stand it, and went back towards the camp.

Milann was watching Pilar Steyne, who was obviously bewildered.

"What *is* it? What is the *matter*?" she was saying. "Why are you all frightened? There's nothing there—nothing but a lot of silly mist... Is it a joke?"

She turned on Jack angrily.

"Are you frightened too? Yes, you are. Come, now, I'll dare you to come down into the place with me. Are you afraid?"

A flush ran into the face of the young man. He was a good-looking, soldierly type of youth, and he started as though stung.

"Afraid, Pilar! No. It seems a detestable sort of place, but I'm not afraid. I will come down."

He moved forward to climb down the cliff, but Milann put out his arm.

"No!" he said, in a cold, quiet voice of complete authority. "The place is *haunted*. Look to the right! That is the body of Burroughs—a thief. He tried to steal the jewels this morning, and he is dead. I will permit no member of this party except Miss Steyne to enter the valley. She alone can do it in safety... Listen! In that valley lie two skeletons—all that is left of the bodies of two men whom I believe to have been Mr. James Westby and Sir Percy Talbot. Near them lies, half-buried, the sack of jewels of which you have all heard. These two men went prospecting in the desert together. They were successful—incredibly successful. Returning, they quarrelled, possibly about the division of their jewels—more probably about Miss Pilar Steyne whom they both loved, and for whose sake mainly they had toiled for the jewels. They quarrelled and fought. Men do strange things after long living together in the wilderness, and both were killed. The jewels remained where they had put them probably when they camped here, or it may be they dug them here. But despite their quarrel, they died filled chiefly with the same desire that Miss Steyne should have the jewels. And from the moment of their deaths they—their spirits, to put it quite simply—have been guarding the jewels from anyone and everyone but—Pilar Steyne. I have put it as simply as possible, so that there should be no misunderstanding. You have all felt, you are all conscious of the lurking terror in the valley, except Miss Steyne. There is not one of you, save Miss Steyne, who would willingly enter the valley. And you are wise, for you would go inevitably to your death. Yet I say that Pilar Steyne can walk in that fearful place, take up the jewels, and bring them away, with no more risk or danger than she would experience in walking across a lawn in some secluded English village. It is for her to choose."

He ceased, and they all stared at him in silence.

Then Pilar Steyne laughed. She had felt nothing of the brooding terror, the loosed menace, of the place, for these things were not directed upon her. The Forces of the Unseen were her friends—were on guard for her sake.

So she laughed, and she was the only one of that company who could laugh.

"Well, I hope the jewels aren't spirit ones, too," she said, incurably frivolous. "But I will see. I don't believe in ghosts"—(It was as though a butterfly said, "I don't believe in battleships.")—"and if they are the ghosts of poor Jimmy Westby and Percy Talbot, I'm quite sure they won't hurt *me!*"

One of the women began to cry softly at that...

But Pilar Steyne ran a few yards along the cliff to a sloping place which gave fairly easy access to the valley floor, and without the slightest hesitation scrambled down, laughing, as children playing on sand cliffs may laugh.

And all the grey and fatal shadows swung up, monstrously, fantastically, veiling her, wrapping themselves about her, so that, it seemed to the watchers on the cliff, she was under a grey bridal veil, as of one who weds the Spectre of Death himself. And the shadows thickened and grew denser and darker, until she was hidden from sight of the watchers entirely.

And at that there hung upon them all one second of vast silence, of unendurable suspense. Pilar Steyne was gone...

And then, while they waited, hardly daring to breathe, a gay, ringing voice came up to them.

"Is it this little sack tied at the corner, Mr. Milann?"

"*Yes!*"

For all his self-control the mediator's voice was hoarse.

"Ah! I have them."

Another pause.

Then the voice came again.

"*Oh! Oh!* What beauties!"...

And then the sentinel shadows, the grey veils, disappeared, floated out like smoke, and the watchers staring down into the sunlit valley saw Pilar Steyne kneeling by the little sack of jewels, pouring them out on the sand, laughing innocently, like a playing child who has passed within an inch of a venomous snake.

Mesmer Milann drew in a long breath.

"She will never know, never realise what has happened... she does not 'believe in ghosts'... not even the poor, faithful, lingering ghosts of those who loved her, and watched over the treasure they gained for her," he said to Tarronhall, smiling oddly.

Tarronhall shook his head, shrugged his shoulders slightly, and threw out his hands, saying nothing.

"How the place has changed! It's bright again—sunny—as though Pilar were the sun," said one of the women as they hurried down to see the jewels.

They would have been glad to laugh after the stress of the last few minutes, but the sight of the skeletons, stark, white, eyeless, sobered them.

Then Pilar Steyne, her eyes lighting on those grim relics, went across to the bones and looked down at them silently for a moment.

"You were always kind to me," she said strangely. "I knew that you would never hurt me, not even frighten me. Thank you, boys!"

Her eyes shone wet as she turned away. Milann liked her the better for that, though her sorrow was quite transient, like all her moods...

Then Pilar Steyne's party went, with the jewels, back to the camp. Mesmer Milann, Tarronhall, and the other men went to examine the pseudo-official Burroughs.

Milann was the only one neither surprised nor horrified to find that practically every bone in the man's body was broken; he must have been whirled out of existence in an instant of time. But Milann was the only one who knew anything at all of the Forces with which Burroughs had come into conflict...

Later they discovered that the forehead of one of the skeletons had been newly pierced, as by a revolver bullet... and the body of Burroughs they buried some distance from the valley, but the skeletons they buried together in the valley. It was Mesmer Milann who ordered this to be done; but he volunteered no reason therefor, and none asked him why. For he was skilled in a lore that was strange and terrible and secret to them; he stood alone, inscrutable, darkling, Egyptian. And they were glad, each man of them, after what they had seen with their own eyes, to leave him in his lonely and terrible eminence. Even Tarronhall.

The newspaper men wrote their "stories" of the affair, but the accounts never appeared as they wrote them. They made the mistake of describing things as they saw and felt them, and since the things they saw and felt seemed in cold print hopelessly incredible, the articles were "edited" into something that satisfied the public without giving the most timorous reader more than a momentary uneasiness.

And the photographic plates which were exposed to take the valley while the shadows were there were found to be empty of anything at all; they were developed with extreme care, but came out simply as transparent sheets of glass. The other pictures were perfect. Some months later the photographer called on Mesmer Milann and questioned him as to this.

Milann took him into another room and showed him a drawer crammed with photographic plates and films.

"These are photographs I have taken under similar conditions," he said.

The photographer-reporter looked at them.

"But they are like mine; they show nothing!" he exclaimed. "What is wrong with them?"

Mesmer Milann closed the drawer.

"Nothing is wrong with them," he said slowly and very gravely. "It is our human vision that is at fault. There are upon those plates pictures—images—of something more than vapour and grey shadows. But it is something that no living eye will ever see. Be glad of that."

"But you—*you* have seen—" began the other excitedly.

"I have seen what I have seen," replied Mesmer Milann solemnly.

And that was the last word.

DR. TAVERNER

in

THE DEATH HOUND

Dion Fortune

Like Algernon Blackwood, Dion Fortune—or Violet Mary Firth (1890–1946) to give her real name—had studied the occult extensively. She was also fascinated by the workings of the mind and became a psychotherapist at the start of the Great War. Her work brought her into contact with the Irish occultist Thomas Moriarty and through him she was introduced to theosophy and the study of ritual magic. In 1919 she joined the Temple of Alpha and Omega, an offshoot of the original Hermetic Order of the Golden Dawn and then transferred to the Stella Matutina Lodge of the Golden Dawn where she developed her skills as a medium. In 1924 she founded her own Community of the Inner Light (now the Society of the Inner Light). Her fascination with the mind led to her book The Machinery of the Mind, *published in 1922, the same year that she began her series of stories featuring Dr. Taverner.*

Taverner runs a nursing home and specialises in mental and psychical afflictions. He is able to probe into individual's ancestral memories, a skill Firth believed she had in her childhood. His exploits are recorded by his colleague Dr. Rhodes who had sought out Taverner because of his own shell shock from the War. Taverner is very much in the mould of John Silence, both able to use profound knowledge and psychic skills to combat problems caused as much by human interference with the occult as with the paranormal itself. The stories were collected as The Secrets of Dr. Taverner *in 1926.*

*Fortune would go on to write several occult novels—*The Demon Lover *(1927),* The Winged Bull *(1935) and* The Goat-Foot God *(1936)—but these fail to have the impact or verisimilitude of the exploits of Dr. Taverner.*

"**W**ell?" said my patient when I had finished stethoscoping him, "have I got to go softly all the days of my life?"

"Your heart is not all it might be," I replied, "but with care it ought to last as long as you want it. You must avoid all undue exertion, however."

The man made a curious grimace. "Supposing exertion seeks me out?" he asked.

"You must so regulate your life as to reduce the possibility to a minimum."

Taverner's voice came from the other side of the room. "If you have finished with his body, Rhodes, I will make a start on his mind."

"I have a notion," said our patient, "that the two are rather intimately connected. You say I must keep my body quiet,"—he looked at me—"but what am I to do if my mind deliberately gives it shocks?" and he turned to my colleague.

"That is where I come in," said Taverner. "My friend has told you what to do; now I will show you how to do it. Come and tell me your symptoms."

"Delusions," said the stranger as he buttoned his shirt. "A black dog of ferocious aspect who pops out of dark corners and chivvies me, or tries to. I haven't done him the honour to run away from him yet; I daren't, my heart's too dickey, but one of these days I am afraid I may, and then I shall probably drop dead."

Taverner raised his eyes to me in a silent question. I nodded; it was quite a likely thing to happen if the man ran far or fast.

"What sort of a beast is your dog?" enquired my colleague.

"No particular breed at all. Just plain dog, with four legs and a tail, about the size of a mastiff, but not of the mastiff build."

"How does he make his appearance?"

"Difficult to say; he does not seem to follow any fixed rule, but usually after dusk. If I am out after sundown, I may look over my shoulder and see him padding along behind me, or if I am sitting in my room between daylight fading and lamp lighting, I may see him crouching behind the furniture watching his opportunity."

"His opportunity for what?"

"To spring at my throat."

"Why does he not take you unawares?"

"That is what I cannot make out. He seems to miss so many chances, for he always waits to attack until I am aware of his presence."

"What does he do then?"

"As soon as I turn and face him, he begins to close in on me! If I am out walking, he quickens his pace so as to overtake me, and if I am indoors he sets to work to stalk me round the furniture. I tell you, he may only be a product of my imagination, but he is an uncanny sight to watch."

The speaker paused and wiped away the sweat that had gathered on his forehead during this recital.

Such a haunting is not a pleasant form of obsession for any man to be afflicted with, but for one with a heart like our patient's it was peculiarly dangerous.

"What defence do you offer to this creature?" asked Taverner.

"I keep on saying to it 'You're not real, you know, you are only a beastly nightmare, and I'm not going to let myself be taken in by you.'"

"As good a defence as any," said Taverner. "But I notice you talk to it as if it were real."

"By Jove, so I do!" said our visitor thoughtfully; "that is something new. I never used to do that. I took it for granted that the beast wasn't real, was only a phantom of my own brain, but recently a doubt has begun to creep in. Supposing the thing *is* real after all? Supposing it really has power to attack me? I have an underlying suspicion that my hound may not be altogether harmless after all."

"He will certainly be exceedingly dangerous to you if you lose your nerve and run away from him. So long as you keep your head, I do not think he will do you any harm."

"Precisely. But there is a point beyond which one may not keep one's head. Supposing, night after night, just as you were going off to sleep, you wake up knowing the creature is in the room, you see his snout coming round the corner of the curtain, and you pull yourself together and get rid of him and settle down again. Then just as you are getting drowsy, you take a last look round to make sure that all is safe, and you see something dark moving between you and the dying glow of the fire. You daren't go to sleep, and you can't keep awake. You may know perfectly well that it is all imagination, but that sort of thing wears you down if it is kept up night after night."

"You get it regularly every night?"

"Pretty nearly. Its habits are not absolutely regular, however, except that, now you come to mention it, it always gives me Friday night off; if it weren't for that, I should have gone under long ago. When Friday comes I say to it: 'Now, you brute, this is your beastly Sabbath,' and go to bed at eight and sleep the clock round."

"If you care to come down to my nursing home at Hindhead, we can probably keep the creature out of your room and ensure you a decent night's sleep," said Taverner. "But what we really want to know is—," he paused almost imperceptibly, "why your imagination should haunt you with dogs, and not, shall we say, with scarlet snakes in the time-honoured fashion."

"I wish it would," said our patient. "If it was snakes I could 'put more water with it' and drown them, but this slinking black beast—" He shrugged his shoulders and followed the butler out of the room.

"Well, Rhodes, what do you make of it?" asked my colleague after the door closed.

"On the face of it," I said, "it looks like an ordinary example of delusions, but I have seen enough of your queer cases not to limit myself to the internal mechanism of the mind alone. Do you consider it possible that we have another case of thought transference?"

"You are coming along," said Taverner, nodding his head at me approvingly. "When you first joined me, you would unhesitatingly have recommended bromide for all the ills the mind is heir to; now you recognise that there are more things in heaven and earth than were taught you in the medical schools.

"So you think we have a case of thought transference? I am inclined to think so too. When a patient tells you his delusions, he stands up for them, and often explains to you that they are psychic phenomena, but when a patient recounts psychic phenomena, he generally apologises for them, and explains that they are delusions. But why doesn't the creature attack and be done with it, and why does it take its regular half-holiday as if it were under the Shop Hours Act?

"Friday, Friday," he ruminated. "What is there peculiar about Friday?"

He suddenly slapped his hand down on the desk.

"Friday is the day the Black Lodges meet. We must be on their trail again; they will get to know me before we have finished.

Someone who got his occult training in a Black Lodge is responsible for that ghost hound. The reason that Martin gets to sleep in peace on Friday night is that his would-be murderer sits in Lodge that evening and cannot attend to his private affairs."

"His would-be murderer?" I questioned.

"Precisely. Anyone who sends a haunting like that to a man with a heart like Martin's knows that it means his death sooner or later. Supposing Martin got into a panic and took to his heels when he found the dog behind him in a lonely place?"

"He might last for half-a-mile," I said, "but I doubt if he would get any further."

"This is a clear case of mental assassination. Someone who is a trained occultist has created a thought-form of a black hound, and he is sufficiently in touch with Martin to be able to convey it to his mind by means of thought transference, and Martin sees, or thinks he sees, the image that the other man is visualising.

"The actual thought form itself is harmless except for the fear it inspires, but should Martin lose his head and resort to vigorous physical means of defence, the effort would precipitate a heart attack, and he would drop dead without the slightest evidence to show who caused his death. One of these days we will raid those Black Lodges, Rhodes; they know too much. Ring up Martin at the Hotel Cecil and tell him we will drive him back with us tonight."

"How do you propose to handle the case?" I asked.

"The house is covered by a psychic bell jar, so the thing cannot get at him while he is under its protection. We will then find out who is the sender, and see if we can deal with him and stop it once and for all. It is no good disintegrating the creature, its master would only manufacture another; it is the man behind the dog that we must get at.

"We shall have to be careful, however, not to let Martin think we suspect he is in any danger, or he will lose his one defence against the creature, a belief in its unreality. That adds to our difficulties, because we daren't question him much, less we rouse his suspicions. We shall have to get at the facts of the case obliquely."

On the drive down to Hindhead, Taverner did a thing I had never heard him do before, talk to a patient about his occult theories. Sometimes, at the conclusion of a case, he would explain the laws underlying the phenomena in order to rid the unknown of its terrors and enable his patient to cope with them, but at the outset, never.

I listened in astonishment, and then I saw what Taverner was fishing for. He wanted to find out whether Martin had any knowledge of occultism himself, and used his own interest to waken the other's—if he had one.

My colleague's diplomacy bore instant fruit. Martin was also interested in these subjects, though his actual knowledge was nil—even I could see that.

"I wish you and Mortimer could meet," he said. "He is an awfully interesting chap. We used to sit up half the night talking of these things at one time."

"I should be delighted to meet your friend," said Taverner. "Do you think he could be persuaded to run down one Sunday and see us? I am always on the lookout for anyone I can learn something from."

"I—I am afraid I could not get hold of him now," said our companion, and lapsed into a preoccupied silence from which all Taverner's conversational efforts failed to rouse him. We had evidently struck some painful subject, and I saw my colleague make a mental note of the fact.

As soon as we got in, Taverner went straight to his study, opened the safe, and took out a card index file.

"Maffeo, Montague, Mortimer," he muttered, as he turned the cards over. "Anthony William Mortimer. Initiated into the Order of the Cowled Brethren, October, 1912; took office as Armed Guard, May, 1915. Arrested on suspicion of espionage, March, 1916. Prosecuted for exerting undue influence in the making of his mother's will. (Everybody seems to go for him, and no one seems to be able to catch him.) Became Grand Master of the Lodge of Set the Destroyer. Knocks, two, three, two, password 'Jackal.'

"So much for Mr. Mortimer. A good man to steer clear of, I should imagine. Now I wonder what Martin has done to upset him."

As we dared not question Martin, we observed him, and I very soon noticed that he watched the incoming posts with the greatest anxiety. He was always hanging about the hall when they arrived, and seized his scanty mail with eagerness, only to lapse immediately into despondency. Whatever letter it was that he was looking for never came. He did not express any surprise at this, however, and I concluded that he was rather hoping against hope than expecting something that might happen.

Then one day he could stand it no longer, and as for the twentieth time I unlocked the mailbag and informed him that there was nothing for him, he blurted out: "Do you believe that 'absence makes the heart grow fonder,' Dr. Rhodes?"

"It depends on the nature," I said. "But I have usually observed if you have fallen out with someone, you are more ready to overlook his shortcomings when you have been away from him for a time."

"But if you are fond of someone?" he continued, half-anxiously, half-shamefacedly.

"It is my belief that love cools if it is not fed," I said. "The human mind has great powers of adaptation, and one gets used, sooner or later, to being without one's nearest and dearest."

"I think so, too," said Martin, and I saw him go off to seek consolation from his pipe in a lonely corner.

"So there is a woman in the case," said Taverner when I reported the incident. "I should rather like to have a look at her. I think I shall set up as a rival to Mortimer; if he sends black thought forms, let me see what I can do with a white one."

I guessed that Taverner meant to make use of the method of silent suggestion, of which he was a past-master.

Apparently Taverner's magic was not long in working, for a couple of days later I handed Martin a letter which caused his face to light up with pleasure, and sent him off to his room to read it in private. Half an hour later he came to me in the office and said:

"Dr. Rhodes, would it be convenient if I had a couple of guests to lunch tomorrow?"

I assured him that this would be the case, and noted the change wrought in his appearance by the arrival of the long wished-for letter. He would have faced a pack of black dogs at that moment.

Next day I caught sight of Martin showing two ladies round the grounds, and when they came into the dining-room he introduced them as Mrs. and Miss Hallam. There seemed to be something wrong with the girl, I thought; she was so curiously distrait and absent-minded. Martin, however, was in the seventh heaven; the man's transparent pleasure was almost amusing to witness. I was watching the little comedy with a covert smile, when suddenly it changed to tragedy.

As the girl stripped her gloves off she revealed a ring upon the third finger of her left hand. It was undoubtedly an engagement ring. I raised my eyes to Martin's face, and saw that his were fixed upon it. In the space of a few seconds the man crumpled; the happy little luncheon party was over. He strove to play his part as host, but the effort was pitiful to watch, and I was thankful when the close of the meal permitted me to withdraw.

I was not allowed to escape however. Taverner caught my arm as I was leaving the room and drew me out on to the terrace.

"Come along," he said. "I want to make friends with the Hallam family; they may be able to throw some light on our problem."

We found that Martin had paired off with the mother, so we had no difficulty in strolling round the garden with the girl between us. She seemed to welcome the arrangement, and we had not been together many minutes before the reason was made evident.

"Dr. Taverner," she said, "may I talk to you about myself?"

"I shall be delighted, Miss Hallam," he replied. "What is it you want to ask me about?"

"I am so very puzzled about something. Is it possible to be in love with a person you don't like?"

"Quite possible," said Taverner, "but not likely to be very satisfactory."

"I am engaged to a man," she said, sliding her engagement ring on and off her finger, "whom I am madly, desperately in love with when he is not there, and as soon as he is present I feel a sense of horror and repulsion for him. When I am away, I long to be with him, and when I am with him, I feel as if everything were wrong and horrible. I cannot make myself clear, but do you grasp what I mean?"

"How did you come to get engaged to him?" asked Taverner.

"In the ordinary way. I have known him nearly as long as I have Billy," indicating Martin, who was just ahead of us, walking with the mother.

"No undue influence was used?" said Taverner.

"No, I don't think so. He just asked me to marry him, and I said I would."

"How long before that had you known that you would accept him if he proposed to you?"

"I don't know. I hadn't thought of it; in fact the engagement was as much a surprise to me as to everyone else. I had never thought of him in that way till about three weeks ago, and then I suddenly realised that he was the man I wanted to marry. It was a sudden impulse, but so strong and clear that I knew it was the thing for me to do."

"And you do not regret it?"

"I did not until today, but as I was sitting in the dining-room I suddenly felt how thankful I should be if I had not got to go back to Tony."

Taverner looked at me. "The psychic isolation of this house has its uses," he said. Then he turned to the girl again. "You don't suppose that it was Mr. Mortimer's forceful personality that influenced your decision?"

I was secretly amused at Taverner's shot in the dark, and the way the girl walked blissfully into his trap.

"Oh, no," she said, "I often get those impulses; it was on just such a one that I came down here."

"Then," said Taverner, "it may well be on just such another that you got engaged to Mortimer, so I may as well tell you that it was I who was responsible for that impulse."

The girl stared at him in amazement.

"As soon as I knew of your existence I wanted to see you. There is a soul over there that is in my care at present, and I think you play a part in his welfare."

"I know I do," said the girl, gazing at the broad shoulders of the unconscious Martin with so much wistfulness and yearning that she clearly betrayed where her real feelings lay.

"Some people send telegrams when they wish to communicate, but I don't; I send thoughts, because I am certain they will be obeyed.

A person may disregard a telegram, but he will act on a thought, because he believes it to be his own; though, of course, it is necessary that he should not suspect he is receiving suggestion, or he would probably turn round and do the exact opposite."

Miss Hallam stared at him in astonishment. "Is such a thing possible?" she exclaimed. "I can hardly believe it."

"You see that vase of scarlet geraniums to the left of the path? I will make your mother turn aside and pick one. Now watch."

We both gazed at the unconscious woman as Taverner concentrated his attention upon her, and sure enough, as they drew abreast of the vase, she turned aside and picked a scarlet blossom.

"What are you doing to our geraniums?" Taverner called to her.

"I am so sorry," she called back, "I am afraid I yielded to a sudden impulse."

"All thoughts are not generated within the mind that thinks them," said Taverner. "We are constantly giving each other unconscious suggestion, and influencing minds without knowing it, and if a man who understands the power of thought deliberately trains his mind in its use, there are few things he cannot do."

We had regained the terrace in the course of our walk, and Taverner took his farewell and retired to the office. I followed him, and found him with the safe open and his card index upon the table.

"Well, Rhodes, what do you make of it all?" he greeted me.

"Martin and Mortimer after the same girl," said I. "And Mortimer uses for his private ends the same methods you use on your patients."

"Precisely," said Taverner. "An excellent object lesson in the ways of black and white occultism. We both study the human mind—we both study the hidden forces of nature; I use my knowledge for healing and Mortimer uses his for destruction."

"Taverner," I said, facing him, "what is to prevent you also from using your great knowledge for personal ends?"

"Several things, my friend," he replied. "In the first place, those who are taught as I am taught are (though I say it who shouldn't) picked men, carefully tested. Secondly, I am a member of an organisation which would assuredly exact retribution for the abuse of its training; and, thirdly, knowing what I do, I dare not abuse the powers that have been entrusted to me. There is no such thing as a straight line in the universe; everything works in curves; therefore it is only a matter of time before that which you send out from your mind returns to it. Sooner or later Martin's dog will come home to its master."

Martin was absent from the evening meal, and Taverner immediately enquired his whereabouts.

"He walked over with his friends to the crossroads to put them on the 'bus for Hazlemere," someone volunteered, and Taverner, who did not seem too well satisfied, looked at his watch.

"It will be light for a couple of hours yet," he said. "If he is not in by dusk, Rhodes, let me know."

It was a grey evening, threatening storm, and darkness set in early. Soon after eight I sought Taverner in his study and said: "Martin isn't in yet, doctor."

"Then we had better go and look for him," said my colleague.

We went out by the window to avoid observation on the part of our other patients, and, making our way through the shrubberies, were soon out upon the moor.

"I wish we knew which way he would come," said Taverner. "There is a profusion of paths to choose from. We had better get on to high ground and watch for him with the field-glasses."

We made our way to a bluff topped with wind-torn Scotch firs, and Taverner swept the heather paths with his binoculars. A mile away he picked out a figure moving in our direction, but it was too far off for identification.

"Probably Martin," said my companion, "but we can't be sure yet. We had better stop up here and await events; if we drop down into the hollow we shall lose sight of him. You take the glasses; your eyes are better than mine. How infernally early it is getting dark tonight. We ought to have had another half-hour of daylight.

A cold wind had sprung up, making us shiver in our thin clothes, for we were both in evening dress and hatless. Heavy grey clouds were banking up in the west, and the trees moaned uneasily. The man out on the moor was moving at a good pace, looking neither to right nor left. Except for his solitary figure the great grey waste was empty.

All of a sudden the swinging stride was interrupted; he looked over his shoulder, paused, and then quickened his pace. Then he looked over his shoulder again and broke into a half trot. After a few yards of this he dropped to a walk again, and held steadily on his way, refusing to turn his head.

I handed the glasses to Taverner.

"It's Martin right enough," he said; "and he has seen the dog."

We could make out now the path he was following, and, descending from the hill, set out at a rapid pace to meet him. We had gone about a quarter of a mile when a sound arose in the darkness ahead of us; the piercing, inarticulate shriek of a creature being hunted to death.

Taverner let out such a halloo as I did not think human lungs were capable of. We tore along the path to the crest of a rise, and as we raced down the opposite slope, we made out a figure struggling across the heather. Our white shirt fronts showed up plainly in the gathering dusk, and he headed towards us. It was Martin running for his life from the death hound.

I rapidly outdistanced Taverner, and caught the hunted man in my arms as we literally cannoned into each other in the narrow path. I could feel the played-out heart knocking like a badly-running engine against his side. I laid him flat on the ground, and Taverner coming up with his pocket medicine case, we did what we could.

We were only just in time. A few more yards and the man would have dropped. As I straightened my back and looked round into the darkness, I thanked God that I had not that horrible power of vision which would have enabled me to see what it was that had slunk off over the heather at our approach. That something went I had no doubt, for half a dozen sheep, grazing a few hundred yards away, scattered to give it passage.

We got Martin back to the house and sat up with him. It was touch-and-go with that ill-used heart, and we had to drug the racked nerves into oblivion.

Shortly after midnight Taverner went to the window and looked out.

"Come here, Rhodes," he said. "Do you see anything?"

I declared that I did not.

"It would be a very good thing for you if you did," declared Taverner. "You are much too fond of treating the thought-forms that a sick mind breeds as if, because they have no objective existence, they were innocuous. Now come along and see things from the view-point of the patient."

He commenced to beat a tattoo upon my forehead, using a peculiar syncopated rhythm. In a few moments I became conscious of a feeling as if a suppressed sneeze were working its way from my nose up into my skull. Then I noticed a faint luminosity appear in the darkness without, and I saw that a greyish-white film extended outside the window. Beyond that I saw the Death Hound!

A shadowy form gathered itself out of the darkness, took a run towards the window, and leapt up, only to drive its head against the grey film and fall back. Again it gathered itself together, and again it leapt, only to fall back baffled. A soundless baying seemed to come from the open jaws, and in the eyes gleamed a light that was not of this world. It was not the green luminosity of an animal, but a purplish grey reflected from some cold planet beyond the range of our senses.

"That is what Martin sees nightly," said Taverner, "only in his case the thing is actually in the room. Shall I open a way through the psychic bell jar it is hitting its nose against, and let it in?"

I shook my head and turned away from that nightmare vision. Taverner passed his hand rapidly across my forehead with a peculiar snatching movement.

"You are spared a good deal," he said, "but never forget that the delusions of a lunatic are just as real to him as that hound was to you."

We were working in the office next afternoon when I was summoned to interview a lady who was waiting in the hall. It was Miss Hallam, and I wondered what had brought her back so quickly.

"The butler tells me that Mr. Martin is ill and I cannot see him, but I wonder if Dr. Taverner could spare me a few minutes?"

I took her into the office, where my colleague expressed no surprise at her appearance.

"So you have sent back the ring?" he observed.

"Yes," she said. "How do you know? What magic are you working this time?"

"No magic, my dear Miss Hallam, only common sense. Something has frightened you. People are not often frightened to any great extent in ordinary civilised society, so I conclude that something extraordinary must have happened. I know you to be connected with a dangerous man, so I look in his direction. What are you likely to have done that could have roused his enmity? You have just been down here, away from his influence, and in the company of the man you used to care for; possibly you have undergone a revulsion of feeling. I want to find out, so I express my guess as a statement; you, thinking I know everything, make no attempt at denial, and therefore furnish me with the information I want."

"But, Dr. Taverner," said the bewildered girl, "why do you trouble to do all this when I would have answered your question if you had asked me?"

"Because I want you to see for yourself the way in which it is possible to handle an unsuspecting person," said he. "Now tell me what brought you here."

"When I got back last night, I knew I could not marry Tony Mortimer," she said, "and in the morning I wrote to him and told him so. He came straight round to the house and asked to see me. I refused, for I knew that if I saw him I should be right back in his power again. He then sent up a message to say that he would not leave until he had spoken to me, and I got in a panic. I was afraid he would force his way upstairs, so I slipped out of the back door and took the train down here, for somehow I felt that you understood what was being done to me, and would be able to help. Of course, I know that he cannot put a pistol to my head and force me to marry him, but he has so much influence over me that I am afraid he may make me do it in spite of myself."

"I think," said Taverner, "that we shall have to deal drastically with Master Anthony Mortimer."

Taverner took her upstairs, and allowed her and Martin to look at each other for exactly one minute without speaking, and then handed her over to the care of the matron.

Towards the end of dinner that evening I was told that a gentle-man desired to see the secretary, and went out to the hall to discover who our visitor might be. A tall, dark man with very peculiar eyes greeted me.

"I have called for Miss Hallam," he said.

"Miss Hallam?" I repeated as if mystified.

"Why, yes," he said, somewhat taken aback. "Isn't she here?"

"I will enquire of the matron," I answered.

I slipped back into the dining-room, and whispered to Taverner, "Mortimer is here."

He raised his eyebrows. "I will see him in the office," he said.

Thither we repaired, but before admitting our visitor, Taverner arranged the reading lamp on his desk in such a way that his own features were in deep shadow and practically invisible.

Then Mortimer was shown in. He assumed an authoritative manner. "I have come on behalf of her mother to fetch Miss Hallam home," said he. "I should be glad if you would inform her I am here."

"Miss Hallam will not be returning tonight, and has wired her mother to that effect."

"I did not ask you what Miss Hallam's plans were; I asked you to let her know I was here and wished to see her. I presume you are not going to offer any objection?"

"But I am," said Taverner. "I object strongly."

"Has Miss Hallam refused to see me?"

"I have not inquired."

"Then by what right do you take up this outrageous position?"

"By this right," said Taverner, and made a peculiar sign with his left hand. On the forefinger was a ring of most unusual workmanship that I had never seen before.

Mortimer jumped as if Taverner had put a pistol to his head; he leant across the desk and tried to distinguish the shadowed features, then his gaze fell upon the ring.

"The Senior of Seven," he gasped, and dropped back a pace. Then he turned and slunk towards the door, flinging over his shoulder such a glance of hate and fear as I had never seen before. I swear he bared his teeth and snarled.

"Brother Mortimer," said Taverner, "the dog returns to its kennel tonight."

"Let us go to one of the upstairs windows and see that he really takes himself off," went on Taverner.

From our vantage point we could see our late visitor making his way along the sandy road that led to Thursley. To my surprise, however, instead of keeping straight on, he turned and looked back.

"Is he going to return?" I said in surprise.

"I don't think so," said Taverner. "Now watch; something is going to happen."

Again Mortimer stopped and looked round, as if in surprise. Then he began to fight. Whatever it was that attacked him evidently leapt up, for he beat it away from his chest; then it circled round him, for he turned slowly so as to face it. Yard by yard he worked his way down the road, and was swallowed up in the gathering dusk.

"The hound is following its master home," said Taverner.

We heard next morning that the body of a strange man had been found near Bramshott. It was thought he had died of heart failure, for there were no marks of violence on his body.

"Six miles!" said Taverner. "He ran well!"

COSMO THOR

in

THE CASE OF THE FORTUNATE YOUTH

Moray Dalton

*Moray Dalton, the alias used by Katherine Mary Dalton Renoir (1881–
1963), had a moderately successful career as a writer of crime fiction,
especially with her novels featuring Inspector Hugh Collier of Scotland
Yard. But she once ventured into the realms of the occult with a short series
featuring Cosmo Thor, a serious student of the occult who is sometimes
consulted by the police when crimes trespass into what Thor calls that "No
Man's Land" between reality and nightmare. In introducing the series
Dalton remarked that Thor's achievements were due to the fact that he
"combined very human sympathies with his considerable fund of knowledge
of things not taught in schools".*

*The series ran to six stories and is one of the rarest in all weird
fiction. The stories were published in* The Premier Magazine *in 1927
and never collected in book form. Copies of the magazine are extremely
uncommon and much of the British Library's run was destroyed in the
Blitz during the Second World War. As a consequence, not only have
the stories never been reprinted, all too few of them have been read
beyond their first appearance. However, fans of Dalton's work would
have encountered Thor again as he reappears in her novel* The Belgrave
Manor Crime *(1935) where he investigates the disappearance of a woman*

only to find himself in dire circumstances—his fate is investigated by his friend, Hugh Collier. It is disappointing that Dalton did not produce a full novel of Thor's exploits but at least we can experience his abilities in this very rare story.

fter dinner Thor had wandered off alone into the grounds. He knew his host very slightly and his fellow guests not at all. Most of them belonged to the younger generation, friends of the daughter of the house, a charming girl of eighteen, whose engagement to a neighbouring squire had just been announced. The lucky man was present at dinner, and had been pointed out to Thor by the lady who sat next to him.

"That is Harry Quinton," she said, "the fair boy on Cynthia Portal's right. We call him the fortunate youth. He has just come into a fortune and one of the most delightful old houses in the county, left to him by a distant relative he had never even seen. Cynthia and he are wildly in love, and everybody approves. Some people seem to have everything, don't they!" and she paid the lovers the tribute of an envious sigh.

Thor was inclined to agree with her when later Cynthia Portal crossed the drawing-room to speak to him.

"Don't you want to play bridge, Mr. Thor? Or billiards? I expect you don't always have to be doing things to amuse yourself. It's rather a proof of a vacant mind, isn't it," she said laughingly. "I have been looking for Harry. He's fearfully keen on meeting you. But he's vanished—"

She stayed with him for a few minutes, and when she went he followed the slim little figure in the childish white frock with his eyes. He did not always approve of the modern girl, but Cynthia was in a class by herself.

He left the house and, crossing the terrace, wandered through the rosary and down a long pleached walk that led between high-clipped hedges of yew to the Dutch garden. The moon had risen above the trees of the plantation. He heard the call of a night bird, and then another sound, the sound of a groan.

He was startled, and for a moment he stood still, listening. He knew that whoever had uttered it was unaware of his presence. There was an opening in the yew hedge a little farther on. He went to it and saw that it led to the bowling-green.

The path that surrounded it was over-shadowed by trees, but he saw a glimmer of white and presently distinguished the figure of a man sitting on a bench, leaning forward, with his face buried in his hands. Thor hesitated, fearing to intrude, and was about to draw back, but the other must have heard him for he raised his head. Thor recognised the fortunate youth.

"I beg your pardon," he said. "I thought I heard something. It sounded like somebody in trouble. I must have been mistaken. Lovely night, isn't it?"

He was preparing to pass on, but Quinton had risen to his feet.

"I'll come with you if you don't mind," he said—"that is, if you're just strolling about."

"I shall be delighted."

They had reached the farther end of the pleached walk when Quinton spoke again.

"The fact is I've been looking forward to the chance of a talk with you, Mr. Thor. I'm—I'm horribly worried," he said unsteadily. Thor was not altogether surprised. He had watched the young man during dinner and had noticed slight but unmistakable signs of nervous tension. He was not surprised, but he was sorry. It was the usual thing, he supposed, some wretched entanglement, some threatened scandal that menaced the lad's new-found happiness.

"If you care to confide in me," he said, "I will try to help you. I may not be able to. It all depends—"

"It is awfully good of you," said Quinton. "I expect you have heard all about my tremendous luck. Six months ago I was a junior clerk in a City office with nothing to look forward to but a possible ten-pound rise in the dim and distant future—if I wasn't fired—and an annual fortnight at Broadstairs or Bexhill. And then a second cousin—I had not even known of his existence—left me Cleeve Manor and quite a lot of money. The Portals were very kind to me from the first, and now Cynthia—"

"Just so," said Thor. "You are very much to be envied."

"Am I?" said Quinton bitterly. "Wait a bit and I will tell you another thing about myself that is not so generally known—" He broke off.

Thor waited, wondering what was coming next. The other resumed with an evident effort.

"I'm going mad!" he said.

Thor received a shock. This was not at all what he had expected. But he answered quickly:

"Rubbish, my dear fellow. What reasons have you for imagining any such thing?"

"I have—delusions."

Thor reflected.

"Have you spoken of this to anyone else?"

"No. I have not had the courage. If they believed me it would mean that I should lose Cynthia. How could they trust a girl to—I must be absolutely sure before I tell them. But I went up to Town last week and saw a man in Harley Street, a mental specialist. He examined me pretty thoroughly and passed me as sound. I—I've never gone off the lines as some chaps do. I don't drink immoderately or take drugs. I've never had a knock on the head, and, so far as I know, there isn't a trace of insanity in my family on either side. Yet the fact remains—"

"Delusions, you said—"

They had turned and were walking back towards the house, and they had emerged now from the dense shadow of walls of yew. They were seen and voices hailed them from the terrace.

"Harry! Harry! Come along, Quinton! We're going to dance—"

Quinton turned to his companion.

"I must go," he said hurriedly. "I'll see you later. I'm staying the night. I shan't be going back to Cleeve until tomorrow afternoon. I—I rely on you—"

"I'll help you—if I can," said Thor.

He held out his hand and the other wrung it hard.

The young people were still dancing in the hall when Thor went up to his room at eleven, and it was not until the house party had scattered, after lunch, the following day that he was approached by Quinton. Cynthia had spilt a cup of coffee over her frock and gone up to change. Quinton, in tennis flannels, with a racket in his hand, strolled casually up to the older man, who sat alone in a wicker chair under the trees at the far end of the lawn.

"I've been thinking," he said, "and I'm going to ask you a favour."

"What is it?"

"I want you to come back with me in the car when I go and spend a couple of days at Cleeve Manor. Will you do that?" he asked.

The words were commonplace, but something in their utterance gave an effect of urgency. Thor, however, chose to ignore the implication and answered with a smile.

"Why not? I should be delighted. I am very fond of old houses. Cleeve Manor is old, isn't it?"

"The main building is Jacobean, but a part of the walls of the left wing and the foundations are pre-Reformation. There's some furniture of the period, too, and a lot of junk that my cousin collected. I thought we might start about five. Can you be ready by then? I'll tell the Portals—"

Thor looked after him thoughtfully as he walked back to the net where his prospective opponents were awaiting the return of Cynthia. A personable young fellow, with pleasant, easy manners and something about him that was thoroughly likable. And apparently not even the girl who loved him had yet realised a fact concerning him which, to Thor, had been obvious from the first. Thor recalled something that had been said to him by the owner of a horse: "Bolted—without the slightest warning!" when Thor had seen the animal trembling and sweating for five minutes before he took the bit between his teeth.

Tea was served on the lawn under the cedar. Afterwards most of the party assembled to see Quinton and his new friend off, and there was a chorus of good-byes as they started.

Quinton drove himself.

"I have not got a chauffeur," he explained. "I've kept on the middle-aged couple who ran the house for my cousin. He cleans the car and does a bit in the garden. Of course, the place needs five or six servants at least, but I'm carrying on for the present. We can make a fresh start when—if—I marry Cynthia."

"Your cousin was a bachelor?"

"Yes. He'd been abroad a lot. He seems to have been a reserved sort of chap. Kept himself to himself. Nobody knew him about here. The house was empty for years before he came home."

A drive of seven or eight miles through the winding country lanes brought them to a wood which Thor had seen dark against the sky as they crossed a patch of moorland. It was one of those woods in which firs predominate and the song of birds is rarely heard, and it made a fitting setting for the old, timbered house whose fantastic chimneys were mirrored in the dark, stagnant waters of the moat among the flat, green lily leaves as the car passed over the wooden bridge. Perfect in its way, thought Thor, but gloomy. Within, it was a maze of low-pitched rooms, panelled in oak, black with age, and of staircases and passages. Mrs. Jakes was waiting to receive them. Her master had called her up to tell her to prepare for a visitor. Dinner was served at seven—quite a recherché little meal, and extremely well cooked. Jakes waited at table, and they talked desultorily on general topics until he had left them.

Thor sipped his port appreciatively.

"A vintage wine," he said.

"Is it? I don't know much about that sort of thing. I believe the cellar is pretty well stocked. My cousin seems to have believed in doing himself well."

The young man's eyes wandered as he spoke. He knocked the ash off the end of his cigarette, and Thor noticed that his hand shook. He thought:

"He's badly frightened. I wonder why?"

He had determined to await developments. At Quinton's suggestion they spent half an hour in the billiard-room knocking the balls about. Neither made any reference to their conversation of the previous evening until Thor, with a yawn, spoke of going to bed.

"All right," said Quinton. "I'll see you up to your room. You might lose your way. These passages are very confusing. I am on the same floor. If you want me turn to the left and then go down to the right after crossing the big landing. Or if you call out I'm sure to hear. The Jakes sleep in the servants' quarters in the old wing. They are shut off by baize doors. The skies might fall and they wouldn't notice. Extraordinary—"

This struck Thor as an odd speech, but he made no comment. His host accompanied him to the door of his room.

"Now, mind!" he said anxiously. "Call if you want me—"

"I will," said Thor, smiling. "But it's not very likely. I sleep well, even in strange beds. Good-night!"

He offered his hand and again the other gripped it vigorously.

Thor undressed leisurely, standing in the little island of light cast by the shaded electric lamp. The walls were panelled in oak and they and the uneven floor of boards, polished by centuries of use, seemed to swallow and absorb the light even there, while the distant corners of the room were thronged with shadows, a sea of shadows in which the great carved four-poster bed with its white curtains rode like a ship at anchor or becalmed. The bedclothes had been turned down and Thor's pyjamas and slippers laid ready. Evidently Mrs. Jakes was an efficient housemaid as well as a remarkably good cook. He wound up his watch and placed it under his pillow before getting into bed.

As he did so something long and black slid off the quilt on the other side. It looked like an old-fashioned bell-rope. For an instant he was startled. He went round the bed to look at it, but there was nothing there, unless, of course, it had slipped under the valance which hung within an inch of the floor. He had only to lift it and look underneath, but—somehow he did not want to do that. He conquered his reluctance and, bending, peered under the bed. There was nothing there.

Nevertheless, it had made him a little uncomfortable. He found himself wishing that the electric switch had been within reach. It was by the door, and if he wanted to get to it in the night he would have to cross the room and fumble about in the dark until he found it. He decided to leave the light burning.

Some instinct prompted him to turn the clothes down to the foot of the bed before he climbed in. There was nothing there, but it seemed to him that there was something decidedly queer about one of the posts that supported the canopy. Its outline appeared to waver. He turned to look at it and found it perfectly solid and immovable, but when he examined it more closely he made a discovery that gave him food for thought. He had supposed the bed to be a genuine specimen of the Jacobean joiner's art with the usual embellishment of stout cherubs, garlands, and true love knots. But the carved design was far more elaborate than that, and less innocent in intention. "Burmese?" said Thor to himself. He was not sure. It was the sort of thing Asiatic craftsmen might turn out if they were shown an illustration of an old English four-post bedstead and told to make one like it. Thor remembered that the late owner of Cleeve Manor had travelled much abroad. No doubt this was one of the treasures he had brought back with him.

Thor arranged his pillows to his liking and lay back. He would not sleep with the light on. Presently he would get out again and switch it off. Meanwhile, he glanced about him, probing the shadows. It was all right, of course. All right—

What was that on the floor on the edge of the little pool of light shed by the shaded lamp? It looked like a rather untidily-coiled ship's cable. God! It was coming undone!

He sat up, staring. Whatever it was it had vanished, gliding off into the darkness. Or—perhaps, after all, it had been nothing more than a trick of light. But he felt no inclination to lie down again. He had an electric torch, but he had discovered while dressing for dinner that the battery needed recharging. It was a pity as it might have been useful.

He thought he heard a faint rustling sound in the far corner of the room. The windows were open. Perhaps a wind was getting up and stirring the blinds. He listened intently, but the night was still with the heavy brooding stillness that presages a thunderstorm. The heat was oppressive, extraordinarily so for England.

He felt for the handkerchief he had pushed under the pillow with his watch and wiped his face. He had been taken by surprise, but he was on his guard now. Some instinct made him look up. The white canopy of the bed was sagging in the middle. Something round and heavy seemed to be settling there in the space, a narrow space, between it and the ceiling.

Thor scrambled out of the bed and ran to the door. As he crossed the room the light went out. Somehow he found the door-handle. Another moment and he was in the passage. He was going to find his host. He tried to recall the directions he had received and to which, at the time, he had paid little attention. Turn to the left—or was it the right?

It was hotter than ever, and more airless. There was a queer, stagnant smell, too, an odour of musk, sickly, almost fœtid, that came to him down the passage like a breath from some foul oven. The moat—yes, of course, the moat. It ought to be drained. He decided that he should turn to the left, and he started, feeling his way and occasionally barking his shins against pieces of furniture ranged against the walls When he came upstairs with Quinton the passage had been lit by one lamp hung high and obscured by a deep red silk shade. The lamp-shade in the room he had just left had been red, too. It struck Thor that this fact was significant. He wondered if they had been there when Quinton entered into his inheritance. As his eyes grew accustomed to the darkness he was able to distinguish the dim outlines of a muniment chest on his right. Beyond it there was a cupboard or wardrobe standing some seven feet high. Some way off, at the far end of the passage, a just perceptible irradiation, coming probably from a window on the landing, became his goal.

The heat was overpowering, and he gasped for breath. It was just then that he became aware that something was moving towards him from the direction of the landing, dragging along the floor. Its length and bulk reminded him of a picture he had seen of a mediæval siege engine, a battering ram made of the trunk of a felled tree. But the horrible odour of musk came with it. For an instant he stood petrified. Then he leapt on to the chest, keeping his foothold by a miracle, for it had a sloping lid, and from thence clambered on to the flat top of the wardrobe. It tilted dangerously, but some instinctive movement of his body balanced it.

The incredible thing below paused, and he was distinctly conscious of its baleful gaze fixed upon him. It exhaled its dreadful odour, the stench of corruption and of the black slime of the mangrove swamps, so that he sickened there, crouching precariously, his cramped body helpless before so awful a manifestation of a malefic power, while his spirit defied and outfaced the enemy.

After a period of agonising strain he felt the pressure of the dark force pitted against him relaxing. The creature below lay silent and motionless. Its outlines grew vague, wavering as though it lay under running water, dwindling inch by inch to a shadow, or to what might have been a black stain on the old oak boards, until, at last, it was gone.

The clock in the hall below struck three. The grey light of dawn was stealing into the house where it could find an entry, through cracks in the shutters, through the window on the landing. Somewhere, far off, a cock crew. The sound affected Thor strangely; it brought tears into his eyes.

He went back to his room, walking feebly, for he was physically spent, threw himself on his bed, and slept heavily until Jakes brought up his hot water at eight in the morning.

His host was already in the dining-room when he went down. He greeted his guest with a nervous attempt to be cheery.

"Another glorious day, what? Did—did you have a good night?"

"Not very," said Thor drily.

Mrs. Jakes was bringing in the bacon and eggs. He waited until she had set down the dish and departed.

"Did you?"

"As a matter of fact, yes. I slept like a log—for once."

Thor helped himself to toast.

"You don't sleep very well here as a rule?" he said. He spoke more as one stating a fact than asking a question.

Quinton had been lifting his cup to his lips. He set it down again, spilling some of his coffee on the cloth.

"My heaven!" he said. "Did you see anything?"

"Why didn't you warn me?" asked Thor with a touch of sternness.

"I thought it was a delusion, that my brain was going. The specialist thought my temperature went up at night. Thor, what is it! Can you explain it?"

"Not yet," said Thor. "But I think I can set your mind at rest on one point. If you are going mad so am I. In fact, I probably saw much more than you have ever seen."

He went on to describe his experiences during the night. Quinton listened, open-mouthed.

"Good heavens!" he said when Thor had done. "That would have finished me. I've never seen anything definite, never been absolutely certain. Shadows, rustlings—" He broke off with a shudder. "What do you think, Thor? Do they come out of the moat? They say it is very deep in places and it has never been known to dry up."

Thor shook his head.

"I don't think so. I won't advance any theory at this stage. Is the house known to be haunted?"

"I don't think so, but I might not have heard. After all, I have only been living here a few weeks," said the young man.

"Jakes and his wife were here in your cousin's time?"

"Yes. I don't think they have ever been disturbed. I don't believe they would have stayed on. But they sleep in the servants' quarters, shut off from the older part of the place."

"Your cousin had travelled a good deal before he settled down here?"

"I believe so. Yes."

"In what part of the world?"

"Pretty well all over, I fancy, but chiefly in Africa, up the West Coast, the Congo, and Liberia. He collected a lot of junk."

"We'll go through it presently," said Thor. "Do you generally ring for them to clear away breakfast?"

"Sometimes."

"Then ring now, will you?"

Quinton obeyed and Jakes answered the summons. He was a meagre little man with thinning hair that was beginning to get grey at the temples. His manner was anxious and subdued.

Thor watched him packing his tray.

"Were you long in the late Mr. Quinton's service, Jakes?"

Jakes looked up as if startled at being addressed and answered deprecatingly:

"Three years, sir, up to the time of his death."

"Did he have many visitors?"

"No, sir. He kept himself to himself more than any gentleman I've ever had to do with."

"What sort of man was he?"

Jakes coughed and glanced at his master.

"All right," said Quinton, reassuringly. "Go ahead. You know I never saw him."

"He was big and stout, with a loud voice, sir, and a bullying way with him. You should have heard him the only time the vicar called. Most insulting. He might have been warning off a chap he'd caught snaring rabbits. I was ashamed, but what could I do? We got good wages and the place suited us in many ways, and he was always civil to us. Mrs. Jakes is a good cook, and he thought a lot of his food, a rare lot."

"Was he ill long before he died?"

"No, sir. He went to bed as usual, and when I took up his hot water in the morning he was dead. Half in and half out of the bed he was. The doctor said it was a fit."

"Did he keep any pets?"

"No, sir, not even a dog. He didn't like animals, and I don't think they liked him. I remember a stray terrier followed one of the tradesmen up the avenue one morning. The master was out and

passed them. The man told me afterwards that the dog gave a yelp
and tore off down the avenue and back into the road. I thought Mr.
Quinton helped it out with the toe of his boot, but he swore it was
never touched."

Jakes waited a moment for further questions, but apparently
Thor's curiosity was satisfied. He waited until the man had left the
room with his laden tray.

"Not popular," he murmured.

"He sounds pretty awful," agreed the other.

"What about his collections?"

"They are in a room called the study. Come and have a look."

The study was airless and gloomy, its one window, set high in the
wall, over-shadowed by the firs that darkened the stagnant waters of
the moat. There was none of the usual furniture, but chests of drawers such as are used for keeping butterflies and geological specimens
were ranged against the walls, and there were a number of packing-
cases, some still unopened, with the labels of the Elder Dempster
Line pasted on the lids. The dust lay thick upon everything.

"Jakes told me they were not allowed in here," said Quinton.
He sniffed. "A bit whiffy, isn't it."

Thor's interest was unmistakable. He moved here and there,
opening and shutting drawers, turning over the contents of one or
two opened cases. The younger man waited, keeping rather near
the door. There was something sinister about this agglomeration of
lumber. He lit a cigarette. Thor had been stooping over a tumbled
heap of brownish fur and gaudy coloured feathers. He held up a
hideous, wrinkled leather mask.

"There's a complete witch doctor's outfit here," he remarked.
He stooped again and uttered an exclamation. "Here we are!"

Quinton came nearer and peered distastefully at what looked like a clumsy pair of furred motoring gloves. Thor turned them over, palm upwards, and revealed that each was furnished with a set of razor-edged claws.

Quinton stared.

"What does it mean?"

Thor dropped the gloves and turned away.

"Come on," he said. "Let's get outside."

He led the way on to the bridge that crossed the moat.

"It means one of two things," he said gravely. "Either your cousin, while in Africa, incurred the enmity of the extremely powerful Leopard Society by assisting the authorities in their attempt to exterminate it, or he went native, as white men sometimes do, and became himself a member. From what we have heard, I am afraid that the latter supposition is the most likely. In that case he probably carried on the secret worship and the secret rites here. That would account for anything you and I have seen. Very big Ju Ju."

"Those gloves—" faltered Quinton.

He was ashy pale.

"Part of the ceremonial. They wear them to tear their victims."

"Good heavens!" muttered Quinton.

"The palms of those gloves we found just now were black and stiff with dried blood."

Quinton groaned.

"What are we to do?"

Thor did not answer immediately.

"This case is unique in my experience," he said. "I don't profess to know much about Ju Ju. Probably no European does. I should advise making a bonfire of all the stuff your cousin brought home, but I think we ought to wait a day or two."

"Why?"

"We must not act hastily. It may be our duty to communicate with Scotland Yard."

Quinton's white lips moved without sound. At last he was able to articulate.

"I don't understand."

"I would rather not say more at present," said Thor. "I must think it over. I may have to spend another night here, but you had better not."

"You'd chance going through that again?" exclaimed Quinton.

"If necessary," said Thor simply. He glanced at his watch. "Wasn't it understood that we were to lunch at the Portals? It is time we started. Not a word to anyone there, of course."

"Oh, of course," echoed Quinton. "I'll get my suit-case packed," he added. "They'll put me up. I can make some excuse." He hesitated. "Thor, the thing that slipped off your bed, and the other—were they real?"

He had lowered his voice, and he glanced uneasily at the moat as they turned away from the bridge.

"Not in the sense you mean," said Thor. "I'm not omniscient. I can only suggest. I should say that they were thought forms materialised through the agency of an evil, discarnate intelligence who, in the earth life, was familiar with the creatures that breed in the slime of the mangrove swamps of West Africa. He formed them almost literally, as the sculptor forms his conceptions out of clay, but the clay in this instance was the living material drawn from the bodies of one or more of the sleepers under your roof. What about that suit-case?"

"Good lord!" said the young man.

Words failed him, and, in any case, it was evident that Thor did not wish to say more just then.

*

They left the Manor a quarter of an hour later, Quinton driving himself, as on the previous day. They passed a ragged old man shuffling along on the grass by the side of the road as they turned out of the gates, and another a little farther on.

"Do you get many tramps in this part of the world?" asked Thor.

"I think we do. There is a union, with a casual ward, at Jessop's Bridge, the market town, seven miles away."

"Perhaps you would drop me there, I may have to run up to town."

Quinton's face fell. He had not realised until then how much he had depended on the older man.

"You won't leave me now?" he said anxiously.

"No, no; you can rely on me. I suppose the Portals won't mind if I turn up again? I may not be in time for dinner. I shall want a few words with you alone. Shall we say the bowling-green, at nine?"

"I shall be there."

At Jessop's Bridge, Thor spent an hour in the office of the local weekly paper, the "Herald," looking through the back files, before he caught the twelve-four express to Waterloo. It was a little after eight when he reached the Towers. He had dined on the train coming down, and had no wish to advertise his presence just then; so he went through the garden without entering the house, and sat down to wait on the seat that overlooked the bowling-green. There was still light enough to read, and he wanted to look over the notes he had made in the pocket-book in which he jotted down the particulars of the cases in which he was engaged. They included the information he had gained partly from the back files of the "Herald" and partly from a friend at Scotland Yard.

During the three years that Quinton's cousin had lived at Cleeve Manor two people had disappeared from the neighbourhood. Both were strangers in the district, and apparently, in each case, very little effort had been made to trace them. The first, a girl of twenty-three named Hilda Parker, had been employed as assistant at a draper's shop in the High Street. She had gone for a ride on her bicycle one Sunday afternoon, and had never returned. She had taken no luggage with her, but her possessions were few and of little value. It transpired that she had told another girl that a gentleman with a car had been taking her for rides, and it was assumed that she had gone off with him. No relatives appeared, and the police had soon dropped the case.

The second was a waiter at the King's Head. He, too, had gone off for a ride on his bicycle, and had not come back. Suicide was suspected, and several ponds were dragged, but without result.

A further inquiry at the union elicited the fact that five vagrants who usually spent a couple of nights in the casual ward in the course of each summer, on their way to and from a famous West Country fair, had apparently chosen some other route.

It was not much to go upon, but among the heap of African junk Thor had turned over in that dark and airless room Quinton had called the study, there had been a dusty and crumpled scrap of cambric—a handkerchief with a hem-stitched border and the initials "H. P."

Thor turned a page. The former owner of Cleeve Manor had died early in the spring, on March 3rd. His heir had come down to the Manor to live on May 29th. On June 17th a girl of sixteen, daughter of a man employed as a gardener at a place called Firshill, had ridden over to Jessop's Bridge to do some shopping and go to the pictures. She had last been seen by a passing motorist at the Honey Pot crossroads. She had got off her bicycle to light her lamp, and she had never been seen since.

Thor, who had bought an ordnance map, noted the fact that Honey Pot was less than half a mile through the woods from the gates of Cleeve Manor.

And Quinton, the elder, had died on March 3rd.

He closed his book and put it away as the man he had come to meet appeared through the opening cut in the yew hedge.

"Well?" he said eagerly.

Thor rose to his feet.

"I am sorry," he said, "I have nothing to tell you at present. You must be patient a little longer. Shall we join the others?"

Quinton was obviously disappointed, but he acquiesced, and they walked back along the yew walk and through the rosary to the terrace, where they found most of the party assembled. The Portals kept open house in the casual modern fashion, and no surprise was expressed or felt at Thor's return. At the Towers guests came and went as they pleased. Cynthia, in her chiffon frock, glimmered like a white moth in the gathering dusk. She looked up to find Thor beside her.

"You startled me! I say, you look awfully ill!" she cried.

"I'm all right," he assured her. "I had a bad night. Do you happen to keep a diary, Miss Portal?"

"A sort of a one," she admitted.

"I wonder if you made an entry on June 17th?"

More than she dreamed of, her whole life's happiness, hung on her answer. Ignorant as she was of the issues something in his tone sobered her.

"Is it important? The seventeenth! Wait a minute! We—we were in Paris. We went over to meet an American friend of mother's and stayed a week. We went on the fifteenth."

"Then during that time, of course, you saw nothing of Mr. Quinton," Thor said, trying to speak cheerfully.

"I saw him every day and all day. He went with us."

"He did? My dear young lady—"

Thor was profoundly relieved, and for once unable to disguise his feelings. Cynthia looked up at him, puzzled.

"What is it all about?"

"Nothing. There's nothing for you to worry about," he said gently. "Go and dance with the others, my dear."

He went up to bed early, and, as he had expected, Harry Quinton followed him up to his room.

"I can't stand this suspense," he said. "What am I to do? Thor, you may think me a coward, but I tell you I daren't go back to the Manor. I've had enough! And what am I to say to people? What will the Portals think?"

"I certainly don't advise you to go back," said Thor gravely.

Quinton had been walking restlessly up and down. He stopped short and looked at the other.

"You said something this morning about Scotland Yard. What did you mean by that? If you had said the Psychical Research Society I should have understood."

Thor reflected a moment. Sooner or later Quinton would have to know the truth, shocking as it might seem to him, and now that his worst fear had been proved groundless there seemed no reason for further delay.

"I need not tell you," he said slowly, "that the power that could produce the unnamable horrors of which you have been vaguely conscious and which I actually saw last night, might manifest in other directions. The Leopard Society is to some extent political, but its secret rites are devil worship and the culminating act is"—he paused—"human sacrifice."

Quinton stared at him.

"You don't think my cousin—"

"I'm afraid so," said Thor. He described the disappearance of the shop girl and the waiter, and his finding of the handkerchief with the initial H.P. among the lumber in the study. "There may have been others, vagrants who might vanish easily without arousing any curiosity."

"Horrible," muttered Quinton. "But—heaven knows I don't want to shield the fellow. If he were living—but he's gone. And nothing we can do can bring his victims back to life."

"I agree," said Thor; "but I haven't finished yet. Another girl, the daughter of a gardener at Firshill, disappeared."

Quinton started.

"Of course, I heard about that. But that was only last month! What are you suggesting?"

"Think over what I said just now," Thor replied. "I told you this morning that to produce the thought forms I saw the discarnate intelligence at the back of all this drew material from the sleepers under the roof of the house it had turned to such vile uses. I have no doubt that it was equally capable of employing one at least of these as an agent when it so desired."

"You mean in a sort of hypnotic trance?"

"Exactly."

Quinton was white to the lips.

"I see," he said very quietly. "Jakes and his wife and I. It—it's not a very big field. You think that one of us inveigled this girl to the house and murdered her. That's it, isn't it? I want to be quite clear."

"Not consciously," Thor reminded him.

He liked the way Quinton was taking it. The boy had pluck.

"Have you been to Scotland Yard?"

"I went to get the information I needed. I didn't tell them anything. That isn't my job, anyway."

Quinton nodded.

"I suppose it may have been me," he said. "How is one to know?"

Thor went over to him and laid a hand on his shoulders.

"By the mercy of God it wasn't. We can prove it, too. The thing happened on the seventeenth and you were in Paris then. I—what's that?"

There was a clamour of excited voices in the passage. Someone knocked at the door and came in. It was Sir James Portal.

"I've been to your room to look for you, Harry," he said hurriedly. "I've just been rung up. I've news for you, bad news. Your house—Cleeve Manor—there's been an outbreak of fire. In fact, from what I can gather, the place has been gutted. The Jessop's Bridge fire brigade got there too late to do much. I am most awfully sorry, my dear fellow. You had better go down to the 'phone. The superintendent wanted to speak to you. They are holding the line—"

Thor followed them down to the hall.

"You'll want to motor over," said Sir James, and bustled away to see about a car.

Quinton took up the receiver.

"Quinton speaking. Yes—yes—I'll come."

After a while he rang off and turned to Thor. Sir James had not yet returned and they were alone.

"They say they think it originated on the ground floor, in a room on the left of the entrance, and that it may have been smouldering for hours. It sounds like the study."

"Very likely. Do you remember lighting a cigarette and throwing the match down. I noticed it at the time, and nearly said something about it being a dangerous thing to do."

Their eyes met. Each was thinking the same thing. Quinton put their thought into words.

"It's the best thing that could have happened," he said, "or it would be if it were not for poor old Jakes. She's all right, but it seems he went in again to fetch his stamp album. The poor old chap collected stamps. And he was overcome by the smoke or something."

"Perhaps even that—" said Thor.

"You think that he—but he was such a decent little fellow! You saw yourself. He didn't like my cousin. He didn't approve of him."

"The unconscious instrument. He was not to blame."

"Can we leave it now?"

"I think so," said Thor. "I'll go over the ground in a day or two and do what I can. There are cleansing rites, you know. But I would not rebuild on the spot if I were you."

Quinton shuddered.

"I shan't."

A year later Thor was motoring through Hampshire, and chance brought him down the unfrequented by-road that led past the ruins of Cleeve Manor. He looked over the low wall and saw the blackened heap of bricks already overgrown with nettles, while the dead firs scorched by the flames were still standing, darkening the stagnant water of the moat. Harry Quinton, he knew, had gone to Canada with his young wife, and talked of settling there.

He drove on. The sun had set, and he had a feeling that he would not care to be there after nightfall.

He turned to his companion, Sir Gavin Steer, the great authority in mental cases.

"That was Cleeve, all that is left of it."

Steer chuckled.

"I remember. You told me about it at the time. The place where you had the nightmare of your life. You gave the show away when you praised the cooking."

Thor smiled good-humouredly.

"Well, I admit that I have very little evidence that would be called evidence in a court of law."

"Of course not," scoffed his old friend. "The whole thing was moonshine."

Thor's smile had faded.

"Some day," he said, "I shall ask you to watch with me. Some night, I should say."

"Done with you," said Steer. "But you needn't hope to convert me."

He laughed again, little dreaming how awfully that promise, so easily given, would be fulfilled.

CRANSHAWE

in

FORGOTTEN HARBOUR

Gordon Hillman

One does not normally expect a writer of crime fiction to become a criminal himself but that is what happened with Gordon Malherbe Hillman (1900–1968). Hillman had had some success as a writer selling stories not only to the pulp magazines but to the higher-class slicks and weeklies such as McCall's, Liberty, *and even* Good Housekeeping. *Some of his stories had been filmed, notably* The Great Man Votes *(1939), about a drunken widower and his children, starring John Barrymore. But the years during the Second World War and beyond reduced his markets and he also turned to drink, finding it harder to sell. Finances were low and he found it difficult to look after his invalid mother. So on the evening of 7 May 1950 he bludgeoned his mother to death. It was he who contacted the police and pleaded guilty yet, surprisingly, he was tried for manslaughter, served a minimal sentence and by 1954 was able to pick up the threads of his life and return to journalism. It was a disturbing episode in what otherwise had seemed a promising life.*

Amongst Hillman's stories was a series for the magazine Ghost Stories. *This was published by the health fanatic Bernarr Macfadden who had founded his fortune on the magazine* Physical Culture, *started in 1899 (and which would have appealed to William Hope Hodgson). Amongst his magazine empire was* True Story, *launched in 1919, which purported* to feature dramatic true stories, often illustrated by mock photographs. Ghost Stories went the same way with the stories usually told in the first person and presented as if the author was retelling the tale from experiences relayed to them. Hillman wrote several stories featuring Cranshawe (we don't learn his first name) billed as "the greatest American authority on poltergeists".

Whenever I hear the roar of the surf, or feel fog on my face, I shudder in terror of the memory that those two wonders of nature bring back to my mind.

It all happened because my friend Cranshawe had been called to Chicago on a case connected with the tax commission. A man there had demanded his taxes be lowered because a house he owned was haunted, and he could neither rent nor sell it. The tax commissioner, very justifiably at his wits' end, had called in Cranshawe, the greatest American authority on poltergeists.

And so I had gone to Forgotten Harbour alone to enjoy a few peaceful autumn days—not knowing that fall in Forgotten Harbour means fog. But then, if I had known that, I should not have gone; and if I had not gone, Forgotten Harbour would have witnessed a tragedy even more horrible than the one which I saw.

Out on the point, a bit away from the rambling town, stood an old hotel that one day soon would collapse into the sea. The summer visitors had all gone, and I was one of the few guests there.

And even those few guests began leaving, some because of the fog; others because of the constant moan of foghorns as fogbound ships sailed up the rocky coast. But most of them left because of the peculiar *feel* of the place.

It was a curious feeling, hard to describe—yet I had felt it from the minute I arrived.

That feeling was even stronger the day I quite innocently asked the proprietor of the hotel, "What's the name of the lighthouse out there on the island?"

"Dead Man's Light!" he said, and he turned oddly silent, as if he did not care to talk about it.

"Curious name, 'Dead Man's Light'," I said.

"They just call it that around here," he told me uneasily. "Used to be known as Eastern Light. Still is, on the government charts."

"Why did they change the name?" I asked.

His eyes flickered, "Oh, I dunno," he said. "It flashes white—flashes every ten seconds."

He was not, I was quite convinced, telling the truth. He knew perfectly well why the light bore that grisly name. Now, I was convinced more than ever that my senses had not betrayed me—that there was something peculiar about the white lighthouse on the shoal.

I was still staring at Dead Man's Light, when one of the waiters rushed up to me. "You're wanted on the phone, Sir," he said.

That was strange, for I knew no one in that part of the country. I picked up the receiver, and the operator's voice came over the wire in a high pitch of hysteria. "Sheriff Fairbarn wants to see you at his office, Sir. Right away! Please, oh, please hurry, Sir!"

Why a sheriff should want to see me, I could not guess, but I hurried to the office as quickly as I could.

The sheriff was nervously pacing up and down in front of a young woman who might have been pretty had her face not been white with terror.

"You're a friend of Mr. Cranshawe's, aren't you?" the sheriff snapped before I had a chance to speak.

I nodded in surprise.

"And Mr. Cranshawe's a ghost-hunter, isn't he?"

"He is," I said, sitting down, "a sort of psychic detective. The only one in America, I believe. Why?"

"We're at our wits' end," the sheriff said suddenly. "We want you to call Mr. Cranshawe here."

"But," I protested, "Mr. Cranshawe is a busy man."

The sheriff pointed toward the window where I could just see the white lighthouse through the fog. "There's trouble out there," he said in a harsh whisper, "—trouble on Dead Man's Light!

"It was about a year ago," he said, "that the light got its name. That was when the first one went!"

"Went?" said I. "Who went?"

"The light-keeper," said the sheriff. "Went like a blown out candle—went like a gust of wind. It was in a fog like this. Tom Thornton was keeper then—an old man who walked with a heavy cane. It was night time and Tom's assistant, Atkinson, was over to the mainland. He left the old man alone with the light—alone in the brutal fog."

He suddenly turned to the white-faced girl. "This young lady," he said, "works in the telephone exchange. She'll tell you what happened that night."

"At one minute to twelve," she said, "a call came in—a call from the lighthouse. I answered it and at first there wasn't any sound at all except a tapping that might have been a man—a man with a heavy cane. Then the line seemed to go dead—only it didn't. There was a scream—just one single scream, and not another thing, though we held the line open." She looked out at the light, then buried her face in her hands.

The sheriff went on in a voice that seemed hollow and dead. "The telephone company called me," he said. "I listened in on the line. At half past twelve, Atkinson began to yell through the phone.

He'd just got back, and Tom wasn't there at all. Atkinson found the phone off the hook, he said, and he wanted me to come right out there. But when I got there an hour later, there was no man—alive or dead—in that lighthouse. Atkinson had gone, too—gone like Tom."

"Disappeared?" I asked.

"Vanished into thin air. There's not a trace of either of 'em been seen since. No bodies found. Nothing!"

I shook my head. "That's a murder, perhaps," I said, "or a double murder. But it's hardly in Mr. Cranshawe's line."

"That isn't all," the sheriff said. Then he turned to the telephone operator. "Tell him what's happened at one minute to twelve every night this week!"

The girl clenched her handkerchief. "The phone from the lighthouse rings," she said shakily, "and we answer it—and there's nothing on the line but slow taps—like—like a lame man walking with a cane. There were lots of taps at first—last night there were only three, and then comes that horrible, ghastly—" She could not finish.

"Scream," the sheriff said huskily, "a scream out of nowhere."

"But there must be men out at the lighthouse now?" I said.

The sheriff nodded. "We've checked up. Neither one of them has touched the phone at night."

"That's odd," I said.

"The whole town's in terror, Sir," he said. "That lighthouse is haunted!"

I still wasn't sure as I left the sheriff's office. Should I call Cranshawe in on what might be a wild goose chase? A practical joke? Or a mere case of nerves on the part of a telephone operator?

Yet, despite my doubts, I felt that strange atmosphere that hung over Forgotten Harbour like its endless fog. It seemed as if the whole town was waiting for something to happen—something unnatural, something ghastly.

I had to think this over. I went into a restaurant, sat down in a booth, and ordered coffee. I could hear a young man's excited voice coming from the booth next to mine.

"I tell you," he was shouting, "I won't stay there much longer! They'll either relieve me or—"

The plump proprietress of the restaurant came to give me my coffee, and jerked her thumb toward the owner of the voice.

"Don't mind him," she said. "He's crazy!"

"Who is he?"

"Him?" she said. "He's one of the keepers out at the light."

"Now, now, Matt," I could hear another and deeper voice say, "you'd better straighten up. There's nothing in what you say! Such things don't happen hereabouts... You'd better get back to Dead Man's Light!"

"That's right," said Matt, louder than before, "that's what it is—Dead Man's Light—the light where dead men don't die! They don't die, I tell you! They don't!"

Then, I saw the owner of the voice, a very lean and bronzed young man with a look of terror in his eyes. A grizzled fisherman was guiding him out of the booth saying, "There's naught in that, Matt! You'll be all right when you're back in your lighthouse!"

"Back there!" screamed the boy. "Back there where that *thing* will get me—that *thing* that comes out of the fog—"

The outside door was slammed and that was all I heard. But it was enough. I practically ran to the railroad station.

"Drop tax matter," I wired Cranshawe. "Hurry here. Most mysterious case of your career. Haste imperative!"

I knew the mere hint of eerie doings would bring Cranshawe

like a shot—and it did. Two days later, he stepped off the train at Forgotten Harbour.

"H'm," he said at once. "Uneasy feeling about this place. Something's going to happen here."

"Something already has," I told him, and as we sat in my hotel room, I recounted the whole story.

Cranshawe listened to the end, then took a pair of field glasses from his bag, and focussed them on the lighthouse and the little island upon which it stood. For perhaps five minutes, he surveyed the sandy ground and then gave a sudden start.

"Here," he said, "look through these. Look at the south end of the island, just beneath the light. Do you see anything?"

For a moment I could see nothing. Then I did see something and I nearly dropped the glasses.

At the very foot of the lighthouse were two odd-shaped mounds—narrow and about six feet long, I should say. In the sharp light of sunset, they seemed to grow and grow—their outlines became firmer. They suggested...

"Graves!" whispered Cranshawe. "Two graves! Watch them! Don't take your eyes off them!"

Though my hands shook, I clung to the glasses. I had looked at the island before, through a telescope, there had been no mounds then—no graves. And these mounds I saw were rapidly losing form—losing shape—disappearing into a flat level of sand—disappearing into nothingness as two men had disappeared a year ago tonight. Had it been the sharp light of sunset that brought out these two graves? Was it a mirage? Was it merely my indignation?

Suddenly, they were completely gone and as I turned to Cranshawe, whose face was as puzzled as mine, a bell began to clang in the town.

It was no ordinary bell. There was something about its ring that brought chills to my spine. And it rang through the fog, rang through the gathering darkness, rang as if each new stroke was a signal of doom.

"My God!" said I. "What's that?"

The bell rang so loudly, I could hardly hear a knock on our door. The door opened and the sheriff burst in.

"Mr. Cranshawe! Mr. Cranshawe!" he called. "For God's sake, do something!"

Of us all, Cranshawe was the only one who remained calm. "Are you Sheriff Fairbarn?" he asked. The sheriff nodded. "Good! Tell me now, are there two graves on the south end of Dead Man's Island? Two graves just in the shadow of the light?"

"No!" said the sheriff. "No, Sir. Some folks say they've seen 'em, but I've looked. There are no graves.

The alarm bell still rang. "What's that?" asked Cranshawe.

"It's the huge bell on the life-saving station," said the sheriff. "It hasn't rung since the *Northern Prince* went down thirty-two years ago."

"Well, why's it ringing now?" I asked. "Is there another wreck?"

"No, Sir!" quavered the sheriff. "Not yet. Nobody's ringing that bell, Sir—nobody human. I've got one of my deputies standing guard beside the bell rope. That bell rope doesn't move—but the bell's ringing—ringing like mad!"

Cranshawe was already putting on his overcoat, slipping a note-book into one pocket, a revolver in the other.

"This noon," the sheriff went on, "two fishermen came to me scared to death. They came in past the lighthouse last night, and they say they saw a lantern in the fog!"

"Good God," I shouted, for my nerves were fast getting the better of me. "A lantern's nothing to worry about."

The sheriff shouted back. "But this one is! It moved about knee-high, slow, as if a man was walking with it—a man who didn't walk very well—but it wasn't on the island—it was on the water!"

"In a boat then?" asked Cranshawe.

The sheriff shuddered. "There wasn't any boat, there wasn't anything out there but the lantern, and the fishermen nearly ran it down."

Cranshawe turned on the sheriff. "Now, Mr. Fairbarn," he said, "there's no use disguising the fact that this is a serious situation and an uncommonly nasty one. I want you to keep your head and answer two or three questions and answer them quickly."

"Okay," said the sheriff.

"First question," snapped Cranshawe, "was there another of those queer telephone calls from the light last night?"

"There was."

"How many times did the dead man's cane tap?"

"Only once. It's been tapping one less time every night now."

Cranshawe frowned. "The time's short," he said. "I should have been called here before. There's a boat due here tonight, isn't there?"

"Yes," said the sheriff. "*Queensland Castle*. Big passenger ship. She'll be due about midnight."

"I knew it! I knew it!" said Cranshawe, half under his breath. Then he turned to the sheriff again. "Mr. Fairbarn, something strange, something horrible is going to happen on Dead Man's Light tonight. I may be able to prevent it; I may not. What I want to know is, will you implicitly follow my orders for the next twenty-four hours?"

The sheriff sighed with relief. "Gladly, Mr. Cranshawe. This business is driving me out of my head, and I'm not the only one. Since that bell's begun to ring, the whole town's in terror. Give me your orders! I'll follow them!"

"First," said Cranshawe, "I want you to make me a deputy sheriff. Second, I want authority to spend tonight at Dead Man's Light!"

"You're practically sworn in," said the sheriff, "but the lighthouse is government property."

Cranshawe spoke slowly, measuring his words. "It may mean disaster if I don't get there tonight."

The sheriff thought for a moment, then said, "As peace officer of Folsom County, I authorise you to stay at the lighthouse as long as you wish. What else, Sir?"

Cranshawe was already at the door. "You stay in town," he snapped. "Put one of your men on the telephone switchboard in the exchange! Have him answer anything from the lighthouse. Don't let him leave his post!

"Station yourself at the life-saving station! Run the surf boat out on the beach! Have every power boat in the harbour ready to move on an instant's notice! Commandeer all available seamen to man them!" The sheriff seemed about to say something but Cranshawe held up his hand for silence. In the distance, the big bell was still booming. "The last time that rang, Sheriff, the *Northern Prince* went down. It went down on Dead Man's Shoal, didn't it?"

The sheriff nodded, his face white as chalk.

Cranshawe spoke to him again as we went down the steps of the hotel. "Remember," he said, "at the slightest sign or hint of anything out of the ordinary at Dead Man's Light, get every available craft started for the shoal." He stopped and then added, "Tell your deputies to load their guns!"

I was completely confused. If Dead Man's Light was haunted, what good would guns do against a ghost? If it wasn't...

The sheriff suddenly shouted to a man across the street, a man who was built like a gorilla, whose face even resembled one.

"That's Roger Wilson, the light-keeper," he hastily said to Cranshawe, as Wilson walked over.

"Wilson, I want you to take these two gentlemen out to the light. They're spending the night there."

The light-keeper's voice was a deep boom. "Can't. Against the rules. It's gov-ment property."

"And," said the sheriff, "you're to take them out now in your boat. If you don't, I'll arrest you for obstructing justice!"

Wilson only nodded his head and led us to the waterfront. In silence, we climbed into his small motor-boat; in silence the sheriff watched us leave. The fog came down again like a pall. Through it we could dimly see that ten second flash of white that meant Dead Man's Light was ahead.

"There've been some queer doings on your light lately?" said Cranshawe smoothly.

The light-keeper shrugged his shoulders. "Some folks say so. Haven't seen 'em myself. You won't see anything, neither."

"Nor hear anything?" asked Cranshawe sharply.

"Nothing to hear," growled the light-keeper. "You've no right to be out there, anyway. I'll report the sheriff to Washington."

Cranshawe leaned forward, his voice cutting like a knife. "I wouldn't," he said softly. "Washington's still interested in what became of its two light-keepers a year ago tonight. So am I!"

Wilson knelt down to do something to the engine. "Oh," he growled, "Secret Service men, huh?"

Cranshawe did not answer. I could quite see why. It would do no harm for the light-keeper to believe we were Department of Justice men; it might do some good.

"Well," shrugged Wilson, as we touched the tip of Dead Man's Island, "you'll find nothing out here."

I wasn't so sure of that. Out here, on the bare little island that boasted only one house and the towering lighthouse itself, the atmosphere was stranger than it had been in town. I shuddered at the thought of what was going to happen.

As we stood on shore, the big light winked at us. In it, I could see a man standing against the little iron railing at the top.

"That's Matt," I whispered, "the assistant keeper. The one I told you about."

Cranshawe nodded and somewhere a clock struck seven. "Five hours till midnight!" snapped Cranshawe. "That doesn't give us much time to find anything. Come on!"

We went across the strip of sand that separated the house from the Light. It was already quite dark, and Cranshawe's flashlight threw a golden ring ahead of us. It shifted once to the very base of the lighthouse. The sand was hard-packed there, smooth and flat. There was no sign of a mound—or a grave.

"But I saw them," I said, "with my own eyes. So did you."

"No matter," said Cranshawe impatiently. "The sheriff says they're only seen at sunset. Hurry!"

We entered the lighthouse and pounded up innumerable rounds of iron stairs. At last, we came to the top where the great lamp wheeled and sent out its rays to pierce the fog. The fog was thicker than ever. Through it, you could hear the sea birds' cries, and occasionally, the faint, far-off whistle of a ship.

"Keep your eyes away from the lamp," Cranshawe said sharply, "or it'll blind you."

At the top, Matt met us. Cranshawe went straight toward him. "Tell me what you know," he snapped. "All you know about Dead Man's Light. Sheriff's orders."

"Oh, government men," said Matt shakily. "It won't do any good. You'll never find anything—never!"

"Now calm down," said Cranshawe, "and tell us what you're afraid of."

Matt leaned toward us and whispered as the great light wheeled and swung, wheeled and flashed. "It's this *thing*," he whispered, "the horrible *thing* that comes out of the fog—a dead man's face—a dead man's footsteps. I don't mind the ghost lantern, nor the noises, but that face, Mister, it's not human—it's not alive—it looks as if…"

I heard a shuffling noise, and there was Wilson standing on the stairway, listening. Suddenly he shouted, "Matt! I'm comin' up to take over."

Cranshawe nodded to me and we went down. As we passed Wilson, he hissed, "Don't mind Matt, he's a little crazy!"

To my surprise, Cranshawe emphatically agreed with him. "Absolutely!" he said.

I followed Cranshawe across the fogbound sands to the house. He opened the door and went in. Downstairs there was a long living-room that smelled of pipe smoke. There were three windows, all facing east. Upstairs, there were two bedrooms. "No one's up there," reported Cranshawe after a search.

The telephone was in the corner of the living room. He motioned me toward it. "Take the receiver off the hook," he commanded, "and tell the sheriff's deputy that nothing's happened yet, but to stand by for trouble."

I picked up the receiver. Above the telephone was a clock, its hands racing toward the hour of eight. "Hello—hello," I shouted into the phone. There wasn't a sound. The line was dead. Then, I could hear footsteps—a lame man's footsteps—the tap-tap of a man with a heavy cane. The noise was coming through the telephone. One tap—two taps—three—four—then silence again. I waited, my ears tense, my nerves jangling for an unearthly scream—the scream of a man in agony—the scream of a man near death.

But no scream came.

Above me, the clock had begun to strike eight.

"Cranshawe! Cranshawe!" I shouted. "There were four taps—four distinct taps—"

My friend nodded as his hand closed on the revolver in his pocket. "Hang up," he said quietly. "Now, try the mainland again. There are just four hours left before something happens here. Tell the sheriff's deputy to have all boats ready to leave the harbour at precisely one minute of twelve!"

This time the line was clear, and I delivered my message.

"Well," I said to Cranshawe, "what now?"

"Wait!" he said.

I must have dozed off, for when I opened my eyes, it was half past eleven and a salt wind was blowing through the door.

Matt stood there, the mist in little beads on his cap and face.

"Wilson sent me back here," he mumbled. "It's almost time—"

"Time for what?" snapped Cranshawe.

"You'll see! You'll see!" said Matt, as he sank down in a chair, his eyes riveted on those three east windows. I looked out the windows, too, but all I could see was fog; all I could hear was the ship's whistle. It seemed almost on top of us now.

Cranshawe slipped the revolver back into his pocket. "I'll take a turn about outside," he said. "Stay by that phone!"

He opened the door and stepped into the fog.

Seconds after Cranshawe left, the lights went out—went out as if some hand had swiftly cut them off. Yet Matt was still sitting in his chair, twenty feet from the switch.

As the lights went out, a great glow from the lighthouse flashed about us, and there, in the window, coming out of the fog was a face—no body—no arms—just a face drifting on the fog. The face of no living man. No human face! It was black, cinder black, as if it had been burned. Its eyelids were closed over what should have been eyes. Slowly, as it pressed against the pane, those eyelids opened… there were no eyes! It was horrible!

Matt suddenly screamed, "It's picking at the glass! It's coming in! The *thing's* coming in…"

Dead Man's Light flashed no longer. It was pitch dark. The face had gone from the now mysteriously opened window. I heard a sharp cry in the dark, the cry of a man being choked. It was Matt's cry.

Though every fibre in me protested, I hurled myself toward Matt, felt something cold flash by my face, something that froze every drop of blood in my body. Suddenly I felt clammy hands on my throat. I fought frantically, but there was nothing, no one there! I was being choked to death by nothing!

In a daze, I dragged myself from that clutch, dragged myself across the floor, found the switch, and the lights went on.

Matt lay on the floor, unconscious. There were ghastly red marks on his throat—the marks of clawing fingers. There was no one else in the room. But in the rug there was a deep, round imprint such as a steel shaft of a heavy cane might make. The window was still wide open; its lock had been broken.

"Cranshawe!" I shouted. "Cranshawe!"

The door opened and he ran in. Without a word, he lifted Matt's head, looked at the scarlet marks on his throat. "There must be some brandy here," he shouted. He found some in a cabinet and poured a little down Matt's throat.

I looked up at the clock. It was two minutes to twelve! And that fog whistle was deafening. The ship must practically be on the island, I thought.

It was still dark outside. Matt, who had regained consciousness, tried to stand up.

"The Light! The light's gone out!" he cried.

Cranshawe and I raced for the door. Above us rose the shaft of the lighthouse, but where there should have been the great flow of the lamp, there was only darkness.

Darkness all around—except to the east. There, barely visible, were the lights of a liner making for the harbour. The ship's whistle blew, frantically, in short, sharp blasts as though calling in panic for the light to flash again.

"Quick!" shouted Cranshawe. "The telephone!"

He was gone in an instant, his revolver in hand, racing toward Dead Man's Light with Matt.

I ran in and reached for the telephone. Above it, the clock said one minute to midnight. I tore down the receiver and jangled the hook.

The steamer's whistle blared again. Closer—closer...

"Hello!" said a voice at the end of the phone. "Hello!"

"The light's out!" I shouted. "The *Queensland Castle* is coming in—she's nearly on the rocks. Get that life-saving crew started!"

The line clicked shut, and as I looked out the door, I could see the light of the steamer drifting toward disaster.

Then, another light flashed. It was a lantern where no lantern should have been—a lantern in the fog—a lantern on the very surface of the sea. It seemed to move slowly, jerkily, but it still moved faster than Cranshawe and Matt. It moved toward the lighthouse, entered it, I saw it through the lighthouse windows, going up—up as if mounting the stairs.

Then, in a sudden burst of glory, Dead Man's Light shone full on my face. The great lamp was blazing, swinging, flashing.

The steamer's siren screamed. I could hear a chorus of shouted commands, "Hard over! Full speed astern!"

There was an instant when her bow shot out of the fog, when it seemed almost to crash down upon me, then it slowed, stopped, and backed away, as the whistle roared and a jangle of bells came from the engine room.

In the dark town beyond, a rocket went up, and I could hear the sirens of boats racing down the bay, as the big alarm bell on the life-saving station boomed and boomed again.

I ran out of the house. To the east, the steamer's lights were slowly swinging away as she took her course up the bay. Above me, Dead Man's Light flashed and flashed again.

And then Cranshawe was beside me, beads of perspiration on his face. "The light-keeper's dead," he said huskily. "Up there in the light. Dead without a mark on him. I wouldn't go to look if I were you. Even before he died, he was being blinded—blinded because as he was dying his face was held close to the light itself!"

"Held?" I gasped.

"Held," said Cranshawe. "You saw the lantern come out of the sea, I suppose. Well, that's that. It's all over now."

It was all over, save for explanations to the sheriff, who came running up the sand.

"My God! Mr. Cranshawe," said the sheriff, after he had heard the tale of that night of terror. "A dead man in the lighthouse.

Another man nearly choked to death! The *Queensland Castle* nearly wrecked! What do you make of it all?"

Cranshawe placidly lit his pipe. As far as he was concerned the case was closed.

"A year ago tonight," he said, "two men disappeared out here. They didn't disappear. They were murdered. There's an old passage-way under the lighthouse. It's sealed up, now. Unseal it and you'll find their bodies—under the sands—under the spot where we saw the two graves at sunset."

"But who murdered them?" gasped the sheriff.

Cranshawe almost smiled. "That's elementary. Roger Wilson murdered them. He wanted this lighthouse job when old Tom Thornton got it. Wilson never forgave him. He waited a year or so for old Tom to die—but old Tom didn't die. So Wilson came here one year ago tonight and killed the old man and hid his body. Then he killed young Thornton. Then he put the bodies in the secret passage, and went away again. Wilson was next in line for the lighthouse job. He took it, never realising that old Tom would come back to haunt the light.

"My God, it's incredible!" the sheriff said.

"Even when he found out Dead Man's Light was haunted," said Cranshawe, "Wilson wouldn't quit. He wouldn't be beaten by a dead man—but he did go mad. He'd already killed two men, he wanted to kill more. He was a homicidal maniac. That's why he tried to wreck the *Queensland Castle*. He would have, too, despite all our efforts, if it hadn't been for—"

The sheriff looked fearfully behind him. "If it hadn't been for a dead man!" he breathed.

"Precisely!" said Cranshawe, as if that were a most commonplace matter. "I don't know how you're going to write that down in the records, Sheriff!"

For once, I thought I had found a flaw in Cranshawe's explanation.

"But why," I asked, "if old Tom—the dead man—wanted revenge on Wilson, why did the *thing* try to strangle Matt?"

"I don't exactly know," said Cranshawe, "but I suspect that before Wilson murdered old Tom, he did a fiendish thing—he held the old man's face toward the light till his eyes were burned out—till he was blinded!"

The sheriff dropped his pipe. "You mean—" he gasped, "the dead man couldn't see!"

"Perhaps!" said Cranshawe, "but that we'll never know!"

Today, the folk of Forgotten Harbour claim that Dead Man's Light is haunted still. They say, too, that a ghost lantern often flickers through the fog. But it does not matter now. After the two bodies were found in the old passageway, the Government abandoned Dead Man's Light. The new lighthouse is on the opposite shoal.

LUCIUS LEFFING

in

IN DEATH AS IN LIFE

Joseph Payne Brennan

Joseph Payne Brennan (1918–1990) had started out writing for the western pulp magazines in 1948 and had he relied solely on their sales he'd probably be long forgotten. But in 1952 he turned to that legendary pulp Weird Tales *and his second appearance there, "Slime" (March 1953) became an instant classic—an evocative tale of the "blob" school of horror. Alas, the original series of* Weird Tales *ceased the following year and Brennan began his own magazine,* Macabre, *in 1957. He kept it going for twenty-three issues—covering almost twenty years—and copies of that little magazine are now extremely rare. It was in the pages of* Macabre *that we first encounter Lucius Leffing, who lived in New Haven, Connecticut, but whose lifestyle and interests were of an English Victorian gentleman. Leffing is befriended by Brennan himself, who chronicles his adventures. Not all the stories are supernatural, though most are unusual, and they are collected in three volumes—*The Casebook of Lucius Leffing *(1973),* The Chronicles of Lucius Leffing *(1977),* The Adventures of Lucius Leffing *(1990)—and one novel,* Act of Providence *(1979).*

I had had no word from my friend Lucius Leffing, the psychic investigator, for many months. My brief notes brought no response; telephone calls were not answered. At length, as a sense of unease grew within me, I decided to pay him a visit.

It was late September. The elm leaves, curled crisp and brown, blew along the walks like summer's husks. Already a faint chill was in the air.

I rang the doorbell at seven Autumn Street and waited. Rang and waited again. And again. I was about to leave when the door opened just a crack. A frosty grey-blue eye squinted out at me.

"Oh, Brennan! Come in! Come in!" The door opened wide and there stood Leffing wrapped in a rather seedy-looking yellow dressing gown. The frost melted from his eyes quickly enough, but his angular face appeared thinner and paler than I had ever seen it before.

"You've been ill?" I inquired, as I followed him down the hall into his Victorian living room.

Sinking into his favourite Morris chair, he shrugged. "An illness of the psyche, Brennan."

As I stood regarding him gravely, he motioned me to another chair. "Sit down, man. Have some brandy."

A decanter stood on a small table next to his chair. It was two-thirds empty.

I accepted a glass of brandy and water and Leffing refilled his own.

Lifting his drink, he surveyed me sombrely. "Here's to the past!" he toasted—and drained the glass.

"Have you seen a doctor?" I inquired.

He waved a hand, wearily, as if to dismiss the subject. "My sickness, as I told you, is of the spirit. I am assailed by a malaise which no physician's prescription can assuage."

He shook his head. "Brennan, I was intended for a different century, another age. I am out of sympathy with the milieu; I am attuned to another time."

Glancing around at the dark mahogany furniture, the marble-topped tables and the gaslight fixtures on the walls, I recalled that he considered himself a pure Victorian born by mistake a hundred years late.

He went on, an edge of bitterness in his voice. "Last week, for the first time in months, I took a long walk about New Haven. I was appalled by the hideous new structures which are arising on all sides—rubble and cement rectangles, ugly unrelieved towers—stark, desolate, dehumanised!"

He refilled his brandy glass. "If I felt depressed before that walk, I felt a thousand times worse afterwards. When I think of the graceful, elegant and irreplaceable structures which have been demolished in this city, decade after decade, to make way for the present hideous piles, I am made sick with the stupidity and senseless greed of our so-called city planners."

I sighed. "I quite agree. New Haven was once a beautiful city—a hundred years ago. But what can we do? To brood about it does no good now."

He lifted his glass. "All we can do is remember—and cherish our regrets."

"There is small nourishment in that," I pointed out.

He ignored the remark. "Think, Brennan, what it would be like," he went on more brightly, "to be walking out under those huge old elms on a summer's day, down venerable brick sidewalks, with smart carriages whirling past, and a good German band playing somewhere down the street!"

I nodded. "You could stop later for sarsaparilla, or a real old-fashioned chocolate soda—or a stein of cold beer and free sandwiches!"

He laughed for the first time. "Brennan, you think too much on comestibles!"

We chatted on for some further time, but he soon lapsed into silence and at length I stood up to leave. His attempt to delay me was polite and perfunctory. As I closed the door, I heard the clink of the brandy decanter.

Leffing's depression and his lapse into heavy drinking surprised and disconcerted me. I had considered him the ideal investigator, the dispassionate man of the world—cool, analytical, detached. I had forgotten that he was human.

Determining to visit him again in the near future, I plunged back into my own hectic routine of tasks. Before I got around to paying another call, I was pleasantly roused by the sound of Leffing's voice at the other end of the telephone line.

"I have a case, Brennan. Would you care to come along?"

I needed no urging. Life had become flat and stale; I welcomed a respite from drudgery.

Two days later I parked my second-hand Studebaker coupe and rang the bell at seven Autumn Street.

After I was seated in Leffing's Victorian living room, he summed up such facts as he possessed concerning the case in question.

He appeared to have completely shaken off the previous mood of lethargy and depression. His angular face seemed animated; his keen blue-green eyes took on the questing look I was later to know so well.

"About two years ago a Mr. Lionel Finchware bought a sturdy but neglected old colonial house in the remoter part of Cheshire. He has spent a considerable sum to have it repaired and restored. With the usual delays, the restoration took nearly a year. At the end of that time Mr. Finchware, his wife, and a nephew who lives with them, moved in. For six months or so all went well. Then various unpleasant incidents occurred."

Leffing leaned forward in his old Morris chair. "One night the nephew awoke in a cold sweat of fear. He recalled fragments of a fearful dream, but said that the fear did not leave him on awakening. He was conscious of impending evil, of *something* nearby so lethal that his throat closed in terror. Gradually the menace receded and he could finally call out."

Leffing paused, reflectively. "Nothing was found, inside the room or out. There was absolutely no sign of forced entry; nothing unusual was found on the grounds."

He went on. "Several times since then, Mrs. Finchware has been nearly frightened out of her wits by the conviction that somebody—or something—was following her about the rooms of the house. Once she *thinks* she caught a glimpse of something in the room behind her, but she cannot describe it clearly.

"You understand, Brennan, that I have these incidents second-hand from Mr. Finchware. But the third chief incident involved Mr. Finchware himself and he has related it to me in some detail.

"Finchware had been reading late in his second-floor room. (He and his wife keep separate sleeping quarters.) At about one o'clock he got up, put down his book and strolled to a window which overlooks a sloping lawn in the rear of the house. He saw nothing unusual at first, but as he gazed at the moonlit scene an indescribable sense of oppression overcame him. He experienced a feeling of despair quite alien to his nature.

"While he stood transfixed by this sudden and inexplicable change in his mood, a grey shape, dim and amorphous, appeared at the far end of the lawn. It moved slowly up the slope toward the house. It seemed to move with effort, in a somewhat zigzag course.

"Finchware averred that this figure, vague and blurred though it was, transfixed him with utter unreasoning terror. He stood frozen, absolutely overwhelmed with fear.

"The figure got halfway up the lawn before he managed to pull himself from the window. He said that he felt that another second would be fatal. When I asked him what he meant, he hesitated and then finally stated that in another second he was convinced that he would see the thing's face—and 'then it would be too late.'

"When I asked 'Too late for what?', he replied that he simply *knew* that a clear view of the shape, particularly its face, would precipitate a horror with which he could not cope.

"After pulling away from the window, he turned up all the lights and switched on a small radio which he keeps near his bed. Oddly enough, he did not lock his bedroom door, although of course he knew the outside house doors were locked.

"When I asked for an explanation, he said he had an instinctive feeling that light and sound would prove a greater barrier to the thing than walls or doors.

"Finchware remained in his room and gradually his feeling of terror, despair and apprehension faded away. There were no further incidents that night, but the next morning both his wife and nephew revealed that they had experienced fearful nightmares."

"It sounds like an unpleasant business," I commented, as Leffing paused.

He nodded. "I fear, Brennan, your remark is an understatement. Finchware is convinced that a focus of evil, an actual lethal entity perhaps, has somehow established itself in the area. After our discussion here, he requested me to visit the premises. Quite probably I will stay overnight. I mentioned the possibility of a companion and he was quite agreeable."

His speculative blue eyes sought out mine and his now familiar smile, a bit crooked, challenging and questioning, relieved the rather severe lines of his high-cheekboned face.

"When do we leave?" I asked.

"There may be danger, Brennan," he warned, resuming a serious expression.

"All the more reason then," I promptly replied, "why I should go along."

He merely nodded, but I knew my answer pleased him.

Drawing out his old-fashioned gold pocket watch, he snapped open the case. "If a taxi called here at two, we could arrive at the Finchware's before three—a good time I think."

"If you are willing to take your chances on a second-hand Studebaker," I said, "you can save the taxi fare and we can leave when we please."

He was slightly disconcerted. He had always maintained—correctly, I think—that taxi fares amounted to less than car maintenance and he felt it would be an imposition if I acted as chauffeur. Only after I had assured and reassured him that I *preferred* to go in my own car would he agree to its use.

He was not communicative during the drive out to Cheshire. He appeared to be inwardly assessing the implications of such information as he possessed concerning the case.

Following directions left by Mr. Finchware, I pulled off the main route and drove up a narrow road screened by overhanging hemlocks. The Finchware house stood on a small hill about a mile up the road.

It was a large clapboarded old colonial, painted white with black shutters and trim. It had obviously been carefully repaired and restored. Several enormous oaks, looking as old as the house, stood nearby, and there was an abundance of evergreen shrubs and smaller trees clustered on all sides.

In spite of its restoration, I felt that the house had an aura of melancholy. It seemed to be imbued with the tragedies of time, with the vanished woes of generations.

Lionel Finchware, an excessively tall and rangy old gentleman, with a thick thatch of streaky white hair, met us at the door. He welcomed us warmly, took our things, and conducted us to the drawing room.

He informed us that there had been no new developments but that both he and his wife were determined to "follow through on the weird business."

Mrs. Finchware, a compact little person with quick black eyes and a resolute bearing, served us tea.

Our host told us that he thought it best we take over his own bedroom, if that was agreeable.

Leffing approved at once and we were soon unpacking our overnight bags in a pleasant enough room on the second floor.

We were served an excellent roast for dinner, but the conversation remained desultory. Both the Finchwares looked strained and worried. Their nephew, we were told, would be back late in the evening.

After a tour of the house, during which we admired the huge old beams, the well-preserved wood panelling and the massive corbelled chimney piers, Mr. Finchware conducted us to the library, where we were offered whiskey and soda.

Leffing refused to drink, explaining that he invariably declined alcohol when there was a possibility that he might encounter psychic manifestations. Any narcotic, he pointed out, tended to dull one's senses. I sipped one drink, without particular relish.

Our host looked more drawn and tired as the evening progressed. Just after nine o'clock, Leffing proposed that we retire.

Although our room contained a large old-fashioned canopy bed as well as a small cot, Leffing suggested that we both sit up and stay awake as long as possible. The antique arm-chairs were comfortable enough and we settled back to await developments.

Conversation ceased; moonlight began its march across the floor and presently I dozed off.

I awoke suddenly and glanced at my watch. It was after midnight. Leffing sat, wide-awake, in a patch of moonlight. His face, sharp-featured in profile, looked alert and expectant. He favoured me with a somewhat frosty smile, but said nothing.

I sighed and settled back, marvelling at his ability to stay awake.

When I woke up the next time, cold sweat was standing on my forehead and my heart was hammering. I seemed to have struggled in a hideous nightmare, but awakening had not dispelled the sense of dread which pervaded me. If anything, it was worse.

Looking quickly around for Leffing, I saw that he was sitting upright in his chair. His face was white and strained and his thin lips were compressed so firmly together his mouth was no more than a slit. He sat staring straight ahead across the room.

I understood that there was something outside the room trying to get in—something so alien and horrible that we might both be doomed if it ever gained entry. I saw nothing and there was absolutely no sound, yet I had the profound conviction that a terrible invasion was underway.

After a moment or two, during which the pressure of some fearful menace seemed steadily to mount, I realised that the alien something was indeed "outside" but not simply outside the room or the house; it was outside our terrestrial laws, outside our earthly environment, seeking entry with whatever diabolical key it possessed or was trying to possess.

As I looked hopefully at Leffing, I realised that he was actively opposing its invasion, not with words or signs or weapons, but simply with the sheer force of his will. He appeared wan and apprehensive and with a sense of shock I concluded that he was losing the deadly duel.

Evil imbued the air; it seemed tangible, something that assailed the throat, the heart, one's very life blood. The sense of some unearthly pressure became nearly unbearable. I heard Leffing sigh; for an instant I thought that he had lost to the enemy; then the awful pressure began to subside and I understood that his sigh had been one of relief and release. The invader had retreated.

We maintained a vigil till nearly dawn, but the enemy made no further attempt to manifest itself. When a cold light began breaking into the room, we both lay down, Leffing on the cot and I on the canopy bed—he insisted on this arrangement. When I awoke hours later, he had left the room.

Breakfast was waiting for me when I went downstairs. A maid told me that the Finchwares had left for town and that Leffing was somewhere on the grounds.

When I went outside, wisps of fog were still clinging about the hemlocks. Leffing was nowhere in sight. I walked around the house and started down the slope at the rear. At the far end of the slope a thick fringe of larch trees screened the area beyond. Pushing through this line of trees, I stopped, startled.

Almost at my feet lay a deep pond. Its waters looked black and forbidding. Not a ripple disturbed its surface, although a few white streamers of fog drifted above it.

"Sinister, isn't it?"

I jumped. Leffing stood a few feet away, partially hidden by a clump of bushes. He strode forward, amused at my state of nerves.

"Hang it, Leffing," I protested, "you might announce yourself!"

He smiled with genuine solicitude. "I am sorry, Brennan. It was a trying night."

"More trying for you than for me," I pointed out. "What did you make of our—almost visitor—last night?"

His expression became sober at once. He shook his head. "There are dark powers at work here, Brennan, dark powers."

"You have an explanation?"

He shrugged. "As yet, only a theory. There is much work to be done."

For a minute or two he stood staring moodily out over the pond. "What do you think of it?" he asked at length. "The mill pond, that is."

"I don't like it at all," I replied. "And how did you know it was a mill pond?"

"Mr. Finchware referred to it in those terms. When I questioned him, he said there actually had been a mill here, nearly two centuries ago."

"Have you told him of our experience last night?"

"I mentioned the imminence of a manifestation, but I did not convey to him the actual horror which I think we both experienced. No need to alarm the Finchwares to the point of panic."

The rest of the day passed listlessly for me. Leffing, becoming uncommunicative, prowled the grounds and the house restlessly for most of the morning. After we had consumed a light lunch, provided by the maid, he slumped in a chair, lost in thought, all afternoon.

The Finchwares, apparently refreshed by their day in town, were better hosts than in the previous evening, but I sensed that Leffing was paying only polite attention to their conversation. The young nephew, John Motson, was cordial but ill at ease.

I was looking ahead to the night hours with no little perturbation. Leffing, I felt sure, shared my foreboding, though perhaps to a lesser degree.

We retired to our room early, as before, and settled down to an expectant and uneasy vigil. Eventually, of course, I fell asleep.

It was long past midnight when I awoke. Leffing sat silently in his chair; he was wide awake.

"No sign of—anything?" I asked.

He shook his head. "Nothing yet."

Rousing myself, I felt constrained to remain awake, at least for a time. Leffing deserved what little moral support I could provide.

Another hour passed uneventfully. I was beginning to yawn, when Leffing sat up suddenly. "What was that?"

"I heard nothing."

Moving soundlessly, Leffing glided to the window. I hurried up beside him.

Cold moonlight gleamed on the grassy slope in the rear of the house. Beyond lay the fringe of larches, looking black in the silvery light.

As we watched, a shrouded figure broke from the shadow of some shrubbery near the house and started down the slope toward the trees.

Leffing gripped my arm fiercely. "Quick, Brennan, down the stairs and out the back door! We must stop her; we have not a second to lose!"

Whirling, he dashed past me, opened the bedroom door and bounded wildly down the stairs. As I rushed after him, I heard another door slam the wall as it was hurled open.

Leffing was already halfway down the slope when I pounded out onto the lawn. As I raced along behind, he plunged through the line of larch trees and disappeared. A moment later I heard a great splash.

Branches lashed my face as I buffeted my way through the trees and emerged on the other side.

Leffing, up to his shoulders in the black waters, was dragging something back towards shore. Gasping for breath, he staggered up the slippery bank and lay his burden on the grass.

It was Mrs. Finchware.

Leffing began applying artificial respiration. After a minute or two, he stopped. "Good. She has taken in very little water. It is, primarily, I think, a case of shock. Quick, Brennan, help me carry her to the house."

Struggling up the slope, slippery now with the night dew, we carried the unconscious woman toward the house. As we approached, Mr. Finchware appeared, hastily tying a robe. He was so agitated he could scarcely speak for a moment. His face worked. "Is she—?"

"She is alive," Leffing assured him. "Fetch warm blankets and some whiskey."

Bundled in blankets on a couch in the library, Mrs. Finchware finally stirred and opened her eyes. Leffing, having hurriedly changed clothes, held a small glass of whiskey to her lips; she managed to sip a few drops.

"Can you tell us what happened?" Leffing asked gently.

For a long minute she looked at him blankly. Then recollection came and an expression of fear and bewilderment crossed her face.

"I woke up," she said, "after a terrible dream. I felt—awful. Depressed. Discouraged with living."

She paused, frowning. "It was—despair. Black despair. There seemed to be no hope for it. I—decided to drown myself in the mill pond."

An expression of shock crossed Mr. Finchware's face. It was obvious that this was the last thing he had ever expected of his wife.

"Can you give any reason for your feeling of despair?" Leffing asked.

The woman shook her head. "No. It was just—a feeling. There is no reason. I must have been mad."

"You were not mad," Leffing told her. "But I think—temporarily—your mind was not your own."

He straightened up. "Try to rest now. You will not be left alone for a minute."

After indicating that he wished me to remain by the woman's side, he drew Mr. Finchware and young Motson out of the room and closed the door.

A muffled conversation ensued; telephone calls were made and presently the three men reentered.

Mrs. Finchware now appeared to be resting more comfortably. Leffing patted her shoulder. "A doctor will be here soon; he will make sure you are all right and then give you something which will induce sleep. Tomorrow you and Mr. Finchware will leave here for a little vacation. Mr. Motson has made plans for out-of-town work."

It was mid-morning before the Finchwares and Motson finally drove away. Leffing and I went to the library and slumped in arm chairs. We had both sat up most of the night.

"Now that they are gone," I told Leffing, "you can tell me what happened to Mrs. Finchware."

Leffing hesitated. "I cannot be sure. But I believe the—intruder—who tried to break down my own mental and psychic resistance the night before, selected Mrs. Finchware as an easier target. I believe there may be some attempt at personality transfer, or at least the transfer of a powerful, an overwhelming emotion, in this instance the emotion of despair. Much remains to be learned. But I feel better with the Finchwares out of the house. Perhaps now we can get to the bottom of this strange business."

The day passed without incident. Leffing roamed about the house and grounds, but appeared to unearth nothing of interest. After dinner, the maid departed; Leffing and I retreated to the library for an hour or so before going up to our bedroom. In spite of my best efforts to stay awake, I caught myself falling asleep at least twice. Leffing sat absorbed in his own thoughts and did not seem to mind.

As we took our chairs in the bedroom, my companion spoke. "We are the only possible targets tonight, Brennan; save for us, the house is deserted."

It was a disquieting thought; in fact it woke me up rather thoroughly. If I were going to be a "target", I decided, I wanted to be an alert one.

Midnight came and went; I began to conclude that our erstwhile visitor would not disturb us. I was preparing to settle down in my chair for a nap, when a kind of pressure, almost imperceptible at first, began to build up in the room. It increased swiftly. Leffing sat up quickly, ready for any eventuality.

A familiar and terrifying feeling of desolation washed over me. I felt as if something powerful and indescribably evil, something as yet a long way off, was rushing toward the room at tremendous speed.

Leffing stood up suddenly, a look of intense alarm crossing his face.

I scarcely had time to rise when the air on the farthest side of the room seemed to ripple. There was a vague but unmistakable undulation, almost as if the wall itself were involved. The whole side of the room seemed to blur before our eyes. It cleared—and the horror was made manifest.

The entity which materialised was something out of nightmare, out of delirium, out of the fright dreams of raging fever. In the very beginning it was somewhat obscured by the undulations which appeared to pulsate through it. But these ceased and the hideous thing stood before us as in the flesh.

It had the form of the corpse of an old man which had lain for an extended period immersed in muddy water. Its blue-white face was horribly bloated, gouged and torn as by innumerable small teeth or claws. Its black lips were broken and putrescent. The shredded, soaked rags of a shapeless brown suit hung muddily about its puffy frame. A matted mass of ravelled hair hung from its head.

But the worst thing about it was its eyes. They should have been the blank filmy eyes of a corpse, but they glared at us with a fiery light of evil and hatred which froze our hearts.

Opening its unspeakable mouth, it gave vent to a kind of muffled yell, a long "Ahhhhhhhhh" of triumph, and lurched toward us. I can recall one other thing clearly; the *squish* made by its water-clogged shoes.

I stood petrified with terror, unable to move. Leffing's voice cut through my frozen immobility like the blade of a knife.

"Toward the door, Brennan! Do not run!"

My mind scarcely functioned, but I obeyed him like a robot. I edged sideways toward the door and saw that he was following.

By the time I slipped through the doorway, the corpse thing had reached the middle of the room. Its face worked with a kind of unearthly fury impossible to describe. It seemed to slobber at us. Emitting a gurgling sort of snarl, it hurled itself in our direction.

Leffing appeared to catapult himself from the room, slamming the door behind him. He nearly knocked me over. As I staggered, we heard a distinct and horribly yielding *thud* as the thing inside struck the door.

"Out of the house!" Leffing commanded.

As we bounded together down the stairs, the bedroom door was wrenched open. An instant later the heavy squishing *thump* of watery footsteps started down the corridor toward the staircase.

Seconds later we were outside and Leffing had turned the Finchware's borrowed key in the lock.

As I hesitated on the porch, he pocketed the key and seized my arm. "Come away!" he said, hustling me down the steps. "Its power may even extend beyond the house!"

My car was parked nearby and we got into it. For one frantic moment the motor faltered; then it caught and we spun away. As we drove down the narrow road through the overhanging hemlocks, Leffing spoke.

"I feel like a craven," he admitted, "fleeing the scene of battle, as it were. But our visitor has obviously built up a terrific reserve of psychic power. I have never seen a materialisation more vivid—and more horrible. I am now convinced that it has lethal capabilities; it would be folly to oppose it, unequipped as we are."

He said little more as we drove along. But at one point he shook his head and sighed. "It was all my fault, Brennan; I underestimated its hellish vitality."

Instead of returning to New Haven, we stopped at a small motel to spend the remainder of the night. Neither of us could sleep. I asked Leffing if he had any plans for the next day.

He sat staring moodily at the wall for long minutes before replying. "I want to look into the history of the Finchware house," he replied finally, "and I may make tentative arrangements for a formal ceremony of exorcism."

After breakfast the next morning—we had eventually managed to get a few hours' sleep—I drove Leffing to the town clerk's office to look up ancient real estate records. He suggested that I stop at the local library; there might be some old town histories available.

I spent the morning turning over area histories and although I found plenty of interest, I did not succeed in locating anything pertaining to the Finchware house.

I picked up Leffing for lunch. He was not particularly communicative, but I sensed that he was on the track of something.

I learned nothing until after dinner when we were ensconced once more in our motel room.

"The local records were not complete," Leffing revealed, "but by a stroke of great good luck I was introduced to a Mr. Bennett Proby, the town's most renowned antiquarian. He edges on ninety-eight but has an excellent memory and possesses a vast fund of information passed along from various forebears."

"What did you learn of the Finchware house?" I inquired, coming directly to the point.

"The house dates from the Revolutionary period. It has of course changed hands a number of times. It would be tedious and I think irrelevant at this time to enumerate the names, occupations and life histories of all the different owners—although Mr. Proby had ample information about all of them."

"You have singled out the source of trouble then?"

Leffing nodded. "I am almost sure that I have. I believe the present evil visitation had its source in the person of a Giles Moray, who was most probably the original owner and first occupant of the house."

I settled back to learn the details and Leffing continued.

"Moray was unquestionably an evil man. The source of his wealth is obscure, but it is believed that it was acquired by some sort of nefarious and illicit trade during the Revolution. After building the house and mill, Moray moved in with an indentured servant girl who promptly disappeared. Over the decades, it appears, indentured wenches, destitute immigrant women and even some actual slaves came and went under the Moray roof. Some remained only months, others for a number of years. When questioned about any of the various disappearances, Moray invariably shrugged off further inquiries by saying that the particular female wretch in question had run away. He even advertised for some of them. But it was rumoured and generally believed that he had murdered most of them when they no longer satisfied his physical appetites.

"Eventually he existed like a hermit, shunned by his neighbours. And finally he lived in the foul clutches of a loathsome disease which, long neglected, became incurable. At length he vanished. His body was never found. It was thought that he had drowned himself in the mill pond behind the house; it is quite deep, however, and grappling operations at the time failed to recover the corpse, if indeed it was there."

"A most unsavoury character," I commented.

"Unsavoury in death as in life," Leffing added. "Since his disappearance, the house and mill pond have become a foci for suicides. According to Mr. Proby, no less than eleven known suicides have occurred on the premises down the centuries. It is a figure which rules out coincidence. Some drowned themselves in the mill pond; others hanged themselves from nearby trees. Several shot themselves in the house."

"You actually believe that Moray's evil spirit caused these acts of self-destruction?" I asked.

"It might be better stated," Leffing replied. "I believe that Moray's lingering influence—a residuum of pure evil—created the conditions, the psychic atmosphere as it were, which triggered the suicides. This influence has apparently strengthened, rather than diminished, over the years. It has become so strong that it could finally seize on the mind and soul of a person to whom suicide—even for good reasons—would be almost unthinkable—Mrs. Finchware."

"It seems incredible!"

Leffing nodded. "Evil is often incredible. I am inclined to think, that in some obscure and malevolent manner of which we remain ignorant, each suicide somehow increased the power of Moray's earthbound apparition. Like an insatiable ghoul, his baleful spirit has fed on suicides over the centuries. Probably, from these poor driven souls, his own entity extracts sustenance. To his lingering personality, they may be a source of psychic energy and renewal."

"It is all too horrible to be accepted by a rational mind!" I objected.

Leffing shrugged rather wearily. "The so-called 'rational mind', my dear fellow, is often the most irrational apparatus on earth!"

"What are your plans now?" I asked presently.

"Tomorrow," he replied, "if you will be kind enough to drive me to the rectory, I intend to look in on Father Muldeen, an old friend of mine."

We arose early the next morning and after a telephone call which confirmed that the priest was in residence and available for an interview, I drove my friend to the rectory.

Father Muldeen met us at the door and welcomed Leffing with unaffected warmth. A tall portly man about sixty who looked as if he had been a professional athlete in his youth, Father Muldeen was blessed with the merriest blue eyes I had ever seen. They seemed to dance and shine and one had the disconcerting sensation that they might actually be peering around inside one's head.

He listened gravely enough, however, as Leffing told his story and he did not interrupt.

Afterwards, he sat musing for a few minutes and then inclined his head. "If the Bishop agrees that a ceremony of exorcism is indicated by the circumstances which you have described to me, I shall be happy enough to perform it."

Leffing seemed satisfied with this reply. Father Muldeen promised to inform us of the decision as soon as possible. After some nostalgic and at times hilarious reminiscing about "the old days"—Muldeen and Leffing had apparently met many years before—we departed.

We spent the rest of the day at the motel waiting for the telephone to ring. Leffing fidgeted, paced the floor and scowled at the wall. I read magazines.

The call did not come until nine o'clock that evening. Father Muldeen informed Leffing that the Bishop had given his consent for the ritual. We were to meet at the Finchware house the next morning at ten o'clock.

We arrived at the Finchware house long before ten and sat waiting in the car for Father Muldeen. At ten minutes after ten a sports car came racing up the Finchware's narrow road and stopped in the driveway.

Father Muldeen got out, slamming the car door. "Sorry I'm a bit late! Had to give last rites in a hurry!"

The ceremony of exorcism, rarely performed, was more elaborate than I had realised. Father Muldeen revealed that he had been fasting for twenty-four hours and informed us that prior to the actual recital of the exorcism text, Mass would have to be said. It was decided that the entire ceremony, including Mass, would be conducted in the room in which Leffing and I had encountered the fearful visitant. Father Muldeen, who had had some previous experiences with psychic materialisations, said that this room might well be a kind of "entrance-way for the unearthly evil one."

Special prayers followed Mass and then the solemn Latin of the exorcism command, awesome in its implication of implacable authority, rang through the room. Every syllable, clearly enunciated, seemed charged with energy and inflexible purpose:

"Adjuro te, serpens antique, per Judicem vivorum et mortuorum, per Factorem mundi, qui habet potestatem mittere te in gehennam, ut ab hac domo festinus discedas. Ipse tibi imperat, maledicte diabole, qui ventis ac mari et tempestatibus imperavit... Audi ergo, Satana, et time, et victus et prostratus recede, adjuratus in nomine Domini nostri Jesu Christi."

The entire ritual proceeded without interruption. Father Muldeen told us afterwards that there could be no guarantee that the ceremony would be fully successful. It might have to be repeated, he said, perhaps several times.

After Leffing's profuse thanks, the priest sped off in his sports car, late for another appointment.

Leffing and I went back to the motel. I was informed that we would return to the Finchware house that evening and spend the night. The day passed in desultory fashion and I think we were both relieved when we started back to the Finchwares' residence.

Some aspects of the exorcism command puzzled me and on the drive I questioned Leffing closely. For instance, the adjuration seemed directed to Satan himself rather than to the departed spirit of Giles Moray.

Leffing answered carefully. "I believe it may be the conclusion of the Church that the visitant is actually possessed by Satan, or by some other demon, or is at least infused with evil energy drawn from malign sources. In other words, the adjuration is addressed directly to the ultimate source of Moray's power. Moray's apparition you might say, is considered only the instrument which conducts and focuses the unearthly energy."

Settled in our room where the exorcism ceremony had been conducted, we awaited developments. The evening hours passed without incident.

It was long after midnight when, in spite of my best efforts, my eyes began to close. Leffing sat nearby, wide-awake and alert. I was roused from a cat-nap by the sound of my name called softly.

Sitting up, I saw that Leffing was standing at one of the windows which faced the sloping lawn in the rear of the house. He beckoned to me.

Joining him at the window, I at first saw nothing unusual. The landscape was silent, silvered with moonlight.

"Near the larch trees," Leffing whispered.

Straining my eyes, I finally saw a vague shape of grey, blurred and amorphous, faintly outlined against the black of the larches. As I waited, it began slowly drifting up the far end of the slope toward the house.

"Moray!" I exclaimed. "Leffing, the exorcism has failed!"

He gripped my arm. "Wait!"

The grey shape, gaining speed, got about halfway up the slope and paused. Veering off at an angle, it circled briefly and then started up again. Once more it stopped. After appreciable seconds during which it remained motionless, it made a sudden dart forward. It not only stopped abruptly but appeared to be thrust backwards, as if it had encountered an invisible yet impassable obstacle.

Again and again it attempted to dart forward. Each time it was thrust further backwards.

As we gazed at this bizarre spectacle, cold with horror and yet fascinated, the thing suddenly gave vent to a howl which literally stirred the hair on our heads. It was a mixture of rage and despair, an unearthly ululation canine in pitch and yet containing a note which was undeniably human.

Even as it howled, it was thrust further down the slope. The howling increased in intensity, a weird wail of utter despair, rising and falling with a desolation indescribable, which froze us into silence.

Forced ever backwards, the thing reached the line of larch trees. Here it appeared to pause momentarily, as if making a supreme effort to halt its remorseless retreat. The howling stopped briefly but then commenced again, if possible with a more abysmal note of absolute despair than before.

The grey shape disappeared into the fringe of larch trees; the fearful howling seemed to die away as if it were fading into infinite distance. At length we could hear it no more. The slope lay before us in the moonlight, empty and silent.

We stayed at the window for long minutes, but the spectre did not reappear. The night remained soundless.

Leffing drew back from the window. "I do not believe these premises will be troubled again. The Finchwares may return whenever they wish. I shall call them tomorrow."

We went back to New Haven the next day. That evening, in spite of the accumulation of work which faced me, I drove willingly enough to seven Autumn Street to avail myself of Leffing's invitation to share a glass or two of his choice brandy. It had become his way of celebrating the successful conclusion of a case.

"One thing puzzles me," I said, after I was comfortably seated in Leffing's gas-lit Victorian parlour. "Moray's apparition appeared to us as an actual flesh-and-blood entity—or corpse!—I could even hear the water in his shoes squish!"

Leffing, fingertips together, remained silent for some time. "The dimensions of space and time," he replied at length, "are not the same to a disembodied spirit as they are to earthbound mortals. And there are many things concerning astral and ectoplasmic projections which remain mysteries to us. Matter in all its various details—or at least the facsimiles of it—can be recreated, as it were, by a psychic entity which possesses sufficient energy and determination. We saw and heard exactly what the spectre of Moray wanted us to see and hear."

I shook my head. "I accept your explanation of course. It is difficult to comprehend, but I can suggest no other."

Leffing sipped his brandy with the appreciation of a satisfied connoisseur. "I can thank the restless spirit of Mr. Giles Moray for one thing. His advent successfully dissipated the morass of despondency into which I had sunk!"

"One would almost have thought," I pointed out, "that his despairing soul had already got hold of you!"

Leffing laughed heartily and insisted on filling my glass again.

As the narrators used to say: "I was nothing loathe."

There is one curious and pertinent footnote to this case which was not revealed until months later. The Finchwares, after learning details of the case, took an intense dislike to the mill pond behind the house. Although there were no further visitations, they decided to do away with the pond. It was drained, dredged and filled with good New England gravel. During the dredging operations the skull fragments and assorted bones of at least nine separate individuals were discovered. They were beyond skeletal reconstruction; no attempt was made to establish identity.

But Leffing told me he had no doubt these melancholy fragments belong to Moray's poor indentured wenches who had "run away", as well as to subsequent suicides over the decades. We both wondered whether the bones of Moray himself were dredged up with those of his victims. We will never know.

After all legal requirements had been met, the bones were incinerated and the ashes interred in some unknown place.

STORY SOURCES

All the stories in this anthology are in the public domain unless otherwise noted. Every effort has been made to trace copyright holders and the publisher apologises for any errors or omissions and would be pleased to be notified of any corrections to be incorporated in reprints or future editions. The following gives the original publication details for each story. They are listed in alphabetical order of author.

"The Fear" by Claude and Alice Askew first published in *The Weekly Tale-Teller*, 22 August 1914, and collected in *Aylmer Vance: Ghost-Seer* (Ashcroft, B.C.: Ash-Tree Press, 1998).

"The Valley of the Veils of Death" by Bertram Atkey first published in *The Grand Magazine*, November 1914.

"A Psychical Invasion" by Algernon Blackwood first published in *John Silence: Physician Extraordinary* (London: Eveleigh Nash, 1908).

"In Death as in Life" by Joseph Payne Brennan first published in *Macabre*, Winter 1963/64 and collected in *The Casebook of Lucius Leffing* (New Haven: Macabre House, 1973).

"The Case of the Fortunate Youth" by Moray Dalton first published in *The Premier Magazine*, August 1927.

"The Death Hound" by Dion Fortune first published in *The Royal Magazine*, October 1922 and collected in *The Secrets of Dr. Taverner* (London: Noel Douglas, 1926).

"Forgotten Harbour" by Gordon Hillman first published in *Ghost Stories*, April 1931.

"The Searcher of the End House" by William Hope Hodgson first published in *The Idler*, June 1910 and collected in *Carnacki the Ghost-Finder* (London: Eveleigh Nash, 1913).

"The Story of the Moor Road" by Kate and Hesketh Prichard first published in *Pearson's Magazine*, March 1898 as by E. & H. Heron and collected in *Ghosts: Being the Experiences of Flaxman Low* (London: Pearson, 1899).